THE HOMESTEADERS

Literature of Canada

Poetry and Prose in Reprint

Douglas Lochhead, General Editor

The Homesteaders

Robert J.C. Stead

Introduction by Susan Wood Glicksohn

UNIVERSITY OF TORONTO PRESS

© University of Toronto Press 1973
Toronto and Buffalo
Printed in Canada
Reprinted in 2018

ISBN 0-8020-2067-4 (cloth)
ISBN 978-0-8020-6196-6 (paper)
LC 73-82583

Preface

Yes, there is a Canadian literature. It does exist. Part of the evidence to support these statements is presented in the form of reprints of the poetry and prose of the authors included in this series. Much of this literature has been long out of print. If the country's culture and traditions are to be sampled and measured, both in terms of past and present-day conditions, then the major works of both our well-known and our lesser-known writers should be available for all to buy and read. The Literature of Canada series aims to meet this need. It shares with its companion series, The Social History of Canada, the purpose of making the documents of the country's heritage accessible to an increasingly large national and international public, a public which is anxious to acquaint itself with Canadian literature — the writing itself — and also to become intimate with the times in which it grew.

DL

Robert J.C. Stead, 1880-1959

Susan Wood Glicksohn

Introduction

Fashions in literature change as inexorably as the height of hemlines and the width of ties and trouser legs. Your parents' favourite bestsellers, like their once-glamorous clothes, seem odd, old-fashioned, ready for banishment to attics or second-hand stores. But Grandmother's shawl and Grandpa's Sunday-best vest — they are quite a different matter. Quaint, certainly, but intriguing, even fashionable again. And what about those books hidden beneath them? Here are Robert Service's poems (a Christmas gift); *The Man from Glengarry*, with its bookplate announcing it was a Sunday School prize awarded to your aunt; some Copp Clark *Narrative and Lyric Poems: For Use in the Lower School*, in their limp green bindings; and another Christmas gift, *The Homesteaders*, by Robert Stead. What earned them their dog-eared pages, in a home that had little time or use for books? What do they have to say to this Canadian-culture-conscious generation? Perhaps it is time they came out of the trunk too.

Who was Robert Stead? Fifty years ago, Canadian readers knew his name and bought his new works. The reviews which praised his detailed accounts of western life told how well he knew that life, born on a farm in Ontario's Lanark County but raised on his parents' homestead near Cartwright, Manitoba. His interest in literature was stimulated by a missionary who lodged one summer at the farm: the Reverend Charles Gordon, internationally famous as the writer, 'Ralph Connor.' By the age of eighteen, Robert Stead had become a successful reporter, editor, and publisher of two weekly newspapers; and in 1908, the respected journalist became a nationally known poet with the publication of *The Empire Builders and Other Poems.*

English-Canadians, enjoying an economic boom as a surge of material progress followed years of depression to open 'Canada's century,' and an accompanying surge of national pride coupled with Imperial fervour, welcomed the optimistic, patriotic tone of Stead's verses. *The Empire Builders,* which went through several editions, was read in Manitoba farm kitchens and Rideau Hall alike; the governor-general, Lord Grey, not only wrote encouragingly to Stead, but recommended that lines from the book be engraved on a Canadian military monument in England. Succeeding collections – *Prairie Born and Other Poems* (1911), *Songs of the Prairie* (1911), *Kitchener and Other Poems* (1917), and *Why Don't They Cheer?* (1918) – also appealed to national sentiment in the ringing manner of Kipling and the popular narrative of Service. Newspapers, lavishing praise on 'The Poet of the Prairie,' added the unofficial title of Canadian Poet Laureate in 1916, when, across the country, they printed his elegy on the death of Kitchener, the first poem deemed important enough to be transmitted in its entirety by Associated Press teletype.

By 1916, however, Stead had also written two of the novels that were to bring him even greater fame in his own generation – and critical appreciation in the next for the one work his contemporaries ignored. *The Bail Jumper* was published in 1914 by Briggs in Canada and by Unwin in England, a firm which secured several reviews in England, Australia, and New Zealand, but apparently little in the way of sales. A melodrama of foul crime and pure love, it seemed chiefly remarkable to reviewers because it featured a prairie setting and a female detective. It is chiefly remarkable to students of Canadian literature, however, for introducing Plainville, Manitoba, a fictional community whose development Stead recorded in three later novels. Though *The Bail Jumper* never became a bestseller, it won Stead a modest reputation as an adventure-writer, and praise for his ability to describe western life convincingly enough to satisfy readers in Cartwright as well as reviewers as far away as Hobart, Tasmania.

The praise increased two years later when Unwin, with Musson in Toronto, published *The Homesteaders.* Through two conventional love stories, Stead explored two important themes: the early settlement of Plainville, with its difficulties and the sense of community they called forth; and the ironic impact upon the pioneers of the dreamed-of prosperity and civilization. The novel first appeared as a serial in the January 1916, issue of *Westminster* magazine, the religious periodical which first published Ralph Connor's early work. It was introduced as 'the kind of fiction Canadian authors ought to write'; and certainly the Canadian public decided that this was the kind of fiction they wanted to read. The first edition sold out by the end of the year, while western papers carried Stead's assurances that a new printing would soon be dispatched to the eager readers who had reserved copies. By 1922, when his popularity was at its height, a fifth edition was issued. Despite the war, reviews appeared throughout the British Empire: in the London *Times, Observer,* and *Post,* in papers in South Africa, Australia, New Zealand, and even in Bangkok, praising the book's vividly-realized background.

No reviewers, however, were more enthusiastic than those of western Canada. The Winnipeg *Telegram* called *The Homesteaders* 'undoubtedly the leading native-born novel of the season,' and found its conflict 'of idealism and Mammon' profoundly moving; the Edmonton *Journal* praised both the 'graphic portrayal of early pioneer life' and 'the beautiful word pictures ... of the magnificent foothill country in Southern Alberta.' The Calgary *Morning Albertan* waxed even more eloquent, declaring: 'This novel has the heady sweetness of the wheat, the clarity of the western atmosphere, and the disingenuousness and practicality of the northern pioneer, and withal it exercises a fascination of plot and character which compels the reader to the end.'

Perhaps the most significant review, because it indicated the nature and scope of Stead's appeal, was that published by an agricultural journal, *Canadian Farm Implements*, in 1917. The editor explained that he had waived the usual policy against reviews of fiction because of *The Homesteaders'* setting and undoubted appeal to farm readers; and the reviewer exclaimed that 'The opening chapter is a masterpiece of the writer's art, and clear through the book runs an engrossing interest that carries to the end with a feeling that this story will live.'

Unfortunately, *The Homesteaders*, and Stead's appeal, would live only as long as the vogue for what another Calgary paper described as 'a story of enthralling romance which holds the reader in a vice-like grip' held sway. Before and after the Great War, Stead's works were high fashion, selling well, reviewed enthusiastically by major dailies and small-town weeklies, and, judging from the social notes in the latter, popular topics for recital and discussion at literary evenings. Wilfrid Eggleston in *The Frontier and Canadian Letters* gives a personal account of cultural life in the early west, when the homesteaders' scanty collections of essential books — 'a Bible, a medical compendium, *The Sky Pilot* perhaps' — were supplemented by the school library, 'commonly stocked with several score of miscellaneous volumes ... a handful of English classics and an occasional title by

L.M. Montgomery, Nellie McClung, Robert J.C. Stead, Charles G.D. Roberts or Ralph Connor.' Stead, then, was one of a small group of Canadian authors whose works were read in a world which read little; and who, therefore, as the pioneering days of the Canadian west ended, recorded and interpreted their reality for all Canadians.

Stead's writing pleased a society which had inherited the frontier's suspicion of the artist as an unproductive member of the community, and the Calvinist-evangelical churches' suspicion of the artist as an immoral being devoted only to worldly concerns. A lingeringly Victorian, prudish society, it demanded pure romance mixed with uplifting morality, an emphasis on the ideals of progress and Christian manliness; and it regarded with horror European and American experiments with 'realism,' associated until well into mid-century with sexuality and corruption.

Nevertheless, 'realistic' descriptions of Canada itself — usually, glowing panegyrics to unspoiled natural beauty, and to the hardy men imposing their marks upon it — appealed to a growing national pride. An enthusiastic audience was assured for Stead's 'beautiful word pictures,' such as his account of John and Mary Harris' Sunday walks beside the river on their homestead, listening

> to the gentle murmur of the water, while fleecy clouds mirrored themselves in its glassy depths ... and a meadow-lark sent its limpid challenge from a neighbouring bush. And at night, when the moon rose in wonderful whiteness and purity, wrapping field and ravine in a riot of silver, the strange, irresistible, unanswerable longing of the great plains stole down upon them, and they knew that here indeed was life in its fulness — a participation in the Infinite, indefinable, but all-embracing, everlasting.

Literary fashion demanded entertainment with an end, whether the moral lessons of Connor and McClung, or an appeal to national consciousness through descriptions of pioneer life which emphasized its spiritual as well as economic importance. Throughout his life, Stead campaigned for a distinctive Canadian literature, as a defence against the tide of American culture sweeping the country, because, as he wrote in *The Canadian Gazette* 1930, 'the nation's traditions become idealized in its literature, and it is that idealization which holds the country together.' In *The Homesteaders* Stead stressed the importance of pioneer life, its heroic and ideal qualities, as part of a unifying national tradition.

Stead's early work, then, followed literary fashion, as most early work does. In 1918, a war-weary public craved idealism and romance; he supplied it in *The Cow Puncher*, a national success (even by modern standards) with over 70,000 copies sold. It was followed in 1920 by the commercially-successful *Dennison Grant*, an uneasy blend of cowboy love story and social theories, expressed in contrived scenes such as that in which the manly hero, having rescued the inevitable rancher's daughter, a free-spirited golden girl of the west, from a prairie fire, sits with her in the moonlight discoursing upon the reorganization of society.

It is to Stead's credit that he did not simply succumb to the demand for hackwork with a prairie background. Instead, it is generally agreed by critics such as Edward McCourt in *The Canadian West in Fiction* that he deliberately abandoned the popular formulas of his early novels and, with developing perceptions and technical skills, 'turned to the serious portrayal of the ordinary men and women of ordinary Western communities in their ordinary occupations.'

As Stead developed as an artist, however, he lost his following as a writer. Ironic — but understandable, given the literary taste of the era. His sixth novel, *Grain* (1926), was a study of a commonplace young man in his unromanticized environment, and of the interaction of the two: a realistic novel published one year after F.P. Grove's *Settlers of the Marsh* had caused a violent moral tempest in the small tea-party of Canadian letters. *Settlers* was withdrawn from circulation; *Grain*, despite some favourable reviews, was simply ignored. It suffered by comparison with Stead's earlier works, including *The Homesteaders;* it was not an adventurous love story, interspersed with lyrical descriptions, like them. Then, as literary tastes changed, interest in Stead and his novels evaporated. What could the prairie romance-spinner who entertained one generation say to its children, the Lost, the Depression, the World War generations? Finally, in the 1960s, growing interest in Canadian literature led to the rediscovery of *Grain* – and the nadir of Stead's literary reputation when Thomas Saunders, introducing the new edition of that novel, dismissed the others as possessing 'little genuine merit' and 'puerile. They did not – and do not – warrant serious critical comment.'

Stead himself withdrew from, but did not abandon the literary life. He had never been in any sense a 'full time' artist; fifty years ago, before Canada Council grants and writer-in-residence appointments, it was almost impossible to support a family on royalty payments alone. After success as a businessman and journalist, Stead finally became a civil servant when, in 1919, he joined the publicity staff of the Department of Immigration and Colonization, and left the west permanently for Ottawa.

His literary contacts and responsibilities increased. In 1923, he became president of the Canadian Authors' Association (a body already under fire as outmoded and stuffy from the new literary generation, and now known primarily as the 'expansive puppets' and 'virgins of sixty who still write of passion' caricatured in

F.R. Scott's satirical poem, 'The Canadian Authors Meet'). Stead continued to write articles on Canadian literature, on his memories of the west, on agricultural developments for farm papers, and, in connection with his later post as superintendent of publicity for the national parks, on Canada's natural beauties. Despite the poor sales of *Grain*, he published one more novel, *The Copper Disc* (1931), and worked on the manuscript of another, *Prairie Farm*, which remained unpublished at the time of his death in 1959.

Stead seems to have regarded with mixed feelings the necessity of ignoring art to earn a living. In an interview published in 1923 by *The Canadian Bookman*, he commented: 'He would have to be a brave (and possibly foolish) man who would try to live by books alone in this country. ... most of us have to do our literary creation at the end of a full day's work, when our vitality is lowered and our power of concentration not at its best.' Yet in 'Origin and Trend of Canadian Literature,' an essay published in 1931, he welcomed the fact that the Canadian writer was forced to support himself by non-literary jobs; this made him less 'professional' than his counterpart in England or the United States, and thus 'saner and more truly representative' of his culture, because he kept in touch with everyday life. 'Writing of that life as he knows it,' Stead continued, 'perhaps it is not remarkable that there is in his work a noticeable lack of that emphasis on sex which is found in much of the current literature of both the United States and Great Britain, and there is a survival of that optimism which has ceased to be popular among many of the professional writers.'

Inspiring, and free of overt sexuality — these were the hallmarks of a literature whose moral complacency and limited scope were mocked by newer writers. In 1928, for example, A.J.M. Smith's 'Wanted: Canadian Criticism' in *The Canadian Forum* criticized the materialism and prudery of a society which mistrusted all art except 'inspiration stuff and he-man Canadiana,' or extravagant local colour 'to be bought from the same patriotic motive that prompts the purchaser of Eddy's matches or a Massey-Harris farm implement, and read along with Ralph Connor and Eaton's catalogue.' Yet it was western romances, Zane Grey north of the forty-ninth parallel, which the public demanded; and Stead, even as he developed artistically, remained sensitive to such demands. In an interview in 1912, for example, he defended his poetry against a charge that it was 'materialistic' rather than artistic. 'Sunsets and rosy dawns have been described by all the poets of the last three thousand years and it is rather foolish for the present generation to attempt to improve on what has already been said,' he argued. 'We have, however, at the present day a condition in Canada which has never existed before and which will never exist again, and it is the province of present-day writers to crystallize that condition and preserve it for posterity. This may be materialism, but the experience of the publishing houses shows it to be what the people want, and after all the people are the best judge.' Stead's works, from *The Bail Jumper* to *Grain*, attempted to balance the artist's desire to record western life and the popular novelist's desire to give the readers the plots and sentiments they enjoyed.

The Homesteaders almost achieves this balance. Certainly, a modern reader will find this account of pioneer life seriously flawed — inevitably flawed, given the circumstances surrounding its creation. The novel opens in Ontario in 1881, with John Harris planning to leave his unrewarding teaching job to homestead in

Manitoba with Mary, his fiancée. This introductory 'masterpiece of the writer's art' now appears mawkish and cliché-ridden. John is introduced, not as a man, but as a symbolic embodiment of the Manly Man, the Connor Anglo-Saxon hero with his 'strong and sunburned face' and 'sober grey eyes' which 'stared unseeing into the forest, while the light wind that stirred the golden maple leaves toyed gently with his unruly locks.' Language is often stilted and overblown: the immigrant train of 1882 is compared to the later tourist sleeper, with 'its dusky attendant, restrained to an attitude of agreeable deference by the anticipation of a gratuity'; a tear is a 'tiny pearl of pathos'; and a meal becomes 'the plying of the viands.' Sentiments, with the language which obscures rather than clarifies them, are lofty and vague; the account of Mary's departure from her home seems particularly quaint. It is not that any modern Canadian would deny the emotion of such a situation, either the mother's grief at losing her daughter forever, or the courage both she and the girl display. It is simply that fashions in language change, and no-one now would express the scene in these terms:

> The bride, glowing in the happy consciousness of her own beauty, and deified by the great tenderness that enveloped her new estate like a golden mist, said her farewells with steady voice and undrooping eyes. Once only, when two frail arms drew her to the great mother-heart that was fighting with joy and unspoken sorrow through its travail of the soul, did their bright rays moisten and tremble like sun-shafts in a pool. ... the mother smiled upon her in a pride that was deeper than her pain. The breed that had not feared, a generation back, to cross the seas and carve a province and a future from the forest, was not a breed to withhold its most beautiful and noble from the ventures of the greater West.

Only a few pages later, however, the language and style become more natural as Stead describes the immigrant train, its aisles 'crowded with standing passengers who stumbled over valises with every pitch in the uncertain roadbed,' with women who fought tears, with children who 'shrieked as they fell between the slippery seats,' and with the occasional established settler like Aleck McCrae, boasting of the west's opportunities:

'Tell us about the crops,' said one of the men passengers. 'What like wheat can ye grow?'

'Like corn,' said the narrator, with great deliberation. 'Heads like ears o'corn. Wheat that grows so fast ye can hear it. Nothin' uncommon to walk into wheat-fields when they's knee-high, an' have to fight yer way out like a jungle.'

People have replaced clichés.

The defects of artificial, heightened language and sentimental thought, which also mar later chapters for a modern reader, mark half of Stead's debt to the literary standards of Canada in 1916. The other half — along with the part-time writer's lack of leisure in which to experiment and innovate — is evident in the clumsily-developed, threadbare plot.

From the opening of Manitoba, shown through the romance of John and Mary, their journey west, and the details of establishing their home, of building a sod hut and ploughing the first furrows, the novel jumps twenty-five years. Two-thirds of the book pictures the equivocal effects of settlement and prosperity through the collapse of John Harris' ideals and his marriage, and his land-hungry journey to the new frontier of Alberta. The abrupt transition itself does not flaw the novel; rather, it emphasizes the changes in the community, and makes more shocking the hero's decay into a materialistic automation. It does indicate, however, Stead's tendency to manipulate the plot obtrusively, rather than let it develop naturally out of itself.

The second part of the novel contains another stock romance between Beulah Harris and Jim Travers (her father reborn, a young man with ideals and ambition) which rapidly develops into a variation on *The Bail Jumper*. As in Stead's other novels, new characters are introduced suddenly to provide a melodramatic ending, basically similar to, but more highly coloured than, the conclusion implied by earlier events. Materialistic Riles and cunning Gardiner, the villains of *The Bail Jumper*, implicate Travers and involve Harris in a complicated land swindle whose details (much as they indicate the extent of Harris' greed) seemed barely credible to reviewers in 1916. Certainly the catastrophe is made to bring about the happy reunion of both generations; but it does not seem, convincingly, to do so. The events of the plot are ultimately irrelevant to the real story, that of John Harris' rediscovery of meaning in his life. Thus the closing pages, obviously meant to grip the reader with the excitement of violent action, sudden disclosures, and obligatory Nemesis at work, seem contrived and anticlimactic. Gardiner's death, for example, has as little effect as his life and one-dimensional villainy on the real drama, the psychological one.

Counterbalancing these flaws, however, is a gift which earned Stead his wide audience in 1916 and which can still attract and reward modern readers: the ability to observe and recreate the life around him. The Stead family had migrated from Lanark County in the early spring of 1882; they had driven 120 miles from Emerson to take up a quarter-section of land which, from Stead's description, closely resembled that claimed by John

Harris on the prairie near the Turtle Mountains; they had known the 'day of faith' when they first broke the land, and the warmth of a community co-operating to build a schoolhouse. Stead brings his family's story, and his own memories, to life. Pioneer conditions are vividly evoked, as are the physical details of life on even a prosperous ranch, the graceless routines which Beulah rejects as 'making little twenty-four hour cycles that don't get us anywhere, except older.' The girl's complaints about her crude life are stifled as 'the scraping of heavy boots on the ploughshare nailed to the block at the door' announces the arrival of the men for their meal:

> The men all wore blue overalls, dark blue or grey shirts, and heavy boots. They were guiltless of coat or vest, and tossed their light straw hats on the water-bench as they passed. There was a quick splashing of greasy hands at the wash-basin, followed by a more effectual rubbing on a towel made from a worn-out grain sack. The hired man paused to change the water and wash his face, but the others proceeded at once to the table, where no time was lost in ceremony. Meat, potatoes, and boiled cabbage were supplied in generous quantities on large platters. ... There was no talk for the first few minutes, only the sound of knife and fork plied vigorously and interchangeably by father and son, and with some regard for convention by the other members of the family. John Harris had long ago recognized the truth that the destiny of food was the mouth, and whether conveyed on knife or fork made little difference.

This picture, more than all Stead's comments, makes Beulah's longing for a life that is not 'just existing' clear. Thus *The*

Homesteaders is, on one level, a fascinating social history, recalled by one who lived it.

In addition to the journalist's ability to select and present interesting facts, however, the book demonstrates the novelist's ability to infuse these facts with life. The immigrants' difficult, hope-filled journey is seen, and shared as well with the sturdy farm woman who, her chest deepened and her imagination cramped 'from years of wrestling with the rocks and timbers of Lanark,' simply cannot believe the good fortune promised to her in Manitoba. 'And is there no stones there, or stumps? ... Has the bush all been cleared away?' she asks, longing to be convinced that 'it has not been all ploughed some time.' Other 'real-life' incidents, such as the bar-room shootout averted by the Mountie, are made real by Stead's command of significant detail and convincing language.

The major importance of *The Homesteaders*, however, is the flesh it moulds onto an abstraction: the tragedy of the pioneer. A theme familiar to any reader of Canadian literature and especially the works of Grove, it is a national version of the Quest theme — the story of a dream that is lost in the finding. The pioneer sets out, a young man with high ideals, to seek both freedom and material success, to rebuild civilization in a new world. The pioneer finds himself, an aging man without the ideals and freedom he lost somewhere in the grinding work of surviving, pursuing a meaningless material success in a civilization whose form he rejects, and which does not need him. Thus Grove's Abe Spalding, in *Fruits of the Earth*, works to make the west 'into a country fit to live in,' to build up a farm 'to leave to my children for them to be proud of.' Yet all his labour (labour which is his master, which brings more money and more land, but never enough), only alienates him from the family he was too busy to know, and creates a more complex civilization which he cannot understand. He creates his own defeat, on a social and personal level.

Stead, too, writes of the decay of dreams. Where Grove's characters are giants and symbols, tragic heroes outside human affairs, John Harris is an ordinary individual. He is thus the more understandable. Rather than awe, the slow erosion of his hopes by age, by the imprisoning round of necessary work, by materialism and by 'success' inspires compassion, and perhaps self-examination. The sentimentality of the opening chapters seem artistically justified in the contrast it presents. Here is the young man, worried about taking his gently-reared bride far from civilization, and determined to create a world with her:

> 'And shall we build our own home, and live our own lives, and love each other — always, — only, for ever and ever?' she breathed.
>
> 'For ever and ever,' he answered.

And here is the middle-aged man, who plans a profitable sale of that home, and who scorns his wife when she begs him to choose 'between life and land':

> 'Now I know where Beulah got her nonsense,' he retorted. 'All this talk about real life is very fine, but you don't get much life, real or any other kind, unless you have the cash to pay down for it. You can't buy beef-steaks with long walks over the prairie, nor clothe yourself and family with sunsets. For my part I want some real success. We've done pretty well here, as you say, but it's only a beginnin' to what we can do, if we set about it, and don't wait until the cheap land is all gone.'

He alone does not realize that his 'real success' is ephemeral, and is destroying the happiness his family knew 'when we lived in the one-roomed sod shanty, with scarcely a cent to bless ourselves.'

John Harris' change embodies the change in the west, as 'the old sense of oneness, the old community interest which had held the little band of pioneers together amid their privations and their poverty, began to weaken and dissolve, and in its place came an individualism and a materialism that measured progress only in dollars and cents. Harris did not know that his gods had fallen, that his ideals had been swept away...'

Such generalized language is rare as, in the central part of *The Homesteaders*, Stead makes social history into human history. The loss of the 'old spirit' which he lamented all his life even in essays welcoming the west's prosperity is documented by the contrast between the early days when the settlers, who 'each had something that his neighbour lacked' gladly exchanged equipment, visited, and organized activities from baseball games to church services; and the unfriendly times of prosperity, in which mean-spirited Mrs Riles demands payment for helping her neighbour by making butter, and successful men like Harris, 'too busy' for religion, see 'in picnics and baseball games only an unprofitable use of time.'

Stead shows even the patterns of settlement changing. Though the opening of the new frontier in Alberta 'revived rich old memories' of 'the courage and the comradeship and the conquering' of his youth in Harris, what Stead presents is a collection of con-men and greedy victims of 'the land fever,' accompanied by wild cowboys and remittance men, answering 'the call of the new land,' rather than the sober pioneers like McCrae who selflessly helped each other to build Manitoba.

Similarly, the character of John Harris is built up by small touches, such as the contrast between the poor man who drove through blizzards from Emerson and lost all his profits buying presents for his pregnant wife; and the rich, but spiritually impoverished man who begrudged his wife the smallest share of the wealth she helped to amass as well as the independence of body and mind it represented.

Without false sentimentality, Stead evokes the pathos of the 'successful' pioneer's life. He makes clear its emptiness and confusion as, still 'sincerely working for the greatest good to his family' but crushed by 'twenty-five years of pitched battle with circumstances' he comes to define that good only in terms of more and more wealth. Not understanding the world he has made, he feels betrayed when his family rejects the ends which have made him, not a father, but 'just the boss — the foreman on the farm.'

Though the secondary characters such as Gardiner, Jim Travers, and the stalwart Mountie, Sergeant Grey, are one-dimensional, the stock figures of western romance, the disintegrating family, and the pressures within it, are well realized. Sympathy is created, not only for Harris, but for Mary in her unwilling rebellion as she realizes that ' "I've slaved and saved until I'm an — an old woman, and what better are we for it?" '; and especially for Beulah, whose stunted life is most fully revealed when she is unable to define the better life she longs for, knowing only it has something to do with the neighbours, the Grants, who use a clean white linen tablecloth and discuss foreign affairs.

Stead controls the pathos of the situation by setting forth its irony. Unconsciously, Harris chooses his own destruction; as Mary comments bitterly, ' "He knows our life isn't complete, and he thinks more money will complete it." ' While he criticizes 'this younger generation' for seeming to reject his values, Harris cannot recognize his own hopes when Beulah repeats them. He even forbids her to relive her parents' life with Jim Travers because, as a wealthy farmer, he wants 'something better' than a farmer, or worse yet a hired man, for his daughter — another proof of the loss of the west's 'old spirit' to false, materialistic values.

Stead the optimist refuses to develop the full implications of this irony, just as he glosses over physical difficulties with the assurance that pioneer life, however hard, 'was also a life of courage, of health, of resourcefulness, of a wild, exhilarating freedom found only in God's open spaces.' The potential tragedy is averted, on the plot level by the shock of the highly-coloured events which close the book, but on the psychological level, more convincingly, by Harris' realization that his old friends, the Arthurs, 'have found something that we missed.' The happy ending may seem an artistic flaw to readers reared on bleaker fictions; certainly it ensures that *The Homesteaders* concludes on a human, not symbolic level. Yet this is Stead's important achievement — that he gives human life to an era and an idea. *The Homesteaders* is less than a great work of art; but it is more than a sentimental relic of a less sophisticated age.

The author's description of *The Bail Jumper*, in a letter to the British publishing house of Unwin in 1912, sums up his second novel as well: 'Although a Western tale there is nothing "Wild West" about it, because the Wild West of literature owes its existence almost entirely to the imagination of certain long-bow novelists. I have simply tried to paint prairie life as true to conditions as my ability will permit.' As a significant part of Canada's social and cultural history, *The Homesteaders* deserves to be taken out of the trunk.

Select Bibliography

POETRY AND NOVELS

The Bail Jumper London: Unwin 1914; and Toronto: Briggs 1914

The Copper Disc New York: Doubleday 1931

The Cow Puncher New York: Harper 1918

Dennison Grant Toronto: Musson 1920 A substantially re-written version, *Zen of the Y.D.*, was offered for serial publication by the Western Newspaper Union in 1923, and was published in London by Hodder and Stoughton (n.d.).

The Empire Builders and Other Poems Toronto: Briggs 1908

Grain Toronto: McClelland 1926 New edition, with an introduction by Thomas Saunders, Toronto: McClelland and Stewart 1963 (New Canadian Library).

The Homesteaders: A Novel of the Canadian West London: Unwin 1916; and Toronto: Musson 1916

Kitchener and Other Poems Toronto: Musson 1916

Neighbours Toronto: Hodder 1922

Prairie Born and Other Poems Toronto: Briggs 1911

The Smoking Flax Toronto: McClelland 1924

Songs of the Prairie Toronto: Briggs 1911

Why Don't They Cheer? London: Unwin 1918

STEAD PAPERS

Stead's papers, donated to the Public Archives by his son, Robert A. Stead, contain a variety of his articles, as well as letters, manuscripts, diaries, and reviews. The articles and ms with most relevance to this introduction are:

'Early Days Out West,' 1925, Stead Papers

'Has Romance Gone from the Canadian West?' 1925, Stead Papers

'Literature as a National Asset,' *The Dome* I: 13, Dec. 1928, 18-19

'Manitoba in the Early Eighties,' *The School*, May 1936

'The Romance of the Royal Mounted,' *The Canada Gazette*, 23 June 1927, 275, 284. Also published in *The Farmer's Advocate*, 30 June 1927; and *The Rotarian*, July 1927

'Origin and Trend of Canadian Literature,' Cornwall (England), *Gazette and News*, 23 Sept. 1931

'Prairie Farm' Unpublished ms. Stead Papers. Public Archives of Canada, Ottawa. This is the final version of a novel existing in several earlier drafts, variously titled 'Dry Water' and 'But Yet the Soil Remains.'

CRITICISM

Bowker, Kathleen K. 'Robert Stead: An Interview,' *Canadian Author and Bookman*, V: 4 (April 1923), 99

Eggleston, Wilfrid *The Frontier and Canadian Letters* Toronto: Ryerson 1957

Elder, A.T. 'Western Panorama: Settings and Themes in Robert J.C. Stead,' *Canadian Literature* 17 (Summer 1963), 44-56

McCourt, Edward A. *The Canadian West in Fiction* rev. ed.; Toronto: Ryerson 1970, 94-100

Saunders, Thomas 'Introduction' to *Grain* Toronto: McClelland and Stewart 1963 (New Canadian Library)

The Homesteaders

Robert J.C. Stead

CONTENTS

THE HOMESTEADERS

PRELUDE

SIX little slates clattered into place, and six little figures stood erect between their benches.

"Right! Turn!" said the master. "March! School is dismissed"; and six pairs of bare little legs twinkled along the aisle, across the well-worn threshold, down the big stone step, and into the dusty road, warm with the rays of the Indian summer sun.

The master watched them from the open window until they vanished behind a ridge of beech trees that cut his vision from the concession. While they remained within sight a smile played upon the features of his strong, sun-burned face, but as the last little calico dress was swallowed by the wood the smile died down, and for a moment he stood, a grave and thoughtful statue framed within the white pine casings of the sash. His sober grey eyes stared unseeing into the forest, while the light wind that stirred the golden maple leaves toyed gently with his unruly locks.

His brown study lasted only a moment. With a quick movement he walked to the blackboard, caught up a section of sheepskin, and began erasing the symbols of the day's instructions.

"Well, I suppose there's reward in heaven," he said to himself, as he set the little schoolroom in order. "There isn't much here. The farmers will pay a man more to doctor their sick sheep than to teach their children. But, of course, they get both mutton and wool from a sheep. I won't stand it longer than the spring. If others can take the chance I can take it too. If it were not for her I would go to-morrow."

The last remark seemed to unlink a new chain of thought. The grey eyes lit up again. He wielded the broom briskly for a minute, then tossed it in a corner, fastened the windows, slipped a little folder into his pocket, locked the door behind him, carefully placed the key under the stone step where the first child in the morning would find it, and swung in a rapid stride down a by-path leading from the little schoolhouse into the forest.

Ten minutes' quick walking in the woods, now glorious in all their autumn splendour, brought him to a point where the sky stood up, pale blue, evasive, through the trees. The next moment he was at the water's edge, and a limpid lake stretched away to where the forests of the farther shore mingled hazily with sky and water. The point where he stood was a little bay, ringed with water-worn stones and hemmed around by the forest, except for one wedge of blue that broadened into the distance. He glanced about, as though expecting someone; he whistled a line of a popular song, but the only reply was from a saucy eavesdropper which, perched on a near-by limb, trilled back its own liquid notes in answer.

"I may as well improve the moments consulting my chart," he remarked to his undulating image in the water. "This thing of embarking on two new seas at once calls for skilful piloting." He seated himself on a stone, drew from his pocket the folder, and spread a map before him.

In a few moments he was so engrossed that he did not hear the almost noiseless motion of a canoe as it thrust its brown nose into the blue wedge before him. The canoe slid with its own momentum gracefully through the quiet waters, suddenly revealing a picture for the heart of any artist. Kneeling near its stern, her paddle held aloft and dripping, her brown arms and browner hair glistening in the mellow sun, her face bright with the light of its own expectancy, was a lithe and beautiful girl. In an instant her eye located the young man on the bank, and her lips moulded as though to speak; but when she saw how unobserved she was she remained silent and up-right as an Indian while the canoe slipped gently toward the shore. Presently it cushioned its nose in the velvety sand. She rose silently from her seat, and stole on moccasined tip-toes along the stones until she could have touched his hair with her fingers. But her eyes fell over his shoulder on the papers before him.

"Always at your studies," she cried, as he sprang eagerly to his feet. "You must be seeking a professorship. But I suppose you have to be always brushing up," she continued, banteringly. "Your oldest pupil must be—let me see—not less than eight?"

He smothered her banter with his affection, but she stole the map from his fingers.

"I declare, if it isn't Manitoba! What next? Siberia or Patagonia? I thought you were still in the Eastern Townships."

"So I am—in school. But out of school I am spending a good deal of my time in Manitoba, Mary."

She caught a grave note in his voice as he said her name. Seizing his cheeks between her hands she turned his face to her. "Answer me, John Harris. You are not thinking of going to Manitoba!"

"Suppose I say I am?"

"Then I am going too!"

"Mary!"

[4]

"John! Nothing unusual about a wife going with her husband, is there?"

"No, of course, but you know——"

"Yes, I know"—glancing at the ring on her finger. "This still stands at par, doesn't it?"

"Yes, dear," he answered, raising the ring to his lips. "You know it does. But to venture into that wilderness means—you see, it means so much more to a woman than to a man."

"Not as much as staying at home—alone. You didn't really think I would do that?"

"No, not exactly that. Let us sit down and I will tell you what I thought. Here, let me get the cushion. . . . There, that's better. Now let me start at the beginning.

"Until you came here last summer—until all this happened, you know—I was quite satisfied to go on teaching——"

"And I have sown discontent——"

"Please don't interrupt. Teaching seemed as good as anything else——"

"As good as anything else! Better than anything else, I should say. What is better than training the tender child, inspiring him with your ideals——"

"Oh, I know all about that. Until I began to have some genuine ideals of my own I was satisfied with it. But now—well, everything is different."

"I know," she answered. "The salary won't support two. There's the rub."

They sat for some minutes, gazing dreamily across the broad sheet of silver.

"And so you are going to Manitoba?" she said at length.

"Yes. There are possibilities there. It's a gamble, and that is why I didn't want to share it with you—at first. I thought I would spend a year; locate a homestead; get some kind of a house built; perhaps break some land. Then I would come back."

"And you weren't going to give me a word in all those preparations for our future? You have a lot to learn yet, John. You won't find it in that folder, either."

He laughed lightly—a happy, boyish laugh. For weeks the determination to seek his fortune in the then almost unknown Canadian West had been growing upon him, and as it grew he shrank more and more from disclosing his plans to his *fiancee*. Had she been one of the country girls of the neighbourhood, a daughter of the sturdy backwoods pioneers, bred to hard work in field and barnyard, he would have hesitated less. But she was sprung from gentler stock. It seemed almost profane to think of her in the lonely life of a homesteader on the bleak, unsettled plains—to see her in the monotony and drudgery of the pioneer life. He had been steeling himself for the ordeal; schooling himself with arguments; fortressing his resolve, unconsciously, perhaps, with the picture of his own heroism in braving the unknown. And she had scaled every breastwork at a bound, and captured the citadel by the adroit diplomacy of apparent surrender.

She had snatched his confession at an unguarded moment. He had not meant to tell her so much—so soon. As he thought over the wheels he had set in motion their possible course staggered him, and he found himself arguing against the step he contemplated.

"It's a gamble," he repeated. "The agricultural possibilities of the country have not been established. It may be adapted only to buffalo and Indians. They say the Selkirk settlers have seen hardships compared with which Ontario pioneers lived in luxury. . . . We may be far back from civilization, far from neighbours, or doctors, or churches, or any of those things which we take as a matter of course."

"Then you will need me with you, John, and I am going."

She could not mistake the look of admiration in his eyes. "Mary," he said, "you are a hero. I didn't think it was in you. I mean I——"

"A heroine, if you please," she corrected. "But I am not that—not the least bit. I want to go because—because to go with you, even to Manitoba, is not nearly so dreadful as to stay at home without you."

"But come," said the girl, springing lightly to her feet, "we have matters of great moment for immediate consideration."

He was at her heels. One hand resting on his strong arm sufficed to steady her firm body as she tip-toed over the stones. Somewhere in the canoe she found a parcel, wrapped in a white napkin. Under a friendly beech she laid her dainties before him.

In a crimson glory the sun had sunk behind the black forest across the lake. The silver waters had draped in mist their fringe of inverted trees along the shore, and lay, passive and breathing and very still, beneath the smooth-cutting canoe. . . . One by one the stars came out in the heavens, and one by one their doubles wavered and mimicked in the lake. A duller point of light bespoke a settler's cabin on the distant shore.

"And we shall build our own home, and live our own lives, and love each other—always,—only, for ever and ever?" she breathed.

"For ever and ever," he answered.

A waterfowl cut the air in his sharp, whistling flight. The last white shimmer of daylight faded from the surface of the lake. The lovers floated on, gently, , joyously, into their ocean of hope and happiness.

CHAPTER I

THE BECK OF FORTUNE

THE last congratulations had been offered; the last good wishes, somewhat mixed with tears, had been expressed. The bride, glowing in the happy consciousness of her own beauty, and deified by the great tenderness that enveloped her new estate like a golden mist, said her farewells with steady voice and undrooping eyes. Once only, when two frail arms drew her to the great mother-heart that was fighting with joy and unspoken sorrow through its travail of the soul, did their bright rays moisten and tremble like sun-shafts in a pool. It was for the moment only; one hallowing kiss on the dear, white cheek; then, with uplifted head, she said good-bye, and the mother smiled upon her in a pride that was deeper than her pain. The breed that had not feared, a generation back, to cross the seas and carve a province and a future from the forest, was not a breed to withhold its most beautiful and noble from the ventures of the greater West.

It had been a busy winter for John Harris, and this, although the consummation of his great desire, was but the threshold to new activities and new outlets for his intense energies. Since the face and form of Mary Allan had first enraptured him in his little backwoods school district, a vast ambition had possessed his soul, and to-day, which had seemed to be its end, he now knew to be but its beginning. The ready consent of his betrothed to share his life in the unknown wilderness between the Red River and the Rocky Mountains had been a tide which, taken at its flood, might well lead him on to fortune. At the conclusion of his fall term he had resigned his position as teacher, and with his small savings had set about accumulating equipment essential to the homesteader. A team of horses, two cows, a few ducks, geese, and hens; a plough, a wagon, a sleigh, a set of carpenter's tools; a gun, an axe, a compass, a chest of medicine, a box of books; a tent, bedding, spare clothing—these he had gathered together at the village store or at farmers' "sales," and the doing so had almost exhausted the winter and his money. Because his effects were not enough to fill a car he had "doubled up" with Tom Morrison, a fine farmer whose worldly success had been somewhat less than his deserts, and who bravely hoped to mend his broken fortunes where land might be had for the taking. Their car had already gone forward, with Morrison's hired man nestling obviously in the hay, and

two others hid under the mangers. When railways were invented they were excepted from
the protection of the Eighth Commandment.

So John Harris and his bride took the passenger train from her city home, while their
goods and chattels, save for their personal bag-
gage, rumbled on in a box-car or crowded
stolidly into congested side-tracks as the exi-
gencies of traffic required.

At a junction point they were transferred
from the regular passenger service to an immigrant train. Immigrant trains, in the spring
of 'eighty-two, were somewhat more and less
than they now are. The tourist sleeper, with
its comfortable berths, its clean linen, its
kitchen range, and its dusky attendant, restrained to an attitude of agreeable deference
by his anticipation of a gratuity, was a grey
atom of potentiality in the brain of an unknown genius. Even the colonist car, which
has done noble service in later days in the
peopling of the Prairie West, was only in the
early stages of its evolution. The purpose of
immigrant trains was to move people. To supply comforts as well as locomotion was an extravagance undreamed of in transportation.

The train was full. Every seat was taken;
aisles were crowded with standing passengers
who stumbled over bundles and valises with
every pitch in the uncertain road-bed; women
fought bravely with memories too recent to be

healed, and children crowed in lusty abandon or shrieked as they fell between the slippery seats. The men were making acquaintances; the communities from which they came were sufficiently interwoven to link up relationships with little difficulty, and already they were exchanging anecdotes in high hilarity or discussing plans and prospects with that mutual sympathy which so quickly arises among those who seek their fortunes together under strange conditions.

One or two of the passengers had already made the trip to Manitoba, and were now on the journey a second time, accompanied by their wives and families. These men were soon noted as individuals of some moment; they became the centre of little knots of conversation, and their fellow-immigrants hung in reverent attention upon every word from their lips. Their description of the great plains, where one might look as far as the eye could carry in every direction without seeing house or tree or any obstruction of the vision, fell with all the wonder of the Arabian Nights upon the eager company. Stories of the trail, of Red River cart and ox-team, of duck shooting by the prairie sleughs, the whiff of black powder from their muzzle-loaders and the whistle of sharp wings against the sky; of the clatter of wild geese which made sleep impossible, and the yelp of prairie wolves snapping up through the darkness; of thunder and lightning, of tempest and rain, of storm and blizzard and snow and cold—cold that crackled in the empty heavens like breaking glass and withered the cheek like fire; of Indians, none too certain, slipping like moccasined ghosts down the twilight, or peering unexpectedly through cabin windows; of hardship and privation and strength and courage and possibilities beyond the measure of the imagination—these fell from the lips of the favoured old-timers, punctuated with jest and prophecy and nicely-timed intervals of silence.

"And is there no stones there, or stumps?" asked a woman, big of bicep and deep of chest from years of wrestling with the rocks and timbers of Lanark. "Has the bush all been cleared away?"

"Bush? There's no bush to clear. The prairie's as bald as yer table—no reflection on yer cookin', ma good woman, but so it is, excep' for the grass that tickles yer fingers as ye walk an' the pea-vine that up-ends ye when ye're no thinkin'. Bush! Ah've burnt more bush from ma ten-acre clearin' than ye'll find in a dozen counties. 'Deed, ye'll think a little more bush 'd be a guid thing when ye have yer house to build an' a hungry stove to keep roarin' from November to April."

"But whereby do they make their fences, if they ha' no cedar rails?" demanded the woman, still unconvinced.

"Fences? An' why for would ye fence a farm, ye unsociable body? To keep the gophers out? Or to keep the badgers in? Seein' ye have all out-doors for yer cattle, an' the days of the buffalo are over, thanks to the white man's powder an' shot, what would ye have with fences?"

"But are ye sure it has no been all ploughed some time?" persisted the woman, who could not bring herself to believe that Nature, unaided, had left great areas ready for the hand of the husbandman. A life of environment amid forests and rocks had sorely cramped her imagination.

"Ah'm no sayin' for sure, but whoever ploughed it took a man's order. It will be a thousand miles long, Ah'm thinkin', an' nobody knows how wide. Pioneers like you an' me ha' been workin' our hands off in Canada" (it was a trick of the old-timers to think only of the Eastern Provinces as Canada), "an' in a hundred years we have no cleared what'd be a garden patch to that farm out yonder. Ah'm thinkin' it was a bigger Hand than yours or mine that did that clearin'."

"Tell us about the crops," said one of the men passengers. "What like wheat can ye grow?"

"Like corn," said the narrator, with great deliberation. "Heads like ears o' corn. Wheat that grows so fast ye can hear it. Nothin' uncommon to walk into wheat-fields when they's knee-high, an' have to fight yer way out like a jungle."

"Is the Injuns werry big?" piped a little voice. "My pa's go'n'to make me a bone-arrow so I can kill 'em all up."

"That's a brave soldier," said the man, drawing the child to his knee. "But Ah know a better way to fight Indians than with bows an' arrows. D'ye want me to tell ye a story?"

" 'S about Moses?"

"No, Ah ain't quite up-to-date on Moses, but Ah can tell ye a story about a better way to fight Indians than with arrows an' powder. Ah fight 'em with flour an' blankets an' badger-meat, an' it's a long way better."

The child climbed up on the friendly knee, and interested himself in the great silver watch-chain that looped convenient to his fingers. "Go on wif your story, man," he said. "I's listenin'."

And big Aleck McCrae forgot the immigrants crowded around, forgot the lurch of the train and the window-glimpse of forests heavy-blanketed with snow, as he ploughed his fertile imagination and spread a sudden harvest of wonderment before the little soul that clung to his great watch-chain.

Harris and his young bride found much to occupy their attention. Their minds were big with plans, nebulous and indefinite but charged with potentiality, which they should put into effect when they had selected their prairie home. To the young girl, naturally of romantic temperament, the journey of life upon which they had so recently embarked together took on something of the glamour of knightly adventure. Through the roseate lens of early womanhood the vague, undefined difficulties that loomed before her were veiled in a mist of glory, as she felt that no sacrifice could really hurt, no privation could cut too deep, while she was fulfilling her destiny as wife and comrade to the bravest and best of men. The vast plains, heart-breaking in their utter emptiness, could only be full to her—full of life, and love, and colour; full of a happiness too great to be contained. She watched the gaunt trees rising naked from the white forest, and her mind flitted on a thousand miles in advance, while on the cold window-sill her fingers tapped time to the click of the car wheels underneath.

Harris, too, was busy with his thoughts. He measured the obstacles ahead with the greater precision of the masculine mind. To him, love was not a magician's wand to dissolve his difficulties in thin air, but a mighty power which should enable him to uproot them from his path. No matter what stood in the way—what loneliness, what hardship, what disappointment and even disillusionment—he should fight his way out to ultimate victory for the sake of the dear girl at his side. As she watched the wintry landscape dreamily through the window he shot quick glances at her fine face; the white brow, the long lashes tempering the light of her deep magnetic eyes; the perfect nose, through whose thin walls was diffused the faintest pink against a setting of ivory; lips, closed and tender as in the sleep of a little child; chin, strong, but not too strong; and a neck full and beautiful, the whole forming a picture of purity, gentleness, and confidence which set his being aglow with the joy of immeasurable possession. As he thought of her love, her faith, her confidence, he swore in his own big heart that neither harm nor want nor sorrow should come upon her; that through every adversity of life he would be her protector, her champion, her defence. And so in the charm and mirage of their young dream they rode dauntlessly, joyously, into the unknown.

With Ned Beacon, the trusty hired man, in charge of the carload of effects, under the direction of Tom Morrison, Harris was relieved of many duties and responsibilities that would have broken in somewhat rudely on his dream. Traffic was congested with the immigrant movement; cars were side-tracked at nameless places for indefinite periods, but stock had to be fed and cared for; bonds had to be provided, and all the conditions of departmental red tape complied with when the effects entered the United States, for in 1882 the All-Canadian railway was a young giant fighting for life with the mighty rocks of the North Shore route, and railway traffic with the New West was, perforce, billed over American roads. These details and a score of others called for patience, for tact, and a judicious distribution of dollar bills. Harris made a mental note of his obligation to Tom Morrison in the matter. He was shrewd enough to surmise that this was the farmer's very practical wedding gift, but he took debit for it nevertheless.

And so the journey wore on. As day succeeded day to the monotonous rumble of the car wheels the immigrants became better acquainted, and friendships took root that in after years were to brave every storm of adversity and bloom forth in the splendid community of spirit and sacrifice which particularly distinguished the pioneers. But the strain of travel drew heavily upon physical endurance; meals eaten stale from lunch-baskets, or hastily snatched at wayside stations; the cramp of days spent in the crowded seats; lack of exercise and lack of sleep; these laid their heavy finger on the strongest and heartiest. But one night the word went round that daylight would see them back on Canadian soil, and the lagging spirit of the travellers was revived. Someone struck up an impromptu song, parodied from a well-known hymn; men, women, and children joined in the chorus as they caught the words, and rolled it forth with a vigour that vibrated every timber of the car.

> " Oh Prairie Land, sweet Prairie Land,
> Where everyone joins heart and hand,"

they sang, and the sociability of the party seemed to swell with the volume of the song. A bond of human interest, human interdependence—perhaps, even, some phase of human suffering, was already linking them together with links of steel that should withstand every shock of the coming years, and bind together the foundations of a mighty land.

In the cold grey of a March morning, when the sun had not yet dispelled the mists of night, and the fringing woods back from the Red River loomed white and spectral through the frost, they re-entered the Empire, and in a few minutes were detraining at Emerson, the boundary town and gateway to the prairies which for a thousand miles stretched into the mysteries of the unknown.

CHAPTER II

INTO THE WILDERNESS

EMERSON was the gateway of the great invasion. Situated just on the Canadian side of the International Boundary, the "farthest west" of rail communication, on the threshold of the prairie country, it seemed the strategical point for the great city which must arise with the settlement and development of the fertile kingdom of territory lying between the Lake of the Woods and the Rocky Mountains, and between the Forty-ninth Parallel and the unknown northern limit of agriculture. Sixty miles northward, at the junction of the Red and Assiniboine Rivers, Winnipeg was throwing street-tendrils out from her main traffic trunk which marked the route the Indian carts had followed for years as they bore their buffalo hides and pemmican to the Hudson's Bay Company's post at Fort Garry. Winnipeg was to be on the main line of the Canadian Pacific Railway—at least, so the promoters of its town-lot activity affirmed; but Selkirk, still farther north, was already flourishing in the assurance that the railway would cross the river at that point. But the

THE HOMESTEADERS

Canadian Pacific Railway as yet existed mainly upon paper; its advance guard were pouring nitro-glycerine into the rocks of the wild Lake Superior fastnesses, and a little band of resolute men were risking financial disaster in an indomitable effort to drive through a project which had dismayed even the Government of Canada. Some there were who said the Canadian Pacific would never be built, and many there were who said that if built it would always be a charge upon the country—that in the very nature of things it could never become self-supporting.

So while Winnipeg and Selkirk indulged their visions Emerson was already enjoying to the full the prosperity which accompanied the inrush of settlers. Although the immigrants were not wealthy as the term is now understood even in an agricultural community, most of them had enough money to pay for their outfitting and place them on their homesteads ready for operations. Accommodation in Emerson was at a premium; hotel space was out of the question, and even the barest rooms commanded mining-camp prices. Those commodities which the settler must needs have had taken their cue from hotel prices, and were quoted at figures that provoked much thoughtful head-scratching on the part of the thrifty and somewhat close-fisted new arrivals from the East.

Harris left his wife with a company of other women in the Government immigration building while he set out to find, if possible, lodgings where she might live until he was ready to take her to the homestead country. He must first make a trip of exploration himself, and as this might require several weeks his present consideration was to place her in proper surroundings before he left. He soon found that all the hotels were full, and had they not been full the prices demanded were so exorbitant as to be beyond his reach; and even had it been otherwise he would have asked her to share the hardships of the exploration trip rather than leave her amid associations which were all too apparent in the hotel section of the town. The parasites and camp-followers of society, attracted by the easy money that might be wrung in devious ways from the inflowing tide of farmers, were already represented in force, and flaunted brazenly the seamy side of the civilization which was advancing into the New West.

Turning to parts of the town which were less openly engaged in business, legitimate, questionable, or beyond question, Harris inquired at many doors for lodgings for himself and wife, or for his wife alone. The response ranged from curt announcements that the inmates "ain't takin' boarders" to sympathetic assurances that if it were possible to find room for another it would be done, but the house was already crowded to suffocation. Great lines of washing in the back yards, and groups of dirty children splashing in the spring mud, bore testimony to the congestion. The March sun was beating down with astonishing fierceness, and the unside-walked streets were a welter of slush. In two hours Harris, notwithstanding his stout frame and his young enthusiasm, dragged himself somewhat disconsolately back to the immigration building with the information that his search had been fruitless.

At the door he met Tom Morrison and another, whom he recognized as the teller of Indian stories which had captivated the children of his car. Morrison was a man of forty, with a dash of grey in his hair and a kindly twinkle in his shrewd eyes; his companion was a bigger man, of about the same age, whose weather-beaten face bore testimony to the years already spent in pioneer life on the prairie.

"And what luck have ye had?" asked Morrison, seizing the young man by the arm. "Little, I'll be thinkin', by the smile ye're forcin' up. But what am I thinkin' of? Mr. McCrae is from 'way out in the Wakopa county, and an old-timer on the prairie. He knows every corner in the town, I'm thinkin'——"

"Aleck McCrae," said the big man. "We leave our 'misters' east of the Great Lakes.

An' Ah'm not from Wakopa, unless you give that name to all the country from Pembina Crossing to Turtle Mountain. Ah'm doing business all through there, an' no more partial to one place than another."

"What is your line of business, Mr. Mc-Crae?" asked Harris.

"Aleck, I said, an' Aleck it is."

"All right," said the other, laughing. "What is your business, Aleck?"

"My business is assisting settlers to get located on suitable land, an' ekeing out my own living by the process. There's a strip of country in there, fifty miles long by twenty miles wide, that Ah know like you knew your own farm down East. It cost me something to learn it, an' Ah sell the information for part of what it cost. Perhaps Ah can do something for you later, along professional lines. Just now, as Tom here tells me, you're hunting a house for the wife. Ah know Emerson too well to suppose you have found one."

"I haven't, for a fact," said Harris, reminded of the urgency of his mission. "I've tramped more mud this morning than would make a good farm in Ontario, but mud is all I got for my trouble."

"It's out of the question," said McCrae. "Besides, it's not so necessary as you think. What with the bad time our train made, an' the good time the stock-train made, an' the fact

that they started ahead of us, they're in the
yards now. That's a piece of luck, to start
with. 'S nothing unusual for settlers to be
held up here two an' three weeks waiting for
their freight, an' all the time bills piling up an'
cash running down in a way that knocks holes
in their pockets."

"But I can't put my wife in a stock-car!"
protested Harris.

"There's worse places," McCrae answered,
calmly worrying a considerable section from a
plug of black chewing tobacco. "Worse places,
Ah should say. Ah've seen times when a good
warm stock-car would have passed for heaven.
But that ain't what Ah have in mind. We'll
all turn in an' get the stock unloaded, hitch up
the horses, pack a load, an' get away. Morrison's hired man'll drive his team, an' Tom'll
stay here himself an' look after the rest of the
stuff. Ah've been making a canvass, an' Ah
find we have six or seven families who can be
ready to pull out this afternoon. An soon as
we get into settled country, perhaps we can
get accommodation, such as it is, along the
way. But my team will go along, with a good
tent an' some cooking outfit. Everyone has
bedding, so we're all right for that. Now, if
we all hustle we can be started by four o'clock,
an' out ten or twelve miles before we pitch
camp. That's far enough for the horses the
first day, anyway. How does it suit you?"

"What do you say, Mr. Morrison?"

"I think Aleck's plan is best. I've my wife and the two girls, and there's no roof for their heads here. I can find a place for myself, but I've got to get them started. Ned is a trusty man; he will drive my team. It suits me."

"But after we get there?" said Harris. "For my part, I don't know where I'm going. Even with Aleck's help it will take some time to look up my land and build a place to live in. Mind you," he said, as if forestalling a question in their minds, "I'm mightily obliged for the kindness of your offer, and it isn't myself I'm thinking about."

"Hoots, man!" said Morrison. "We ken who you're thinkin' about, right well. And a poor man ye'd be if ye didn't, for a bonnier lass never came out of Canada, and that's saying somethin'. But she'll be all right out there, and a deal better than if you left her here. There's not many settlers with houses in the country yet, Aleck tells me, but there's a few, and it's wonderful the e-las-ticity of a shanty on the prairie."

"Tom's right," said McCrae. "We haven't many of the conveniences of civilization out there yet, but we haven't the narrowness or vices either, an' your wife'll be both welcome an' safe in any farmer's home. Now, if it's all settled," continued McCrae, who had the leader's knack of suppressing indecision at the psychological moment, "we'll all turn in with the unloading of the stock."

Harris ran to tell his wife that they were to join a party for "the front" that very afternoon. She received the news joyously. Her only fear had been that she would be left behind during the weeks in which her husband made his exploration of the country.

In a few minutes all hands, both men and women, were busy at the cars. The horses, stiff and sore after their long journey, stalked rheumatically down the gangway. Feeling solid ground beneath their feet, they shook their heads vigorously, as though to rid them of the rumble of the cars, and presently were rolling and stretching in the warm sun. Dogs jumped with muddy paws and boisterous affection upon masters and mistresses; cows lowed, roosters crowed, and pigs emitted little grunts of that supreme happiness peculiar to their race. Many hands made the work light, and by mid-afternoon six sleighs were loaded for the journey. All the women and children were to go with the party; Morrison and one or two hired men would remain in Emerson, complete the unloading, and take charge of the effects until the teams should return from their long journey. McCrae, on account of his knowledge of the town and of the needs of the journey, was chosen to secure the supplies. His own team, which had wintered at Emerson, was to take the lead, and in his sleigh were a large tent, some cooking equipment, and an assortment of eatables, consisting mainly of dried meat, lard, beans, molasses, bread, flour, oatmeal, and tea. McCrae provided his team and equipment without charge; the cost of the provisions was reckoned up and divided among the immigrants in their various proportions to the whole party.

Each settler's sleigh carried that which seemed most indispensable. First came the settler's family, which, large or small, was crowded into the deep box. McCrae made them pack hay in the bottom of the sleigh-boxes, and over this were laid robes and blankets, on which the immigrants sat, as thickly as they could be placed. More robes and blankets were laid on top, and sacks stuffed very full of hay served the double purpose of cushioning their backs and conveying fodder for the animals. Such space as remained was devoted to grain for the horses, bundles of clothing and boxes of dishes, kitchen utentils, and family effects. In one of the sleighs a pig was quartered, and in another was a crate of hens which poked their heads stupidly through the cracks, blinking at the bright light. Behind the sleighs were tethered the cattle.

Morrison came up to Harris's sleigh, and gave it an approving inspection.

"You will all be fine," he said, "and a great

deal better than wearyin' about here. Besides, you're just as well to be away," he added, in a somewhat lower voice. "McCrae tells me if this sun keeps up the roads will be gone before we know it, and that means a delay of two or three weeks. There's been a tremendous snow this winter, and a steady thaw, what with these north-runnin' rivers, means floods on the low-lyin' lands, and perhaps in the town itself, McCrae tells me he's none too sure about the bridge."

At this moment McCrae himself joined the group. "There's only two in your party, Harris," he said, "an' while Ah don't want to interrupt your honeymoon, there's another passenger to be taken care of. Dr. Blain is going with us, and Ah'm going to put him in your charge. He's a bit peculiar, but Ah don't think he'll give you any trouble. It's just a case of being too much of a good fellow. One thing Ah know—he's a doctor. Saw him last fall on a scarlet fever job. Settler's sod shack, twenty miles from nowhere. Three children down, mother down, father frantic. Well, Ah know that Blain camped right there in the thick of it; doctored, nursed, cooked, kep' house—did everything. An' they're all of 'em alive an' well to-day, or were when last Ah saw them. So he's worth more'n a speaking acquaintance, Harris; you may know that better some day. Ah'm going up town for him now; you can shift your stuff a little an' make room."

The whole party were ready for the road and waiting before McCrae appeared again. When he came a companion staggered somewhat uncertainly by his side.

"I'm aw'right, McCrae," he was saying. "I'm aw' right. Shay, whash thish? Shildren 'v Ishrul?"

"Come now, Doctor, straighten up. Ah want to introduce you."

"Introdush me? Thash right. Make me 'cquainted wish the ladish. How juhdo, Princhessh?" he said, stopping and gesticulating before an imaginary figure. "Thish is Dr. Blain, late of—late of—wash that, McCrae? Oh, very good. I'm aw' right."

Half leading and half pulling, McCrae at last brought the doctor to Harris's sleigh. "Sorry he's in this shape," he whispered. "He'll likely go to sleep, an' be all right when he wakes up. Ah can't take him in my sleigh, an' Ah feel sure you can handle him."

"I'll do the best I can," said Harris, though he was little pleased with the prospect.

"Straighten up, Doctor," said McCrae, giving him a good poke in the ribs. "This is Mr. Harris, who you will travel with—Jack Harris. An' Mrs. Harris."

The doctor had glanced only casually at Harris, but at the mention of the woman's name he straightened up and stood alone.

"Glad to meet you, madam," he said. "And it's only proper that the pleasure should be all mine." There was a little bitterness in his voice that did not escape her ear.

"But indeed I am glad to meet *you*," she answered. "Mr. McCrae has been telling us something of your work among the settlers. We are very fortunate to have you with us."

He shot a keen look into her face. She returned his gaze frankly, and he found sarcasm neither in her eyes nor her voice.

"Help me in, McCrae," he said. "I'm a bit unsteady. . . . There now, my bag. Don't move, Mrs. Harris. . . . I think we are quite ready now, are we not?"

"Most remarkable man," whispered McCrae to Harris. "Wonderful how he can pull himself together."

McCrae hurried to his own sleigh, called a cheery "All ready!" and the party at once proceeded to get under way. This was not accomplished without difficulty. The cattle showed no disposition to follow the sleighs, but hung back, pulling on their ropes with amazing strength. One or two, in an excess of stubbornness, sat down in the snow and had to be dragged bodily. The settlers had three or four dogs along, but it was not considered safe to let them get at the cattle, lest the frightened animals should break their ropes and occasion further delay. The situation was only relieved by a number of men following behind, prodding vigorously and twisting the tails of the most recalcitrant. Presently the cows began to swing along, and, finding that no harm befell them, they soon settled into a slow but steady gait, and gave no more trouble until they began to tire with their travel.

The horses, too, had their own difficulties. Jaded and nervous with their long trip in the cars, and strange to the air and surroundings, they fidgeted and fretted, and soon the sweat-line was creeping up their backs. The sleigh trails stood high over the level of the surrounding prairie, and the horses were continually slipping off. The snow packed in hard balls under their feet, and at intervals the drivers were obliged to get out and clear it away. The March sun, which had shone down with such fierce heat during the middle of the day, now swung far to the westward, facing the travellers over an ocean of snow stretching away into the unknown. The day grew colder; women and children drew blankets tighter about them, and huddled lower in the sleighs to escape a sharp wind that slipped silently down from the north, carrying a ground-drift of icy particles in its breath.

Harris's thoughts were on his team, on the two cows trudging behind, and on the multiplicity of arrangements which his new life would present for decision and settlement. But his wife gazed silently out over the ocean of snow. The rays of the sun fell gratefully on her cheeks, pale and somewhat wan with her long journey. But the sun went down, and the western sky, cloudless and measureless, faded from gold to copper, and from copper to silver, and from silver to lead. Turning uncomfortably in her crowded seat the girl could see, far beyond the last of the teams, the road over which they had travelled, stretching away until it lost itself, a point in the gathering darkness. To the west it lost itself over the shoulder of the prairie. . . . The men had ceased to shout to each other; the cattle plodded uncomplainingly; silently they moved in the midst of a silence expanding into the infinite. It was her first sight of the prairie, and a strange mixture of emotions, of awe, and loneliness, and a certain indifference to personal consequences, welled up within her. Once or twice she thought of home—a home so far away that it might have been in another planet. But she would not let her mind dwell on it for long. She was going to be brave. She had talked with the other women on the train and in the town. They were women from Ontario farms, some of them well into middle life, women who had known the drudge of unremitting toil since childhood. Their speech was faulty; their manners would not have passed muster amid her old associations; but their quiet optimism was unbounded, their courage was an inspiration. She too would be brave! For the sake of the brave man who sat at her side, guiding his team in the deepening darkness; for the sake of the new home that they two should build somewhere over the horizon; for the sake of the civilization that was to be planted, of the nation that must arise, of the manhood and womanhood of to-morrow—she would be brave. Deep in her heart she swore she would be brave, even while a recreant tear stole forth unbidden and froze into a little pearl of pathos on her cheek.

A bright star shone down from the west; one by one they appeared in the heavens. . . . It grew colder. The snow no longer caked on the horses' feet; the sleigh-runners creaked and whined uncannily.

Suddenly a strange sound came down on the north wind—a sound that made the girl who had just been vowing to be brave nestle still closer to the big man at her side, and his arm fell protectingly about her. It was a succession of sharp barks like those of a dog, but the barks presently ran together in a long, doleful howl that rose in a high crescendo on the night air, and then slowly died away into a minor note that seemed to echo back and forth across the plain. As it died out in one point of the compass it was taken up in another, until the little party wending its way in the darkness seemed altogether surrounded by it.

"What is it?" whispered the girl. "What is it, Jack? Do you know?"

"I don't know," said the man. "It sounds like—wolves."

"Don't be alarmed, Mrs. Harris," said a quiet voice. Looking around they found the doctor sitting up in the sleigh. He had fallen asleep as soon as the journey started, and they had almost forgotten his presence.

"Don't be alarmed," he repeated. "Their howl is the only terrifying thing about them. Prairie wolves are very different from their cousins of the woods. They fill the night air with their howling, but they are cowardly brutes and would rather run than fight."

"I suppose you have had some strange experiences with animals of the prairies," said the girl, with a brave effort to appear at ease, but before the doctor could answer the team came to a sudden stop. The sleigh in front was obstructing the road, and the party closed up in solid formation.

"Camp Number One," called Aleck McCrae, from the head sleigh. "The horses and cattle are tired, an'——"

"And the captain is hungry," put in Ned Beacon. "Isn't that right?"

"Well, Ah *am* nursing a young appetite," admitted Aleck, exhibiting the slack of his belt. "Now, run these sleighs up in two rows," and Aleck indicated where he wanted them placed. "It's hard on the horses an' cattle, after the warm cars, but they'll stand it to-night if they're well blanketed. To-morrow night we'll be among the Mennonites, with a chance of getting stable room."

Under Aleck's direction the sleighs were run up in two rows, about twenty feet apart, facing the north. Two sleighs were then run across the opening at the north end, so that altogether they formed a three-sided court. Men with shovels quickly cleared the snow from the northerly portion of the court, and there the tent was pitched. On the south side of the tent, where they were sheltered from the north wind, the horses and cattle were lined up as closely as they could be crowded. Horse blankets, buffalo robes, rag carpets, and even family bedding, were tied about the animals. The horses were supplied with hay and oats and the cattle with hay alone, and after eating they lay down for the night, and were soon blowing and heaving in a warm fog of comfort.

Meanwhile inside the tent was a scene of great activity. The ground was covered with blankets, robes, and bedding. A lantern from the centre pole sent wedge-shaped shadows darting back and forth; the camp stove was set up, and a fire from wood which McCrae had brought along was soon crackling in it. Pots and pans were produced; women eager to be of service swarmed about the stove, and children, free at last of their muffling wraps, romped in high-laughtered glee among the robes or danced back and forward with the swinging shadows.

"Now this won't do at all," said McCrae, returning from an inspection of affairs outside. "Too many cooks, you know. Ah want one woman here. Everybody else sit down."

The captain's word was recognized as law. He selected an able-looking settler's wife as assistant cook, while the others, men, women, and children, sitting down, seemed to fill the tent to the limit of its capacity.

Savoury smells soon were coming from hot frying-pans, as sliced ham, with bread and gravy, was served up in tin plates and passed about the tent. Everybody—married men and women, maidens and young men, girls, boys, and little children—was ravenously hungry, and for a few minutes little could be heard but the plying of the viands. But as the first edge of hunger became dulled the edge of wit sharpened, and laughter and banter rollicked back and forward through the tent. The doctor, now quite sober, took a census, and found the total population to be twenty-eight. These he classified as twelve married, eight eligible, seven children, and himself, for whom he found no classification.

"You have a head for figures, Harris, I think," he said. "How much space can be allotted to each?"

Harris found that the tent was twelve by eighteen feet, and that about eight feet of floor space would be available for each person, if they moved the stove out.

"The space is sufficient, but the ventilation isn't," said the doctor, as he set about opening ventilator flaps. "If I am to be responsible for your health there are just two rules to follow. Do whatever Aleck McCrae tells you, and don't be afraid of fresh air, even with frost in it."

The tin plates had gone back to McCrae, and were returning, loaded this time with bread and molasses. A steaming cup of tea accompanied each plate. Fortunately there was milk for the children, two of the cows having contributed this important item of the commissariat.

When the meal was over and the dishes washed and packed, Aleck made another round of the camp before settling down for the night. Meantime mothers gathered their families about them as best they could; the little ones sleepily mumbled their prayers, and all hands, young and old, nestled down like a brood of tired chickens under the white wings of the protecting tent. Outside the ground-drift sifted gently about the sleighs, the cows sighed in contentment, and the wolves yapped to each other in the distance.

CHAPTER III

THE afternoon that has just been described was typical of the days that were to follow as the immigrant party laboured its slow pilgrimage into the Farther West. True, they entered on the very next day a district having some pretence of settlement, where it was sometimes possible to secure shelter for the women and children under hospitable Mennonite roofs. The peculiar housekeeping principles of this class of settlers, however, which involved the lodging of cattle and horses in the same building with the human members of the family, discouraged too great intimacy with them, and for the most part the new-comers preferred the shelter of their own tent. They soon emerged from the Red River Valley, left the vast, level, treeless plain behind them, and plunged into the rolling and lightly wooded Pembina region. Here clumps of small willows and, where repeated fires had not destroyed them, light bluffs of slender poplars afforded a measure of protection, and from the resources of the few scattered settlers already in the country they were able to replenish their supplies of fodder for the stock, and even to add to their own larder. Fortunately the wind continued to blow from the north, and, although the sun shone with astonishing fierceness in the middle of the day, the snow thawed but little and the trail remained passable. Other parties of settlers, wending, their way westward to the region where homesteads were still available, or moving in to lands located the previous year, were overtaken; and again the party were themselves overtaken by more rapid-moving immigrants from behind, so that in the course of four or five days their cavalcade stretched far ahead and far to the rear. Acquaintanceships were made quickly—no one stood on ceremony; and as the journey wore on the Harrises began to feel that they already possessed many friends in the country, and that life on the prairie would not be altogether lonely.

After numerous consultations with McCrae, Harris had arranged that his immediate destination should be in a district where the scrub country melted into open prairie on the western side of the Pembina. The Arthurses, who were also of the party, had homesteaded there, and Fred Arthurs had built a little house on the land the year before. Arthurs was now bringing his young wife to share with him the privations and the privileges of their new home. A friendship had already sprung up between

Mrs. Arthurs and Mrs. Harris, and nothing seemed more appropriate than that the two women should occupy the house together while Harris sought out new homestead land and Arthurs proceeded with the development of his farm. It was McCrae, whose interest in every member of the expedition was that of a father, that dropped the germ of this suggestion into Arthurs' receptive ear, and it was with paternal satisfaction he found the young couples speedily work out for themselves the arrangements which he had planned for them all along.

After the crossing of the Pembina the party began to scatter—some to homesteads already located; others to friends who would billet them until their arrangements were completed. As team after team swung out from the main road a certain sense of loss was experienced by those who were left, but it was cheery words and good wishes and mutual invitations that marked each separation. At length came the trail, almost lost in the disappearing snow, that led to Arthurs' homestead. A quick handshake with McCrae, Ned Beacon, and the doctor, and a few others who had grown upon them in the journey, and the two young couples turned out to break their way over the little-used route that now lay before them.

Darkness was settling down—darkness of the seventh night since their departure from Emerson—when, like a mole on the face of the plain, a little grey lump grew on the horizon. Arthurs rose in his sleigh and waved his fur cap in the air; Harris sent back an answering cheer; the women plied their husbands with questions; even the horses took on new energy, and plunged desperately through the frozen snow which one moment supported their weight and the next splintered in broken ice-cakes beneath them. Slowly the mole grew until in the gathering shadows it took on indistinctly the shape of a building, and just as the rising moon crested the ridge of the Pembina hills the travellers swung up at the door. Arthurs had carried the key of the padlock in his hand for the last mile; everybody was out of the sleighs in a moment, and the next they were stamping their cramped feet on the cold wooden floor of the little shack. Arthurs walked unerringly to a nail on the wall and took down a lantern; its dull flame drove the mist slowly down the glass, and presently the light was beating back from the glistening frost which sparkled on every log of the little room.

"Well, here we are in Hungry Hall," said Arthurs. "Everything just as I left it." Then, turning to his wife, "Come, Lil," he said. "Jack, perhaps you have an engagement of your own." He took his wife in a passionate embrace and planted a fervent kiss upon her lips, while Harris followed his example. Then they sat down on the boxes that served for

chairs, amid a happiness too deep for words.
. . . So the minutes passed until Mrs. Arthurs
sprang to her feet. "Why, Mary," she exclaimed, "I do believe you're crying," while
the moisture glistened on her own cheek.
"Now, you men, clear out! I suppose you
think the horses will stable themselves? Yes,
I see you have the box full of wood, Fred.
That's not so bad for a start. Leave some
matches, and say, you might just get our boxes
in here. Remember we've lived in these clothes
for the best part of two weeks."

The young men sprang to their task, and as
soon as they were out of the house the girls
threw their arms about each other and wept
like women together. It was only for a moment; a quick dash of the hand across the eyes,
and both were busy removing coats and wraps.
The door opened, and their "boxes," as well as
other equipment from the sleighs, were carried
in, and the men disappeared to the little stable
at the back of the house. After several attempts the girls succeeded in starting a fire in
the rusted stove, and soon its grateful heat
was radiating to every corner of the room. As
they busied themselves unpacking dishes and
provisions they had opportunity to take observations of the new place that for one was to
be a home and for the other a very welcome
haven in a strange land.

The house was built of poplar logs, hewed

and dovetailed at the corners with the skill of
the Ontario woodsman. It was about twelve
by sixteen feet in size, with collar-beams eight
feet from the floor. The roof was of two thick-
nesses of elm boards, with tar-paper between.
The floor was of poplar boards. The door was
in the east side, near the south-east corner; the
stove stood about the centre of the east wall.
The only window was in the south; six panes
of eight-by-ten glass sufficed for light. Through
this window another lantern shone back from
the darkness, and the flickering light from the
stove danced in duplicate. A rough board
table sat under the window; a box nailed in the
south-west corner evidently served as cupboard. No tools or movables of any value had
been left in the place, Arthurs having stored
such effects with a neighbour, some dozen miles
away, lest they be stolen from the cabin by
some unscrupulous traveller during his absence.

"I like the plan of it very much," said Mrs.
Arthurs, after a general survey of the room.
"Don't you think Fred has shown good judgment in the design? This"—indicating the
door—"will be my reception-room. And this,
a little further in, is the parlour. The kitchen
and pantry are right at hand—so convenient
for the maid in serving, you know. And then
our rooms. Fred and I will have the long room
in the north-west wing, while you, of course,

will occupy the guest-chamber in the northeast. Do not be alarmed, my dear; if the silence of the prairies weighs too heavily upon you we shall be within call. The bath may be reached from either room with equal convenience."

Both laughed, but Mary, more serious and sober-minded, was already slicing ham and greasing a frying-pan. "We need water, Lil— get some snow while I find the tea. The bread is hard, but there'll be coals presently, and we shall have toast. Lucky there were baked potatoes left over from last night's camp; they'll fry up fine along with this——" But already Lil was outside gathering snow.

She returned in breathless excitement. "Oh, Mary, I've just had a great thought. All my wedding china—presents, you know—is in that box, and I have my wedding clothes, too. Have you yours?"

"Of course. But why——"

"Why, dear, don't you see? The men are busy shovelling a path into the stable. It'll be an hour yet before they are in. Let's put on our wedding dresses, and set the table with our best dishes and best linen, just for a kind of post-nuptial. Let's!"

"But ham and friend potatoes!"

"And toast. Didn't you promise toast? And tea. And I'll wager there's some jam among these provisions. Oh, let's hurry."

An hour later, when the hungry men returned after making their horses and cattle comfortable, they stopped in amazement at the sight that confronted them. Snowy linen, delicate china, and sparkling glass returned the soft light from one of those great lamps such as are bought only for presentation; and beside the table, like fairies spirited from a strange land, stood two beautiful women, robed in the delicate draperies of their bridal hour. Exclamations of surprise were drowned in a flood of tender associations, and never in palace or banquet-hall did sweeter content and happiness reign than among these four young pioneers as they sat down to their first home-served meal in the new land.

The days that followed were days of intense activity for both men and women. There was much to do, inside and out. In the interior of the little house an extraordinary change was wrought; simple draperies and pictures relieved the bareness of the walls; shelves were built for the accommodation of many trinkets dear to the feminine heart; a rag carpet covered the centre of the floor; plain but appetising dishes peeked enticingly from behind the paper curtain that now clothed the bare ribs of the cupboard; and a sense of homeliness pervaded the atmosphere. The two men, in their own realm, had found much to occupy them, although for some days the range of their activi-

ties was limited owing to the necessity of giving the horses a much-needed rest before
putting them back into the harness.

A week had passed, and no sign of life, other
than that of the little party itself, had been seen
about the Arthurses' homestead, when one day
Harris's eyes already becoming keen to the
prairie distances, espied a dark point on the
horizon. It grew slowly from a point to a spot,
from a spot to an object, and at length was de-
fined as a man on horseback. Presently Aleck
McCrae drew up at the door.

"Hello, farmers," he cried, "how goes the
battle? An' the good wives? Building a little
Eden in this wilderness, I'll warrant. Tell
them to put another name in the pot, an' a
hungry name at that. I haven't seen a white
woman's meal I don't know when."

The friends gathered about the old-timer,
plying him with questions, which he answered
or discussed until the meal was over, holding
his own business quietly in the background.
But with supper ended, his pipe in his teeth and
his feet resting comfortably in the oven, he
broached his subject.

"Ready for the road in the morning, Jack?
Don't want to break up your little honeymoon,
y' know, but the month is wearing on. Nothing but horseback for it now, an' they do say
the settlers are crowding up something wonderful. The best land's going fast. Most of

them will hold up now, with the roads breaking, but by slipping out on our horses we can locate an' file before the real spring rush opens. You should get some kind of shelter up before the frost is out of the ground, so's to lose no time from ploughing once the spring opens."

Harris needed no urging, and in the early morning the two men, with blankets and provisions, started out on horseback for the still farther West. The snow was now going rapidly; water stood in a thousand pools and ponds on the face of the prairie, or ran with swift noiselessness in the creeks and ravines, although the real "break-up" of the streams would not occur until early in April. By avoiding the sleigh-trails and riding over the open prairie fairly sound footing was found for the horses and a good opportunity given to observe the land. Harris soon found that more judgment was required in the selection of a prairie farm than he had supposed, and he congratulated himself upon having fallen in with so experienced a plainsman as McCrae. On the first day they rode over mile after mile of beautiful country, following the survey stakes as closely as possible, and noting their location from time to time by the lettering on the posts.

"This is good enough for me," said Harris at length, as their horses crested a little elevation from which the prairie stretched away in all directions, smooth as a table. "Isn't it magnificent! And all free for the taking!"

"It's pretty to look at," said McCrae, "but I guess you didn't come West for scenery, did you?"

"Well, what's the matter with it? Look at that grass. If the soil wasn't all right it wouldn't grow native crops like that, would it?"

"The soil's all right," answered McCrae. "Nothing better anywhere, an' you can plough a hundred and sixty acres to every quarter-section. But this is in the frost belt. They get it every August—sometimes July. Shouldn't wonder but it'll be all right in time, when the country gets settled up, but most homesteaders can't afford to wait. We've got to get further West yet, into the higher land of the Turtle Mountain slopes. I know there's good stuff there that hasn't been taken."

And so they pressed on, until, in the bright sunshine, the blue line of the Turtle Mountain lay like a lake on the western horizon. Here McCrae began paying more minute attention to the soil, examining the diggings around badger holes, watching out for clumps of "wolf willow," with always a keen eye for stones and low-lying alkali patches and the general topography of the quarter.

"This is more rolling country, with more land broken up by sleughs an' creeks, but it's good stuff," he said. "It's early to make predictions, but I'll risk one guess. There are two classes of people coming into this country—men who are looking for wheat land, nothing but wheat land, an' men who want some wheat land an' some stock land. I predict that in twenty-five years the wheat farmers will be working for the mortgage companies, an' the stock farmers will be building up bank accounts. Now stock must have water, an' if you can get natural shelter, so much the better. A creek may break your land a little, but it's worth more than it costs."

Many times in their explorations they passed over sections that Harris would have accepted, but McCrae objected, finding always some flaw not apparent to the untrained eye. Once, where a little river had worn its way across the plain, they came on a sod shack, where a settler was already located. "Nice spot," said McCrae, "but too sandy. His farm'll blow away when he breaks the sod. There's an easy crossing there' though, an' perhaps he thinks the railway will hit him when it comes. That's all a gamble. It may go north of the lake; if it does we only bet on the wrong horse. We've got to take our chance on that."

But at length they rode over a quarter where McCrae turned his horse and rode back again. Forward and back, forward and back, they rode the whole hundred and sixty acres, until not a rood of it had escaped their scrutiny. On the south-east corner a stream, in a ravine of

some depth, cut off a triangle of a few acres'
extent. Otherwise it was prairie sod, almost
level, with yellow clay lying at the badger holes.
Down in the ravine, where they had been sheltered from fire, were red willows, choke-cherry
bushes, and a few little poplars and birches;
a winding pond marked the course of the
stream, which was running in considerable
volume. Even as they stood on the bank a
great cracking was heard, and huge blocks of
ice rose to the surface of the pond. Some of
these as they rose turned partly on their edge,
showing two smooth sides.

"Good!" exclaimed McCrae. "There's
some depth of water there. That pond hasn't
frozen solid, or the ice wouldn't come up like
that. That means water all winter for stock,
independent of your well—a mighty important
consideration, which a lot of these land-grab-
bers don't seem to reckon on. Now there's a
good quarter, Jack. I don't say it's the best
there is; they'll be opening up new land that'd
make your teeth water twenty-five years from
now. But we can't explore the whole North-
West, an' you're far enough from the railroad
here. This coulee will give shelter for your
stock in raw weather, an' there's a bench looks
at though it was put there for your little house.
There's light timber to the north, fit for fuel
an' building, within fifteen miles, an' there'll be

neighbours here before the summer's over, or I'm no prophet. What do you say?"

"The quarter suits me," said Harris. "And the adjoining quarter is good stuff too. I can take pre-emption right on that. But there's just one thing I'm in doubt about."

"What's that?"

"How I'm going to square it with you for the service you have given. My cash is getting low, and——"

"Don't worry about that. I generally size up my customer an' bill him accordingly. If he has lots of money, an' seems likely to part with it foolishly, I put as much of it as I can in safe keeping. But there isn't any money fee as far as you're concerned. Fact is, I kinda figure on trading this bill out with you."

"Trading it out? How?"

"Well, I expect to be roving this country, east an' west, for some years to come, an' I've a little policy of establishing depots here an' there—places where I can drop in for a square meal an' a sleep an' a bit of Western hospitality. Places, too, if you like, where there are men to say a good word for Aleck McCrae. How's that suit you?"

Harris took his friend's hand in a warm grip. He rightly guessed that McCrae was not bartering his services for hospitality, but was making it easy for Harris to accept them by appearing to bargain for a service in return. So they shook hands together on the side of the bank overlooking the little coulee, and as they looked in each other's eyes Harris realized for the first time that McRae was still a young man. A sense of comradeship came over him—a feeling that this man was more of a brother than a father. With admiring eyes he looked on McCrae's fine face, his broad shoulders, his wonderful physique, and the question he asked sprang from his lips before he could arrest it.

"Why don't you get married, Mac?"

"Who, me?" said McCrae, laughing; but Harris detected a tone in his voice that was not all happiness, and the thought came to him that McCrae's craving for hospitality might root deeper than he supposed.

"It's a long ride to the land office," continued McCrae, "an' you can't file a minute too soon. We'd better find a corner post an' make sure of the number of this section, an' put as much road behind us as we can to-night."

CHAPTER IV

ROUGHING IT

A FTER filing at the land office Harris returned at once to the Arthurses' homestead. The news that the Harrises were to be neighbours within forty miles was received with enthusiasm by both Fred and Lilian Arthurs. But Harris was now consumed with a burning energy; he allowed himself only a precious half-day at the home of the Arthurses, bade his wife an affectionate farewell, and, with a cheery good-bye to the warm friends on the homestead, he was away down the trail to Emerson. By this time the sleighing was gone, and as his wagon was left with the car he rode one horse and led the other, carrying with him harness and such equipment as was absolutely necessary on the road. He expected some trouble from the streams, which were now breaking up in earnest, but he was determined that at all costs he would get his wagon, plough, and tools to the homestead before the frost came out of the ground and left the sod trails absolutely impassable.

On arrival at Emerson one of the first men he met was Tom Morrison. The two pioneers shook hands warmly, and in a few words Harris told of having selected his claim, waxing enthusiastic over the locality in which his lot was to be cast.

"I must get out there myself," said Morrison.

"Do," Harris urged. "There are some other fine quarters in the neighbourhood, and nothing would be better than to have you on one of them."

"Well, we'll see. Now, I've got your wagon loaded ready for the road. I couldn't get all your stuff on, but I loaded what you'll want first, and the balance can come with the rest of mine, so you won't have to make another trip. Ned has been back for some days, and we're ready to pull out too. And the sooner the better. The river is risin' real dangerous like, and if it keeps on this town's goin' to be under water before it knows it. Indeed, it wouldn't surprise me if the bridge went out. So we took the rest of the stuff—yours and mine—out a day's haul on the road. It's in safe hands there, and we can get it later even if the bridge does go. We thought we might as well do that while waitin' for you."

"Waiting for me?" repeated Harris. "You don't mean to say you have stayed here just on my account?"

"Oh, no; you see, we wanted to get all the stuff out of danger."

But Harris read between the words that honest Tom had valued his interests equally with his own.

The west-bound trip was made in good time, although not without difficulty at some points in the road, and before the 10th of April Harris was back under the shelter of Arthurs' roof. He was for pressing on alone in the morning, but he found that his wife had made all her plans to accompany him and would listen neither to persuasion nor reason.

"No, Jack," she said, gently but firmly setting all his entreaties aside. "I'm not going to let you do all the pioneering. I'm going with you."

"But, Mary, there's no house, and no shelter, and no neighbours—nothing but sky and grass as far as you can see."

"All the more reason I should go," she answered. "If you have to rough it in the open you at least deserve your meals cooked for you, and such other help as a woman can give. We will take the cows—one of them is milking now; the calf will have to go in the wagon; but we'll have lots of milk, and I'm sure we'll get along. But I really must be with you. I really must, John, and you know—I'm going."

So at last he consented. The supplies of provisions were increased; room for the calf was found somewhere in the wagon, and together they set out to wrestle their fortunes from the wilderness.

On arrival at the homestead the young wife immediately gave evidence that she intended to bear her full share of the pioneer's duties. A comparatively dry spot was found among the little poplars, and here she built a tent with blankets and a bit of rag-carpet that came in most handy for such purposes. Their stove was set up, and although it smoked stubbornly for lack of draught, it furnished heat for cooking, and when Jack returned from tethering the horses the smell of frying ham and hot tea struck his nostrils.

"Well, that's better than rustling for myself, I will admit," he said, as she placed his supper on an improvised table. "But it's mighty rough on you."

"No, it isn't, either. I'm healthy—why, this prairie air gives me an appetite that city people would pay thousands for, and I'm strong—and happy."

He drew her to him, thrilled with the pride of her courage.

That night, before the darkness had gathered too deep, they selected the site of their house on the very bench that McCrae had indicated. It was about an acre in extent, and stood halfway between the prairie level and the bottom of the coulee, where a small river was now running. . . . They would face their house eastward, so it would look over the pond fifty yards from the door, and the bank behind would

shelter it from the north-west winds of winter.
. . . It was quite dark when they sought the
cover of their little tent, and the wolves were
howling far down the ravine.

Presently they were startled by a crashing
noise, as of some big animals rushing upon
them through the poplars, and the horses, in
headlong haste, almost swept over their sleep-
ing-place. On recognizing their master the
animals stood, snorting and shivering.

"That wolf howl put the fear into the silly
brutes," said Harris, speaking calmly, although
his own flesh was creeping just a little. "I
suppose they've ripped their tether ropes to
pieces. Well, we'll tie them down here, where
they'll have company." And he led them back
a short distance into the bushes.

A moment later, suddenly, as if congealed
out of thin air, on the bank right above them,
silhouetted against the dim light in the western sky, stood a horse and rider. Instantly
into Harris's mind came a warning of McCrae:
"Sleep with one eye open when your horses are
tethered out."

Harris had no proof that the strange rider
was a horse thief, but it struck him at the moment that the terror of the horses might not
have been due altogether to wolves. Sometimes these noble animals have an uncanny
instinct for detecting danger.

He stole silently toward the tent. There

was a gun there, loaded with shot for any possible game on the prairie. As he moved in the deep darkness of the valley he stumbled over a root and fell. The same moment came a flash of light on the bank, and Harris heard the "thuk" of a ball burying itself in the sod. He lay perfectly still. The stranger peered into the darkness for a full minute; then, dismounting, began to come cautiously down the hillside. Harris would have rushed for his gun, but he feared to reveal the whereabouts of his wife. So he lay still, and the stranger came on, the glint of his gun-barrel showing in the darkness. It was evident he thought his bullet had found its mark, and he proposed still to possess himself of the horses. But he was taking no chances. Presently he discerned Harris's body on the ground, and again raised his gun to his shoulder. Harris lay in an agony of suspense, praying that the aim would be faulty, and that his assailant would advance until he could spring up and disarm him. Then came another flash, a loud report, a yell from the intruder, who half fell to earth, then scrambled to his feet, rushed up the bank, pulled himself somewhat limply on his horse, and rode into the darkness.

"Oh, Jack, are you killed?" cried the girl, rushing in his direction.

"Not even hurt," he answered; and she fainted in his arms.

He carried her to the tent and applied water to her forehead. As he was engaged in restoring her his hand fell on his gun. The barrel was hot.

He raised her face to his, and kissed her again and again.

In the morning they found a few drops of blood on the grass at the top of the bank.

Harris and his wife allowed themselves no time for nerve-strain over the experience of their first night on their homestead. It was fortunate for them there was so much to do, and that they were thrown entirely upon their own resources. Their little store of money was running very low, and they decided their house must be of the cheapest possible construction. Harris had already discussed his buildings with McCrae, who advised him to make use of sods, and gave general directions how to do so; and he now set about to put McCrae's suggestions into effect. Some fifteen miles north of the homestead was a valley in which grew trees of sufficient size for building purposes—poplars, cottonwoods, elms, and oaks. Farther down the valley, at the head of a lake, was a saw-mill, where boards and shingles might be bought— if one had money.

So this morning, after caring for their cows, they hitched the horses to the wagon, took an axe, a saw, their gun, and a lunch, and set out for the valley, returning late at night with sufficient logs and poles for the framework of their house and stable. The next day construction was commenced. Four stout posts were set on end, enclosing a rectangle twelve by sixteen feet. The tops of the posts were connected by logs laid upon them, dovetailed at the corners after the fashion of woodsmen, and held in position by wooden pins driven in auger-holes. Lengthwise along the centre, to form a ridge-pole, another stout log was laid and the whole framework supported by additional posts, among which were two on the east side to enclose the door. Small poles were then placed on end, sloping slightly inwards, and resting against the plate-logs. Similar poles were laid from the plate-logs to the ridge-pole to support the roof.

Harris found a southern slope where the frost was out enough to admit of him ploughing some sods. He knew he would not get as good a sod here as later in the season might be found in some low-lying spot, but his first consideration was to get some kind of permanent shelter. So he ploughed the sods, three inches thick and fourteen inches wide, and cut them into two-foot lengths with his axe, to the sad injury of its cutting edge. These sods were then built into a wall like bricks, resting gently against the framework of poles, from which, however, they were separated by a padding of grass, which Harris cut in a sleugh with his scythe, and small willows from the ravine. This mattress of grass and willows prevented any earth shaking through into the house itself. A framework made of a hewn log was inserted in the south wall to leave space for a window, which should be bought when the family finances could afford such luxuries. For the time being it would be left open in fine weather and covered with canvas when the elements were gruff or unruly. The rag-carpet, when no longer needed as a tent, would be draped in the doorway, pending the purchase of boards to make a wooden door.

For a roof grass was laid on the poles and covered tightly with sods. Then Harris found a sticky, yellow clay in the side of the ravine, and two or three inches of this he spread carefully over the sods, like icing on a great cake. The greasy clay soon hardened in the sun, and became so impervious to water that the heaviest rains of summer made no impression upon it.

When, save for the missing door and window, the house was finished, they stood in the centre and admired. It was absolutely the product of their own labour, applied to such scanty resources as the prairie provided. But it was warm and snug, and, as they later on learned, the wall and roof of sod were almost perfect non-conductors of either heat or cold. The floor was of earth, but Mary Harris knew the difference between earth and dirt, although the words are frequently confounded, and her house was from the first a model of cleanliness and order.

By this time the snow was all gone, except in north-facing nooks along the ravine, and the frost was out of the sod in all places deep enough to admit of plouging. As the stock were taking no harm from the open air, thanks to the shelter of the ravine, Harris decided to delay the construction of his stable until after seeding and to proceed at once with the plough-ing of his land. He had also to make a trip to Arthurs' for seed grain, and to borrow a couple of sections of drag harrows. With it all, by the middle of May he had sown fifteen acres of wheat, and notwithstanding a heavy snowfall about the 23rd, by the 1st of June he had added ten acres of oats. With his help Mary had planted a small garden of potatoes and vegetables, and a few flowers were springing up at the door of the house.

It was a life of hard, persistent work—of loneliness, privation, and hardship. But it was also a life of courage, of health, of resource-fulness, of a wild, exhilarating freedom found only in God's open spaces. They had learned to know the animals of the field—the cheeky gopher; the silent, over-industrious badger; the skunk, unchallenged monarch of his imme-diate circle; the sneaky coyote, whose terror is

all in his howl; the red fox, softly searching
amid the grass for the nests of ducks or prairie
chicken; and the rabbit, curious but always
gracefully elusive. Then there were the waterfowl, infinite in number. The stuffed ducks on
the dinner-table were limited only by the
amount of powder and shot which Harris cared
to spend on the pond at their door. At night,
when the horses had been unharnessed and
dusk was setting in, he would slip his gun under
his arm and walk down among the willows. It
was necessary only to wait. Two graceful
forms, feeding under a grassy bank, hearing a
slight rustle above, would shove with quick,
silent stroke into the supposed safety of their
native element. Harris would peer through
the dusk for the brighter markings of the male,
for only a game-murderer shoots the female in
the nesting season. Then, as they separated a
little, his gun would speak; a sudden splashing
of water; a sharp whistle of rapid wings cutting
the air; a form, paddling an uncertain circle in
the pond, then lying strangely flat upon the surface. Harris as yet had no dog, and often it
meant stripping and a sharp plunge in the ice-
cold water to bring in the trophy; but the
strong, athletic young man counted that only
part of the sport. At other times the nights
were clamorous with the honking of wild geese,
and in the morning Harris, slipping quietly
over the bank of the coulee, would see the

prairie white as from new-fallen snow with the backs of countless thousands of "wavies." Sometimes the geese, secure in the supposedly unsettled wilderness, relaxed the vigour of their military guard, and on such occasions he could get within range. But if there is one quality the goose lacks it is that which is most attributed to him—foolishness. On his marches through the unmapped desert of the air he moves with the precision of an army in the field, scouting out all the land, taking aerial observations before making camp, and immediately throwing out sentries around his feeding ground. But long-continued immunity from attack breeds carelessness, even in a goose, and the price of such neglect frequently adorned the table in Harris's cabin.

The prairie flowers, too, were a never-ending delight to the heart of the young woman. She knew some of them by name, but many were peculiar to the prairie. The first few warm days of spring had clothed all the wilderness with a magic carpet of pale-purplish blossoms, and the advancing season brought new blooms to view with every passing week. On Sundays, when there was total relaxation from their regular labours, the two, arm in arm, would stroll along the bank of the ravine, or walk, ankle-deep in strawberry blossoms, far over the undulating plain to the west. Returning, they would find their way to the edge of the stream, where, in the shallow crossing, the suckers would dart in all directions in panic at their appearance. Here they would sit and listen to the gentle murmur of the water, while fleecy clouds mirrored themselves in its glassy depths, and plovers ran whistling up and down the bank, and a meadow-lark sent its limpid challenge from a neighbouring bush. And at night, when the moon rose in wonderful whiteness and purity, wrapping field and ravine in a riot of silver, the strange, irresistible, unanswerable longing of the great plains stole down upon them, and they knew that here indeed was life in its fulness—a participation in the Infinite, indefinable, but all-embracing, everlasting.

CHAPTER V

T HE summer was a season of great activity
and development. Harris did not sow
any crop after the 1st of June, but applied himself then to the construction of his
stable, which was built after the same fashion
as the house. The shelter of its cool walls and
roof was gratefully sought by the cows in the
heat of the day, and its comparative freedom
from mosquitoes was a haven to the horses in
the evenings. Then there was more land to
plough, and Harris's soul never dulled to the
delight of driving the ploughshare through the
virgin sod. There was something almost sacred in the bringing of his will to bear upon soil
which had come down to him through all the
ages fresh from the hand of the Creator. The
blackbirds that followed at his heel in long,
respectful rows, solemnly seeking the trophies
of their chase, might have been incarnations
from the unrecorded ages that had known these
broad fields for chase and slaughter, but never
for growth and production. The era of the
near vision, demanding its immediate reward,
had passed away, and in its place was the day

[67]

of faith, for without faith there can be neither seed-time nor harvest.

But it was not only on Harris's homestead that development was taking place. As Mc-Crae had predicted, there was a considerable movement of settlers into the district, and at several points their tents or rude houses now broke the vast sweep of the horizon. Tom Morrison had found land to the satisfaction of his heart within three miles of the Harris homestead, and his big log-house, eighteen by twenty-four, assumed the proportions of a castle by comparison with the smaller homes springing up around. Some miles to the east Dick Matheson, straight from the lumber camps of the Madawaski, had pitched his tent, and a few miles farther on was his friend of the shanties, John Burton. To the west were the Grants, and to the north Hiram Riles and his wife, Eliza. A mixed community they were, drawn from many corners, and all of them more or less under the heel of poverty; but they were filled with enthusiasm, with resourcefulness, and an indomitable determination to face and overcome all obstacles. A missionary had in some way spied out the field, and held monthly Sunday services at Morrison's house; and Dr. Blain, when not in one of his unfortunate debauches, had his headquarters at the new town of Plainville, which consisted of Sempter's general store and a "stopping-place," and which had sprung up near the junction of two streams in anticipation of the railway.

None of these pioneers was possessed of a complete farming equipment, but each had something which his neighbour lacked, and they made common cause together in their struggle with Nature. Thus Harris had no mower, but when haying season came he was able to borrow Morrison's, at the same time lending his plough to Riles, who simultaneously accommodated Morrison with his hay-rack. Among the women exchanging became something of an exact science. Mrs. Grant was the proud possessor of a very modern labour-saver in the shape of a clothes-wringer, as a consequence of which wash-day was rotated throughout the community, and it was well known that Mrs. Riles and Mrs. Harris had to do their churning alternately. But it was Mrs. Morrison's sewing-machine that was the great boon to the community, and to it, perhaps, as much as the open-hearted hospitality of honest Tom and his wife, was due the fact that their house became the social centre of the district.

Nor was the settlement deprived of its share of sport and amusement. On one of his periodical visits McCrae donated a baseball, and Harris quickly shaped a bat from the trunk of a stout willow he found by the river-bed. They had all outdoors to play in, and it was a simple matter to mow the grass from a stretch of level prairie and turn over the sod at points to mark the bases. Unfortunately, there were not enough men in the community to make two baseball teams, but a species of game was devised in which the players batted in turn, and when not batting or base-running were always on the "out" side. Harris developed considerable ability as a pitcher, throwing the powerful straight ball which in those days was a greater menace to the bare hands of the catcher than to the batter at the plate. On the occasion of his monthly visits the missionary, who was an ardent ball-player, generally contrived to reach Morrison's by Saturday afternoon, and so was able to take part in the Saturday night game. And although he never took advantage of his association with the young men to "preach" to them, except on Sundays, a sense of comradeship sprang up, and a standard of sport was established which bore fruit in the community many years later.

And so the first summer wore away and the first harvest was at hand. Any disappointment which had been occasioned by backward conditions earlier in the season was effaced by the wonderful crop which now crowned the efforts of the pioneers. On their finest Eastern farms they had seen nothing to equal the great stand of wheat and oats which now enveloped them, neck-high, whenever they invaded it. The great problem before the settlers was the harvesting of this crop. It was a mighty task to attempt with their scythes, but there was no self-binder, or even reaper, within many miles.

Finally Morrison solved the problem for the whole community by placing an order, at a fabulous figure, for a self-binder from the United States. It was a cumbrous, wooden-frame contrivance, guiltless of the roller bearings, floating aprons, open elevators, and sheaf carriers of a later day, but it served the purpose, and with its aid the harvest of the little settlement was safely placed in sheaf. The farmers then stacked their grain in the fields, taking care to plough double fire-guards, with a burnt space between, as a precaution against the terrifying fires which broke over the prairie as soon as the September frosts had dried the grass. A community some twenty miles to the eastward boasted a threshing mill, and arrangements were made for its use after it had discharged the duties of its own locality. The machine was driven by horse-power, and in the dawn of the crisp November mornings the crescendo of its metallic groan could be heard for miles across the brown prairie. It, too, with its hand feed, its open straw-carriers, its low-down delivery, which necessitated digging a hole in the frozen earth to accommodate the bags,and its possible capacity of six hundred bushels a day, bears mean comparison with its modern successor; but it threshed grain at a lower cost per bushel, and threw less into the straw than has ever been accomplished by the mighty steam and gasoline inventions which have displaced it.

When Harris's threshing was done he found he had six hundred bushels of wheat and seven hundred bushels of oats in cone-shaped piles on his fields. The roads were fine and hard, and no snow had yet fallen, so he determined to begin at once with the marketing of his wheat. His last cent had been spent months before; indeed, it had been only through the courtesy of the storekeeper at Plainville, who was also postmaster, and who had stretched the law to the point of accepting hen eggs as legal tender in exchange for postage stamps, that Mary Harris had been able to keep up the brave, optimistic series of letters written "home." So Harris decided that he would at once market some of his wheat. Most of the oats would be needed for his horses and for seed, and what remained would command good prices from new settlers the following spring, but some of the wheat must be turned into money at once. During the latter part of the summer they had lived exclusively on the produce of their farm; on vegetables from the garden, fish and ducks from the stream, prairie chickens, and an occasional rabbit from the fields. The wild geese had deserted them early in the spring, and returned only after harvest. But now they should have a change on their table. Mary had accepted the pioneer fare of the summer without complaint, but of late Harris had discovered a strange longing in her eyes, and more than once she had arrested herself in the words "I wish we had——" Then two penitent little tears would steal softly down her cheeks, and she would bury her head in his arms as he soothed her with loving words and promised that "after threshing things would be different."

So now he set out for Emerson with the best load his horses could draw. The first few miles he drove in silence, for there was a heavy weight at his heart as he thought of the little wife alone with the responsibilities of the farm. . . . That she would be faithful to every responsibility he knew beyond question. . . . But he was not quite satisfied. A strange moodiness had come over her, and even with him at home she had at times given way to fits of downheartedness which seemed altogether alien to her nature.

But this morning as he drove the well-worn trail, a burnished sun mounted higher and higher ahead of him, and with it his own spirits rose until he found himself whistling and boyishly building castles in the air. But his castles, as he told himself, had solid foundations; indeed, they were not even speculations, but already might be accepted as assured accomplishments. Some things he certainly must do for Mary. First of these was the purchase of a glass window for the house, and next to that he promised enough boards for a door, and perhaps enough to floor part of their little room. Then there should be sugar, and tea, and flour, and warm boots, and some much-needed kitchen utensils. True, he needed some things himself, but his needs could wait. And then there were other things. Oh, he knew what to get. He hadn't been having little conferences with Mrs. Morrison for nothing. . . . A tender smile gently suffused his face, and his cheery whistle soared above the rumble of the wagon-wheels on the hard lumps of the trail.

Ten days later he retraced his course in the teeth of a blinding blizzard. A dozen times he had been lost in the last forty-eight hours, but he had developed the prairie-dweller's sense of direction, and had always been able again to locate the trail. The Arthurs would have detained him, almost by force, but the thought of a pale, patient face, wrung with an agony of anxiety not for itself, made him adamant in his resolve to go home at whatever cost. The roads were almost impassable; he left his lumber at Arthurs', but carried with him his window, a few boards for a door, and a little bundle of drygoods. Everything else had gone by the way, surrendered in exchange for food and shelter for himself and horses.

It was not dreadfully cold, but the sky seemed only a vast turmoil of snow. The north-west wind pelted the flakes in his face, where they melted with the warmth of his skin and again drooped in tenacious icicles from his eyebrows and moustache. The horses, too, were half blinded with the storm, and the empty wagon dragged laboriously through the deep drifts. Darkness came down very early, but at last Harris began to recognize familiar landmarks close by the trail, and just as night was settling in he drew into the partial shelter of the bench on the bank of the coulee. The horses pulled on their reins persistently for the stable, but Harris forced them up to the house. His loud shout was whipped away by the wind and strangled in a moment, so he climbed stiffly from the wagon and pulled with numbed hands at the double thickness of carpet that did service for a door. He fancied he heard a sound, but could be sure of nothing; he called her name again and again, but could distinguish no answer. But at last the fastenings which help the carpet gave way, and he half walked, half fell, into the house.

The lantern burned dimly, but it was not at the lantern he looked. In the farthest corner, scarcely visible in the feeble light, stood his wife, and at her shoulder was the gun, trained steadily upon him.

"Mary, Mary, don't you know me?" he cried.

She dropped her weapon to the floor, where it went off, harmlessly burying its charge in the sod wall.

"Thank God, oh, thank God!" she exclaimed.

He threw off his wet overcoat and rushed to her side. But she sat silent on the bed, staring absently at the light flickering uncertainly in the wind from the open door.

He hastily rearranged the carpet, then, returning to her, he took her hands in his and rubbed them briskly. But she still stared vaguely at the light.

Suddenly a thought came to him. He rushed outside, to find that the horses, of their own accord, had taken shelter beside the stable. Here from the wagon he drew a little bundle and hurried back to the house.

She was sitting where he left her, shivering slightly and watching the play of the light as it flickered up and down the wall. He tore the package open and spread its contents before her.

At first she took no notice, but gradually her eyes found the outline of soft cloth and dainty feminine devices. With a great joy he watched the colour returning as her set face relaxed in a smile of ineffable tenderness. She raised her face to his and slipped her arms about his neck, and he knew that for the moment he had snatched her out of the valley of the shadow.

Harris made no more attempts to market his wheat that winter. His wife's health now became his first consideration, but, even had there been no such problem, experience had shown that nothing was to be gained by making the long and expensive trip to Emerson. The cost of subsistence of man and team on the way devoured all the proceeds of the wheat; indeed, there were instances on record in the settlement where men who attempted such trips during the winter actually came back poorer than they left, while those who could show a gain of a bag of sugar, a sack of flour, or a box of groceries were considered fortunate indeed.

"What shall we eat?" said Harris to his wife, when, after a full discussion, it was decided that no more grain could be marketed until spring.

"Oh, we shall not suffer," was her calm reply. "We have over five hundred bushels of wheat."

"But we can't eat wheat!"

"I'm not so sure of that. I heard Mr. McCrae say that lots of families had wintered on wheat. Indeed, boiled wheat is something of a delicacy. Even the best city families rarely have it, although it is more nutritious than flour and much easier to prepare."

Harris thrilled with joy over his wife's vivacity. The strange gloom that oppressed her so much of late had cost him many anxious hours.

"Besides," she continued, "we are well off to what some of them are. We have a good supply of vegetables, and one of the cows will milk most of the winter, and we have half a dozen laying hens. Then you will be able to shoot a rabbit now and again."

"Yes, we'll be all right," he agreed. "Perhaps I will get a day or two out at the lake. They say there is fine fishing all winter where some of the springs keep the ice open. And then, there's always a chance to pick off a deer."

So, in high spirits, they planned for their winter. There were long hours, and little diversion, and the desolation of bleak, snowbound prairies on every side, but through it all they kept up their courage and their hopefulness. Mary spent much time with her needle, from which John, when he felt she was applying herself too closely, beguiled her to a game of checkers or an hour with one of their few but valued books. To supplement their reading matter Mrs. Morrison sent over her little library, which consisted of "The Life of David Livingstone" and a bound number of "The Gospel Tribune." And there were frequent visits and long evenings spent about a cosy fire, when the Morrisons, or the Grants, or the

Rileses, dropped in to while away the time. The little sod house was warm and snug, and as the men played checkers while the women sewed, what cared the pioneers for the snow and the cold and the wind whistling across the plains?

At last came the crisis. At four in the afternoon Harris kissed his wife an affectionate farewell, hitched his horses to the sleigh, and started out posthaste for Plainville. The sun, hanging low to the western horizon, was banded by a great ring of yellow and gold, bulging into two dull reflected glows at either side. A ground-drift of snow whipped keenly across the hard crust, and the north-west wind had a rip to it, but overhead the sky was clear and the blue amazingly deep. Harris drove by way of the Morrisons, where a few low words sent Tom to the stable at a trot to hitch his own team, while the good wife bustled about in the "room," almost overwhelmed with the importance of her mission.

"I will go for the doctor, Jack, and you go back and take the wife with you," was Morrison's kindly offer, but Harris would not agree. It was dark by this time, and he felt that he could trust no one else to make the journey to Plainville. Besides, there was more than a chance that Dr. Blain might be incapable, and in that case it meant a drive of thirty miles farther.

"It's good of you, Morrison," he said, "but you are more used to your wife's bidding than I am, and you can be of good service there, if you will." And without waiting to argue he sprang into his sleigh again and was whipping his team into the darkness.

Dr. Blain, when at home, was to be found at the stopping-place. Harris tied his team at the door and went in, shaking the snow and frost from his great-coat. The air inside was close and stifling with tobacco, not unmixed with stronger fumes. A much-smoked oil lamp, hung by a wall-bracket, shed a certain sickly light through the thick air, and was supplemented in its illumination by rays from the door of a capacious wood stove which stood in the centre of the room, and about which half a dozen men were sitting.

"Night, Harris," said the landlord, who had a speaking acquaintance with every settler within twenty miles. "Ye're drivin' late. Ye'll have a bite supper, an' stable the team?"

"No, Hank, not to-night, thanking you the same. But I'm after Dr. Blain, and I'm in a hurry. Is he here, and—is he fit?" There was an anxiety in the last words that did not escape the host.

"Nothin' ser'ous, I hope? Frost, or somethin'?" Then, without waiting for reply, he continued: "Yes, doctor's here. Upstairs, bed to the right as ye go up. Just got in a little back. As for fit—dig 'im out an' judge for yourself."

Harris lost no time in scaling the ladder which led to the upper half-storey of the building. It was a garret—nothing better—where the cold stars looked through knot-holes in the poplar shingles, and the ends of the shingle-nails were tipped with frost. Another wall-lamp burned uncertainly here, flickering in the wind that whistled through the cracks in the gables, and by its light Harris found "the bed to the right." The form of a man lay diagonally across it, face downward, with arms extended above the head, and so still that Harris paused for a moment in a strange alarm. Then he slipped his hand on the doctor's neck and found it warm.

"Come, Doctor," he said, "I want you with me." But the sleeping man answered with not so much as a groan.

"Come, Dr. Blain," Harris repeated, shaking him soundly. "I want you to go home with me." He might have been speaking to the dead.

In sudden exasperation he seized the doctor by the shoulders, and with one heave of his mighty arms set him upright on the floor and shook him vigorously.

Dr. Blain opened his eyes and blinked uncertainly at the light. "Whatche doing, Harris?" he said at length, and the recognition brought a thrill of hope. " 'S no use. . . . Gotta sleep it off. 'S no use, Harris. 'S no use." And he crumpled up in the bed.

But Harris was desperate. "Now I'm not going to fool with you," he said. "You get up and come with me or I'll take you. Which is it?"

But the doctor only mumbled " 'S no use," and fell heavily to sleep.

Throwing open his coat to get free motion for his arms, Harris in a moment wrapped the sleeping man in a couple of blankets from the bed, threw him over his shoulder, carried him down the rickety ladder, and deposited him, none too gently, in the sleigh. There was a mild cheer from the men about the stove over these heroic measures, and one of them thoughtfully threw the doctor's satchel into the sleigh. The next moment all were lost in the darkness.

Harris drove for an hour, watching the trail keenly in the whitish mist of the winter's night, and urging the horses to the limit of their exertions. He had almost forgotten his passenger when he felt a stir in the bottom of the sleigh. Looking down closely he found the doctor trying to extricate a flask from one of his pockets. With a quick wrench he took it from him, and would have thrown it into the snow, but the thought struck him that it might be needed, and he put it into his own pocket.

The doctor struggled to his feet. "Say, Harris, you're friend o' mine, but don't take too many liberties, see? 'S no use tryin' without it. Jush give me that bottle now, or I'll get out an' go home."

Harris was so pleased at the signs of returning coherence that he could have hugged the doctor, but he only said, "You've had enough for to-night. And you won't get out, because if you try to I'll knock you senseless in the bottom of the sleigh."

Then the doctor changed his tactics. He threw his arms about Harris's neck, and genuine tears coursed down his cheeks.

"Say, Harris, you don' know anything about it. You don' know what I'm up agains'. Jush got in from Wakopa to-day, and I haven't had my closh off for week. 'S right! I tell you, Harris, you don' know. . . . Oh, I know I'm a fool—yes, don' tell me. But th' engineer knows it too when he ties down th' shafety valve t' make th' grade. Dosh it jush th' same. Thash jus' like me. Come on, Harris, hand it over. I got t' have it, or I can't make the grade."

"Well, you'll make the grade first to-night," said Harris.

After that the doctor remained silent for some time. Then suddenly he demanded: "Shay, Harris, where you takin' me to, anyway?"

"I'm taking you home."

"Home? What home? I got no home, jus'
a——"

"I'm taking you to my home."

"Wha' for? You're all right, I guess. . . ."
Suddenly the doctor stood erect.

"Harris, is your wife sick?"

"That's why I came for you."

"Well, why the devil didn't you say so?
Here, give me that whip. Harris, Harris, what
did you waste time arguing for?"

"I didn't waste much. The argument was
mostly on your side."

"Harris," said the doctor, after a long silence, "you think I'm a fool. You're right. It
isn't as though I didn't know. I know the
road I'm going, and the end thereof. . . . And
yet, in a pinch, I can pull myself together.
I'm all right now. But it'll get me again as
soon as this is over. . . . Any good I am, any
good I do, is just a bit of salvage out of the
wreck. The wreck—yes, it's a good word that
—wreck."

Just as the dawn was breaking he knelt beside her. Her eyes were very large and quiet,
and her face was white and still. But she
raised one pale hand, and the thin fingers
fondled in his hair. She drew his face very
gently down, and big silent tears stood in his
eyes.

"We will call him Allan," he said.

CHAPTER VI

A QUARTER of a century is a short time as world history goes, but it is a considerable era in the life of the Canadian West. More things—momentous things—than can be hinted at in this narrative occurred in the twenty-five years following the great inrush of 1882. The boundless prairie reaches of Manitoba were now comparatively well settled, and the tide of immigration, which, after a dozen years' stagnation, had set in again in greater flood than ever, was now sweeping over the newer lands still farther west. Railways had supplanted ox-cart and bob-sleigh as the freighters of the plains; the farmer read his daily paper on the porch after supper, while his sons and daughters drove to town in "top" buggies, tailor-made suits, and patent-leather shoes. The howl of the coyote had given way to the whistle of the locomotive; beside the sod hut of earlier days rose the frame or brick house proclaiming prosperity or social ambition. The vast sweep of the horizon, once undefiled by any work of man, was pierced and broken with elevators, villages, and farm buildings, and the whiff of coal smoke was blown down the air which had so lately known only the breath of the prairies. The wild goose no longer loitered in the brown fields in spring and autumn, and the wild duck had sought the safety of the little lakes. The pioneer days had passed away, and civilization and prosperity were rampant in the land. There were those, too, who thought that perhaps the country had lost something in all its gaining; that perhaps there was less idealism and less unreckoning hospitality in the brick house on the hill than there once had been in the sod shack in the hollow.

Mary Harris hurried about her capacious kitchen, deep in the preparation of the evening meal. The years had taken toll of the freshness of her young beauty; the shoulders, in mute testimony to much hard labour of the hands, had drooped forward over the deepening chest; the hair was thinner, and farther back above the forehead, and streaked with grey at the temples; the mouth lacked the rosy sensuousness of youth, and sat now in a mould, half of resolution, half submission. Yet her foot had lost little of its sprightliness, and the sympathy in her fine eyes seemed to have deepened with the years.

A moist but appetizing steam rose from the vegetable pots on the range, and when she threw back the iron door to feed more coal the hot glow from within danced in reflection along the bright row of utensils hanging from the wall, and even sought out the brass plate on the cream separator at the far end of the big room. Through the screen door came the monotonously redundant clic . . . a . . . clank of the windmill, and a keen ear might have caught the light splash of water as it fell in the wooden horse-troughs from the iron nozzle of the pump.

Mary stuck a fork in a potato to ascertain if the "bone" was all gone, meanwhile shielding her face from the steam with the pot lid, held aloft in an aproned hand. Having satisfied herself that the meal was making satisfactory progress, she stepped to the door and sent a quick look across the fields, to where a streak of black smoke was scrawled along the sky.

"Beulah," she called, turning toward the interior part of the house. "Come, Beulah, set the table. They're coming from the field."

In a moment a girl of twenty, plainly attired in a neat calico dress, entered the kitchen. She was fresh and beautiful as her mother had been that first summer in the sod house on the bench, and something in her appearance suggested that with her mother's beauty and fine sensibility she had inherited the indomitable spirit which had made John Harris one of the most prosperous farmers in the district. She moved in an easy, unconscious grace of self-reliance—a reliance that must be just a little irritating to men of old-fashioned notions concerning woman's dependence on the sterner sex—drew the long wooden table, with its covering of white oilcloth, into the centre of the kitchen, and began placing the dishes in position.

"I don't see why we can't have supper in the dining-room," she protested at length. "Before we built the new house we were always talking about how fine it would be to have a separate room for our meals, and now we don't eat in it once a week.

"I know," said the mother, in a quiet, tired voice. "But you know what your father thinks about it. You know how down he is on style."

"It's no great style to eat in a dining-room," continued the girl. "What did he build it for? To take off his boots in? That's about all he does there, nights before he goes to bed."

"Now, Beulah, don't be unreasonable. You know we always have meals there Sundays. But your father likes the kitchen best when it ain't too hot. And besides, I can hardly take them into the dining-room while the ploughing's on. You know how greasy they are with the engine."

"They're ploughing over at Grant's, too, and when I dropped in there yesterday the dinner was set in the dining-room, and a clean white linen cloth on the table, and napkins set for the men, and I guess they use the same kind of grease as we do," persisted the girl. "And I noticed when they came in to dinner Mr. Grant and the boys, and the hired man too, all put their coats on—not their working coats, but coats they had hanging in a closet handy. It didn't take a minute, but it looked different."

"Now, Beulah, you know your father would never stand for putting on airs like that. He——"

" 'Tisn't putting on airs. It's putting on clothes—clean clothes to eat in. Susy Grant never has to feel—I hate to say it, Mother—*ashamed* if any of her friends drop in at meal-time. And I couldn't help thinking how fine Harry looked——"

" 'Pon my word, Beulah, I'm beginning to think you must be a bit soft on Harry Grant. I had thought perhaps your weakness was toward Jim, but perhaps I'm mistaken."

"Can't a girl say a fellow's fine-looking without being soft about it?" she continued. "As for Jim——"

But at this moment the conversation was cut short by the scraping of heavy boots on the ploughshare nailed to the block at the door, and John Harris, followed by Allan and the hired man, Jim, walked into the kitchen. The farmer's frame was heavier than in his younger days, and his hair, too, was streaked with grey,

7

but every muscle in his great body seemed to bulge with strength. His face was brown with the prairie sun and wind of twenty-five summers, and lines of worry and care had cut their tracings about the mouth and eyes. Beside him stood Allan, his only son, straighter and lither of figure, but almost equally powerful. The younger man was, indeed, a replica of the older, and although they had their disagreements, constant association had developed a fine comradeship, and, on the part of the son, a loyalty equal to any strain. The hired man, Jim, was lighter and finer of feature, and his white teeth gleamed against the nut-brown of his face in a quiet smile that refused to be displaced in any emergency, and at times left the beholder in considerable doubt as to the real emotions working behind.

The men all wore blue overalls, dark blue or grey shirts, and heavy boots. They were guiltless of coat or vest, and tossed their light straw hats on the water-bench as they passed. There was a quick splashing of greasy hands at the wash-basin, followed by a more effectual rubbing on a towel made from a worn-out grain sack. The hired man paused to change the water and wash his face, but the others proceeded at once to the table, where no time was lost in ceremony. Meat, potatoes, and boiled cabbage were supplied in generous quantities on large platters. A fine stack of white bread tiered high on a plate, and a mountainous pile of Mary Harris's famous fresh buns towered on another. All hands ate at the table together, although the hired man was usually last to sit down, owing to his perverse insistence upon washing his face and combing his hair before each meal. Although this loss of time sometimes irritated Harris, he bore it in silence. There was no better farm hand in the country-side than Jim Travers, and, as Harris often remarked, employers nowadays couldn't afford to be too particular about trifles.

Harris helped himself generously to meat and vegetables and, having done so, passed the platters to his son, and in this way they were circulated about the table. Mary poured the tea from a big granite pot at her elbow, and whenever a shortage of food threatened Beulah rose from her place and refilled plate or platter. There was no talk for the first few minutes, only the sound of knife and fork plied vigorously and interchangeably by father and son, and with some regard for convention by the other members of the family. John Harris had long ago recognized the truth that the destiny of food was the mouth, and whether conveyed on knife or fork made little difference. Mary, too, had found a carelessness of little details both of manner and speech coming over her, as her occasional "ain't" betrayed, but since Jim had joined their table she had been on her guard. Jim seldom said anything, but always that quiet smile lay like a mask over his real emotions.

When the first insistent demands of appetite had been appeased, Harris, resting both elbows on the table, with knife and fork trained on opposite corners of the ceiling, straightened himself somewhat and remarked:

"Allan an' me's goin' to town to-night; anything you want from Sempter's store, Mary?"

"That lets me in for the cows," said Beulah. "You were in town night before last, too, and it was half-past nine before I got through milking."

"Oh, well, Jim was away that night," said Allan.

"Jim has enough to do, without milking cows after hours," returned the girl. "What do you want to go to town for again to-night, anyway?"

"Got to get more coal," said Harris. "We'll take two teams, an' it'll be late when we get back."

"Try and not be too late," said the mother, quietly. "You have to be at work so early in the morning, you know."

"I think it's all nonsense, this day-an'-night work," persisted Beulah. "Is there never going to be any let-up to it?"

"Beulah, you forget yourself," said her

father, "If you'd more to do you'd have less time to fret about it. Your mother did more work in one summer than you have in all your life, an' she's doin' more yet."

"Oh, Beulah's a good help," interposed Mary. "I hope she never has to work like I did."

"I guess the work never hurt us," said Harris, helping himself to preserved strawberries. "Just the same, I'm glad to see you gettin' it a bit easier. But this younger generation—it beats me what we're comin' to. Thinkin' about nothin' but fun and gaddin' to town every night or two. And clo'es—Beulah there's got more clo'es than there were in the whole Plainville settlement the first two or three years."

"I got more neighbours, too," interjected the girl. Then springing up, she stood behind her father's chair and put her arm around his neck.

"Don't be cross, Dad," she whispered. "Your heart's in the right place—but a long way in."

He disengaged her, gently enough. As Beulah said, his heart was all right, but a long way in. Twenty-five years of pitched battle with circumstances—sometimes in victory, sometimes in defeat, but never in despair; always with a load of expense about him, always with the problem of income and outlay to be solved—had made of Harris a man very different from the young idealist of '82. During the first years of struggle for a bare existence in some way the flame of idealism still burned, but with the dawn of the "better times" there came a gradual shifting of standards and a new conception of essentials. At first the settlers attached little value to their land; it was free for the taking, and excited no envy among them. The crops of the early years were unprofitable on account of the great distance to market; later, when the railway came to their doors, the crops were still unprofitable, owing to falling prices and diminishing yields due to poor cultivation. Then came a decade during which those who stayed in the country stayed because they could not get out, and it became a current saying that the more land a man farmed the deeper he got in debt. Homesteads were abandoned; settlers flew by night "across the line" or to more distant districts to begin their fight over again. And yet, in some way, Harris kept his idealism amid all the adversity in which the community was steeped; reverses could neither crush his spirit nor deflect it from its ambitions.

Then came the swing of the pendulum. No one knows just what started it prosperity-wards. Some said it was that the farmers, disheartened with wheat-growing, were applying themselves to stock, and certain it is that in "mixed farming" the community eventually found its salvation; others attributed the change to improved agricultural implements, to improved methods of farming, to greater knowledge of prairie conditions, to reductions in the cost of transportation and enlarged facilities for marketing, or to increasing world demand and higher world prices for the product of the farm. But whatever the causes —and no doubt all of the above contributed— the fact gradually dawned upon the settlers that land—their land—was worth money.

It was the farmers from the United States, scouting for cheaper lands than were available in their own communities, who first drove the conviction home. They came with money in their wallets; they were actually prepared to exchange real money for land. Such a thing had never before been heard of in Plainville district. At first the settlers were sceptical. Here were two facts almost beyond the grasp of their imagination: that farmers should buy land with money, and the farmers should have money with which to buy land. True, a few of them had already bought railway lands at three or four dollars an acre, but they bought on long terms, with a trifling investment, and they aimed to pay for the lands out of the crops or not at all.

But 'a few transactions took place; lands were sold at five dollars, six dollars, eight dollars an acre. The farmers began to realize that land represented wealth—that it was an asset, not a liability—and there was a rush for the cheap railway lands that had so long gone a-begging. Harris was among the first to sense the change in the times, and a beautiful section of railway land that lay next to his homestead he bought at four dollars an acre. The first crop more than paid for the land, and Harris suddenly found himself on the way to riches.

The joy that came with the realization that fortune had knocked at his door and he had heard was the controlling emotion of his heart for a year or more. But gradually, like a fog blown across a moonlit night, came a sense of chill and disappointment. If only he had bought two sections! If at least he had proved up on his pre-emption, which he might have had for nothing! He saw neighbours about him adding quarter to quarter. None of them had done better than himself, but some had done as well. And in some way the old sense of oneness, the old community interest which had held the little band of pioneers together amid their privations and their poverty, began to weaken and dissolve, and in its place came an individualism and a materialism that measured progress only in dollars and cents. Harris did not know that his gods had fallen, that his ideals had been swept away; even as

he sat at supper this summer evening, with
his daughter's arms about his neck, he felt that
he was still bravely, persistently, pressing on
toward the goal, all unaware that years ago
he had left that goal like a lighthouse on a
rocky shore, and was now sweeping along with
the turbulent tide of Mammonism. He still
saw the light ahead, but it was now a phan-
tom of the imagination. He said, "When I
am worth ten thousand I will have reached
it"; when he was worth ten thousand he found
the faithless light had moved on to twenty-
five thousand. He said, "When I am worth
twenty-five thousand I will have reached it";
when he was worth twenty-five thousand he
saw the glow still ahead, beckoning him on
to fifty thousand. It never occurred to him to
slacken his pace—to allow his mind a rest
from its concentration; if he had paused and
looked about he might, even yet, have recognized the distant lighthouse on the reef about
the wreck of his ideals. But to stop now
might mean losing sight of his goal, and John
Harris held nothing in heaven or earth so
great as its attainment.

So, gently enough, he disengaged his daughter's arms and finished his supper in silence.
As soon as it was ended the men started for
the barn, and in a few minutes two wagons
rattled noisily down the trail.

Beulah helped with the supper dishes, and

then came out with the milk-pails to the corral where the cows, puffing and chewing, complacently awaited her arrival. But she had not reached the gate when the hired man was at her side and had slipped one of the pails from her arm.

"Now, Jim, I don't think that's fair at all," she said; and there was a tremor in her voice that vexed her. "Here you're slaving all day with coal and water, and I think that's enough, without milking cows at night."

But Jim only smiled and stirred a cow into position.

"Yes, that's like you," she continued. "Pick Daisie first, just because you know she's tough as rubber. Say, Jim, honest goods," she demanded, pausing and facing him, milk stool in hand, "why do you let father put this kind of stuff over on you?"

"Your father doesn't put anything over on me," he answered. "I'm very fond of milking."

"Yes, you are—not," she said. "You do it on my account, because you're too big-hearted to quit before I'm through. . . . " There was a tuneful song of the tin pails as the white streams rattled on their bottoms.

"Jim," she said, after a while, when the noise of the milking was drowned in the creamy froth, "I'm getting near the end of this kind of thing. Father's getting more and more set on money all the time. He thinks I should slave along too to pile up more beside what he's got already, but I'm not going to do it much longer. Mother stands it—I guess she's got used to him, and she won't say anything, but if there's anything I'm not strong on it's silence. I'm not afraid of work, or hardship either. I'd live in a sack if I had to. I'd——"

"Would you live in a shack?" said Jim.

She shot a quick look at him. But he was quietly smiling into his milk-pail, and she decided to treat his question impersonally.

"Yes, I'd live in a shack, too, if I had to. I put in my first years in a sod-house, and there was more real happiness romping up and down the land then than there is now. In those days everybody was so poor that money didn't count. . . . It's different now."

Jim did not pursue the subject, and the milking was completed in silence. Jim finished first, and presently the rising hum of the cream separator was heard from the kitchen.

"There he goes, winding his arm off—for me," said the girl, as she rose from the last cow. "Poor Jim—I wish I knew whether it's just human kindness makes him do it, or whether——" She stopped, colouring a little over the thought that had almost escaped into words.

When the heavy grind of the separating was finished Jim went quietly to his own room, but the girl put on a clean dress and walked out through the garden. Rows of mignonette and lobelia bordered the footpath, and sweet, earthy garden smells filled the calm evening air. The rows of currant and gooseberry bushes were heavy with green fruit; the leaves of the Manitoba maples trembled ever so little in the still air. The sun was setting, and fleecy fragments of cloud were painted ruddy gold against the silver background of the sky. From the barnyard came the contented sighing of the cows and the anxious clucking of a hen gathering in her belated brood. The whole country seemed bathed in peace—a peace deep and unpurchasable, having no part in any of the affairs of man.

At the lower gate she stooped to pick a flower, which she held for a moment to her face; then, toying lightly with it in her fingers, she slipped the latch and continued along the path leading down into the ravine. It was dark and cool down there, with a touch of dampness in the grass, and the balm-of-Gileads across the stream sent a fine moist fragrance through the air. To the right lay the bench where the sod-house had stood, not so much as a mound now marking the spot; but the thoughts of the girl turned yearningly to it, and to the days of the lonely but not unhappy childhood which it had sheltered.

Presently she reached the water, and her quick ear caught the sound of a musk-rat slipping gently into the stream from the reeds on the opposite bank; she could see the widening wake where he ploughed his swift way across the pond. Then her own figure stood up before her, graceful and lithe as the willows on the bank. She surveyed it a minute, then flicked the flower at her face in the water, and turned slowly homeward. She was not unhappy, but a dull sense of loss oppressed her —a sense that the world was very rich and very beautiful, and that she was feasting neither on its richness nor its beauty. There was a stirring of music and poetry in her soul, but neither music nor poetry found expression. What she felt was a consciousness that great things were just beyond the horizon of her experience, things undefined and undefinable which, could she but grasp them, would deepen life and sweeten life and give a purpose to all her being. And as she walked up the path and the fragrant night air filled her nostrils, something of that wilder life seemed borne in upon her and sent a fresh spring to her ankle. And presently she discovered she was thinking about Jim Travers.

Her mother sat in the dining-room, knitting by the light of the hanging lamp. Her face seemed very pale and lovely in the soft glow. "Don't you think you have done enough?"

said the girl, slipping into a sitting posture on the floor by her mother's knee. "You work, work, work, all the time. I suppose they'll have to let you work in heaven."

"We value our work more as we grow older," said the mother. . . . "It helps to keep us from thinking."

"There you go!" exclaimed the girl; but there was a tenderness in her voice. "Worrying again. I wish they'd stay home for a change."

The mother plied her needles in silence. "Slip away to bed, Beulah," she said at length. "I will wait up for a while."

Late in the night the girl heard heavy footsteps in the kitchen and bursts of loud but indistinct talking.

CHAPTER VII

NOTWITHSTANDING Harris's late hours the household was early astir the following morning. At five o'clock Jim was at work in the stables, feeding, rubbing down, and harnessing his horses, while Allan and his father walked to the engine, where they built a fresh fire and made some minor repairs. Even at this early hour the sun shone brightly, its rays mellowing in a sheen of ground-mist that enveloped the prairie, but there is a tang in the Manitoba morning air even in midsummer, and the men walked briskly through the crisp stubble. A little later Beulah came down to the corral with her milk-pails, and the cows, comfortably chewing where they rested on their warm spots of earth, rose slowly and with evident great reluctance at her approach. A spar of light blue smoke ascended in a perpendicular column from the kitchen chimney; motherly hens led their broods forth to forage; pigs grunted with rising enthusiasm from near-by pens, and calves voiced insistent demands from their quarters. The Harris farm, like fifty thousand others, rose from its brief hush of rest and quiet to the sounds and energies of another day.

Breakfast, like the meal of the night before, was eaten hurriedly, and at first without conversation, but at length Harris paused long enough to remark, "Riles is talkin' o' goin' West."

"The news might be worse," said Beulah. Riles, although a successful farmer, had the reputation of being grasping and hard to a degree, even in a community where such qualities, in moderation, were by no means considered vices.

Harris paid no attention to his daughter's interruption. It was evident, however, that his mention of Riles had a purpose behind it, and presently be continued:

"Riles has been writin' to the Department of the Interior, and it seems they're openin' a lot of land for homesteadin' away West, not far from the Rocky Mountains. Seems they have a good climate there, and good soil, too."

"I should think Mr. Riles would be content with what he has," said Mary Harris. "He has a fine farm here, and I'm sure both him and his wife have worked hard enough to take it easier now."

"Hard work never killed nobody," pursued the farmer. "Riles is good for many a year yet, and free land ain't what it once was.

Those homesteads'll be worth twenty dollars an acre by the time they're proved up."

"I wish I was sure of it—I wouldn't think long," said Allan. "But they say it's awful dry; all right for ranchin', but no good for farmin'."

"Who says that?" demanded his father. "The ranchers. They know which side their bread's buttered on. As long's they can get grazin' land for two cents an acre, or maybe nothin', of course they don't want the homesteader. They tell me the Englishmen and Frenchmen that went out into that country when us Canadians settled in Manitoba have more cattle now than they can count—they measure 'em by acres, Riles says."

Breakfast and Harris's speech came to an end simultaneously, and the subject was dropped for the time. In a few minutes Jim had his team hitched to the tank wagon in the yard. The men jumped aboard, and the wagon rattled down the road to where the engine and ploughs sat in the stubble-field.

"What notion's this father's got about Riles, do you suppose, mother?" asked Beulah, as the two women busied themselves with the morning work in the kitchen.

"Dear knows," said her mother wearily. "I hope he doesn't take it in his head to go out there too."

"Who, Dad? Oh, he wouldn't do that.

8

He's hardly got finished with the building of this house, and you know for years he talked and looked forward to the building of the new house. His heart's quite wrapped up in the farm here. I wish he'd unwrap it. a bit and let it peek out at times."

"I'm not so sure. I'm beginning to think it's the money that's in the farm your father's heart is set on. If the money was to be made somewhere else his heart would soon shift."

"Mother!" exclaimed the girl. In twenty years it was the first word approaching disloyalty she had heard from her mother's lips, and she could hardly trust her ears. It was nothing for Beulah to criticize her father; that was her daily custom, and she pursued it with the whole frankness of her nature. But her mother had always defended, sometimes mildly chiding, but never admitting either weakness or injustice on the part of John Harris.

"Well, I just can't stand it much longer," said the mother, the emotions which she had so long held in check overcoming her. "Here I've slaved and saved until I'm an—an old woman, and what better are we for it? We've better things to eat and more things to wear and a bigger house to keep clean, and your father thinks we ought to be satisfied. But he isn't satisfied himself. He's slaving harder than ever, and now he's got this notion about going West. Oh, you'll see it will come to that.

He knows our life isn't complete, and he thinks more money will complete it. All the experience of twenty years hasn't taught him any better."

Beulah stood aghast at this outburst, and when her mother paused and looked at her, and she saw the unbidden wells of water gathering in the tender eyes, the girl could no longer restrain herself. With a cry she flung her arms about her mother's neck, and for a few moments the two forgot their habitual restraint and were but naked souls mingling together.

"It's a shame," exclaimed Beulah at length. "We're not living; we're just existing. When I get among people that are really living—like the Grants, over there—you don't know how mortified and mean I feel. And it's not that alone—it's the sense of loss, the sense that life is going by and I'm not making the best of it. You know we are missing the *real thing;* we are just living on the husks, and father is so blind he thinks the husks are the grain itself."

"Your father is hungry, too," said the mother. "Hungry—hungry, and he thinks that more land, more money, more success, will fill him. And in the meantime he's forgetting the things that would satisfy—the love that was ours, the little devo——Oh, child, what am I saying? What an unfaithful creature I am! You must forget, Beulah, you must forget these words—words of shame they are!"

"The shame is his," declared the girl, defiantly, "and I won't stand this nonsense about homesteading again—I just won't stand it. If he says anything more about it I'll—I'll fly off, that's what I'll do. And I've a few remarks for him about Riles that won't keep much longer. The old badger—he's at the bottom of all this."

"You mustn't quarrel with your father, dearie, you mustn't do that."

"I'm not going to quarrel with him, but I'm going to say some things that need saying. And if it comes to a show-down, and he must go—well, he must, but you and I will stay with the old farm, won't we, mother?"

But the mother's thought now was for quelling the storm in the turbulent heart of her daughter. Beulah's nature was not one to lend itself to passive submission, nor yet passive resistance. She was the soul of loyalty, but with that loyalty she combined a furious intolerance of things as they should not be. She had not yet reached the philosophic age, but she was old enough to value life, and to know that what she called the real things were escaping here. At night, as she looked up at the myriad stars spangling the heavens, the girl's heart was filled with an unutterable yearning; a sense of restriction, of limitation, of loss—a sense that somewhere lay a Purpose and a Plan, and that only by becoming part of that Plan could life be lived to the fullest. Her mother was of a different nature, not less brave, but more resigned; content to fill, without question, the niche to which fate assigned her; accepting conditions as a matter of course. Yet at times she had inklings of those deeper questions which arose in persistent interrogations before her child, and she guessed that if Beulah once became convinced that she saw the Plan, not all her loyalty could dissuade her from following it. So she strove to control the sudden outburst in her own heart lest the fire lighted in Beulah's should break forth in conflagration.

"There, there now," she said, gently stroking her daughter's hair. "Let us forget this, and remember how much we have to be thankful for. We have our health, and our home, and the bright sunshine, and—I declare," she interrupted, catching a glimpse of something through the window, "if the cows haven't broken from the lower pasture and are all through the oat-field! You'll have to take Collie and get them back, somehow, or bring them up to the corral."

Perhaps it was part of the Plan that the diversion should come at that moment, but the rebellion in Beulah's heart was by no means suppressed. Pulling a sun-bonnet upon her head she called the dog, which came leaping upon her with boisterous affection, and hurried down the path to the field where the cows stood almost lost in a jungle of green oats. She soon located the breach in the fence, and, with the help of the dog, quickly turned the cows toward it. But alack! just as victory seemed assured a rabbit was frightened from its hiding-place in the green oats, and sailed forth in graceful bounds across the pasture. The dog, of course, concluded that the capture of the rabbit was of much more vital import- ance to the Harris homestead than driving any number of stupid cattle, and darted across the field in pursuit, wasting his breath in sharp, eager yelps as he went. Whereupon the cows turned oatward again, not boisterously nor in- solently, but with a calm persistence that steadily wore out the girl's strength and pa- tience. They would not move a foot toward the pasture unless she drove them; they would move only one at a time; as she drove one the others pushed farther into the oat-field, and when she turned to pursue them the one she had already driven followed at her heels. The sun was hot, the oats were rank, the wild buckwheat tripped her as she ran; her appeals to the dog, now seated on a knoll looking somewhat foolishly for the rabbit which had given him the slip, and her commands to the cattle alike fell on unheeding ears. She was in no joyous mood at best, and the perverseness of things aggravated her beyond endurance. Her callings to the cattle became more and more tearful, and presently ended in a sob.

"There now, Beulah, don't worry; we will have them in a minute," said a quiet voice, and looking about she found Jim almost at her elbow, his omnipresent smile playing gently about his white teeth. "I was down at the creek filling the tank, when I saw you had a little rebellion on your hands, and I thought reinforcements might be in order."

"You might 've hollered farther back," she said, half reproachfully, but there was a light of appreciation in her eye when she dared raise it toward him. "I'm afraid I was beginning to be very—foolish."

She tripped again on the treacherous buckwheat, but he held her arm in a strong grasp against which the weight of her slim figure seemed but as a feather blown against a wall. The life of the plains had bred in Beulah admiration for physical strength, and she acknowledged his firm grip with an admiring glance. Then they set about their task, but the sober-eyed cows had no thought of being easily deprived of their feast, and it was some time before they were all turned back into the pasture and the fence temporarily repaired behind them.

"I can't thank you enough," Beulah was

saying. "You just keep piling one kindness on top of another. Say, Jim, honest, what makes you do it?"

But at that moment the keen blast of an engine whistle came cutting through the air —a long clear note, followed by a series of toots in rapid succession.

"I guess they're running short of water," said Jim. "I must hustle." So saying he ran to the ford of the creek where the tank-wagon was still standing, and in a minute his strong frame was swaying back and forth to the rhythmic clanking of the pump. But it was some minutes before the tank was full, and again the clarion call of the whistle came insistently through the air. Hastily dragging up the hose, he uttered a sharp command to the horses; their great shoulders socketed into the collars; the tugs tightened, quivering with the strain; the wheels grated in the gravel, and the heavily-loaded wagon swung its way up the bank of the coulee.

Meanwhile other things were transpiring. Harris had returned from town the night before with the fixed intention of paying an early visit to the Farther West. He and Riles had spent more time than they should breasting the village bar, while the latter drew a picture of rising colour of the possibilities which the new lands afforded. Harris was not a man who abused himself with liquor, and Riles, too, rarely forgot that indulgence was expensive, and had to be paid for in cash. Moreover, Allan occasioned his father some uneasiness. He was young, and had not yet learned the self-control to be expected in later life. More than once of late Allan had crossed the boundary of moderation, and John Harris was by no means indifferent to the welfare of his only son. Indeed, the bond between the two was so real and so intense that Harris had never been able to bring himself to contemplate their separation, and the boy had not even so much as thought of establishing a home of his own. Harris sometimes wondered at this, for Allan was popular in the neighbourhood, where his good appearance, strength, and sincere honesty made him something of a favourite. The idea of homesteading together assured further years of close relationship between father and son, and the younger man fell in whole-heartedly with it.

"We'll hurry up the ploughing, Dad, and run West before the harvest is on us," Allan said as they rode home through the darkness. "We can file on our land and get back for the fall work. Then we will go out for the winter and commence our duties. The only question is, Can they grow anything on that land out there?"

"That's what they used to ask when we came to Manitoba," said his father. "And there were years when I doubted the answer myself. Some parts were froze out year after year, and they're among the best in the country now, and never think of frost. The same thing'll happen out there, and we might as well be in the game."

To do him justice, it was not altogether the desire for more wealth that prompted Harris. It was the call of new land; the call he had heard and answered in the early eighties; the old appetite that had lain dormant for a quarter of a century, but was still in his blood, waiting only a suggestion of the open spaces, a whiff from dry grass on the wind-swept plains, the zigzag of a wagon-trail streaking afar into the horizon, to set it tingling again. The thought of homesteading revived rich old memories—memories from which the kindly years had balmed the soreness and the privation and the hardship, and left only the joy and the courage and the comradeship and the conquering. It was the call of the new land, which has led the race into every clime and flung its flag beneath every sky, and Harris's soul again leaped to the summons.

So this morning father and son were especially anxious that not a moment of their ploughing weather should be lost, and it was particularly aggravating when the hired man's long delay resulted in a bubbling sputter followed by a dry hiss from the injector, warning the engineer that the water-tank was empty. Allan shot an anxious glance down the road to the coulee, but the water team was not in sight. Seizing the whistle cord, he sent its peremptory summons into the air. Harris looked up from the ploughs, and the two exchanged frowns of annoyance. But the water stood high in the glass, and Allan did not reduce the speed, although he cut the link action another notch to get every ounce of advantage from the expansion. Down the field they went, the big iron horse shouldering itself irresistibly along, while the ploughs left their dozen furrows of moist, fresh soil, and the blackbirds hopped gingerly behind. But the water went down, down in the glass, and still there was no sign of a further supply. Allan again cut the air with his whistle, and at length, with a muttered imprecation, he slammed the throttle shut and jumped from the engine.

His father ran up from the ploughs. "What do you think of that?" the younger man exclaimed. "Jim must have had trouble. Bogged, or broke a tongue, or something. Never fell down like that before."

"Keep a keen eye on your fire," said Harris, "and I'll go down and see what's wrong with him." So the farmer strode off across the ploughed field. The delay annoyed him, and he felt unreasonably cross with Travers. As he plodded on through the heavy soil his temper did not improve, and he was talking to himself by the time he came upon Travers, giving his team their wind at the top of the hill leading up from the creek.

"What kept you?" he demanded when he came within a rod of the wagon. "Here's the outfit shut down waiting for water, and you——"

"I'm sorry, Mr. Harris——"

"That ain't what I asked you. You can't make steam with sorrow. What have you been foolin' about?"

"I haven't been fooling. As to what delayed me—well, you're delaying me now. Better jump on and ride up with me."

"So you won't tell me, eh? You think you can do what you like with my team and my time, and it's none of my business. We'll see whose business it is."

Harris came threateningly toward the wagon, but was met only by the imperturbable smile of his hired man. He thrust his foot on a spoke of the wheel and prepared to spring on to the tank, but at that moment the horses stirred and his foot slipped. Seeing that the farmer was about to fall Travers seized him by the collar of his shirt, but in so doing he leaned and lost his own balance, when the weight of the falling man came upon him, and the two tumbled on to the grass in each other's arms.

Allan, having satisfied himself that the engine would take no harm, had followed his father, and came over the crest of the ridge above the coulee just in time to see Jim apparently strike his employer and the two struggling on the grass together. In an instant the young man's hot blood was in his head; he rushed forward, and just as Jim had risen to his knees he struck him a stinging blow in the face that measured him again in the grass.

It was only for an instant. Travers sprang to his feet, a red line slowly stretching down his cheek as he did so. Allan came upon him swinging a tremendous blow at the jaw; but Jim guarded skilfully, and answered with a smash from the shoulder straight on the chin, which laid his adversary's six feet prostrate before him.

Allan rose slowly, sober but determined, and for a moment it looked as though a battle royal were to be fought on the spot, both men strong, lean, rigid, hard as iron, and quick as steel; Allan angry, careful, furious; Jim calm, confident, and still smiling. But Harris rushed between them and seized his son by the arms.

"Stop it, Allan; stop, I say. You mustn't fight. Jim didn't hit me—I'll say that for him. Now quit it. As for you" (turning to Jim), "I'm sorry for this, but you have yourself to blame. I'll give you one more chance to answer me—what kept you?"

"I don't choose to answer," was Jim's reply, spoken in the most casual tone. His eye was rapidly closing where Allan's blow had fallen on it, but his white teeth still glistened behind a smile.

"All right," said Harris. "You can go to the house and tell Mrs. Harris to pay you what is coming." And the farmer climbed on to the wagon and took the reins himself.

When Jim entered the kitchen he was received with astonishment by Mrs. Harris and Beulah. "Why, whatever has happened?" they exclaimed. "Has there been an accident? You're hurt!"

But Jim smiled, and said: "No accident at all. I have merely decided to go homesteading." And he went up the stairs to pack his belongings.

CHAPTER VIII

HARRIS and Allan drove straight to the engine, never looking back to see what became of the hired man. On the way the farmer explained to his son what had taken place; that words had passed between them, but no blows had been struck, until Allan appeared on the scene.

"Well, if that's the way of it, I'm sorry I hit him," said the young man, frankly, "and when I see him I'll tell him so. I plugged him a good one, didn't I?—though, to be honest, he was hardly on his feet. But he sure landed me a stem-winder on the chin," he continued, ruefully rubbing that member, "so I guess we're about even."

"He might 've broke your neck," said Harris. "You're too hot-headed, both of you. . . . I can't make out what got into Jim, that he wouldn't answer a civil question. Jim was a good man, too." Perhaps the disturbing suggestion entered Harris's mind that the question had been none too civil, and he was really beginning to feel that after all Jim might be the aggrieved party. But he crushed down

[119]

such mental sedition promptly. "It don't matter how good a man he was," he declared, "as long as I pay the piper I'm goin' to call the tune."

"It puts us up against it for a water-man, though," said Allan, thoughtfully.

"So it does," admitted Harris, who up to that moment had not reflected that his hasty action in dismissing Travers would result in much more delay than anything else that had occurred. "Well, we'll have to get somebody else. We'll manage till noon, and then you better ride over to Grant's or Morrison's. They'll be able to lend a man or one of the boys for a day or two." It was significant that although Harris was planning a considerable venture with Riles, when he wanted a favour his thought instinctively turned to his other neighbours, Grant and Morrison.

At noon Jim's chair was vacant, and the family sat down to dinner amid a depressing silence. No mention was made of the morning's incident until the meal was well advanced, when Harris, feeling that he ought in some way to introduce the subject, said: "Is Jim gone?"

"Yes, he's gone," blazed Beulah. "You didn't expect he'd wait to kiss you good-bye, did you?"

"One in the family is enough for that treatment," put in Allan, whose swollen chin and stiff neck still biassed him against Travers.

"He didn't, either. And if he did it's none of your business, you big——"; she looked her brother straight in the face, her swollen eyes telling their own story, and repeated deliberately, "you big coward."

Allan bit his lip.

"You're about the only person, Beulah, that could say that and get off with whole skin. I suppose he told you I hit him before he was on his feet."

"Well, he didn't. He didn't say you hit him at all, but he couldn't deny it, so we knew the truth. And we knew you must have taken some mean advantage, or you'd never have got near enough to leave a mark on him."

"Jim's quite a hero, all right. It's too bad he's gone."

"It's a good job he's gone," said Harris. "By the way Beulah talks things have gone far enough. I don't want my daughter marrying a farmer."

"Her grandmother's daughter did," said Mary Harris.

"Yes, I know, but things are different now. I look for something better for Beulah."

It was characteristic of Harris, as of thousands of others, that, although a farmer himself, he looked for "something better" for his daughter. He was resigned to Allan being a farmer; his intimate, daily relationship with his son shrank from any possibility of separation. But for his daughter—no. He had mapped out no career for her; she might marry a doctor, lawyer, merchant, tradesman, even a minister, but not a farmer. It is a peculiarity of the agriculturist that, among all professions, he holds his own in the worst repute. As a class he has educated himself to believe that everybody else makes an easy living off the farmer, and, much as he may revile the present generation for doing so, he is anxious that his children should join in the good picking. In later years has come a gradually broadening conception that farming, after all, calls for brain as well as muscle, and that the man who can wrestle a successful living from Nature has as much right to hold up his head in the world as the experimenter in medicine or the lawyer playing hide-and-seek with Justice through the cracks in the Criminal Code. Herein is a germ of the cityward migration: the farmer himself is looking for "something better" for his children.

"Jim was a good man," persisted his wife. "Don't you think you were—well, perhaps, a little hasty with him?"

Harris sat back. It was his wife's business to agree. For twenty years and more she had been faithful in the discharge of that duty. That she should suggest an opinion out of harmony with his indicated a lack of discipline, not very serious, perhaps, but a seed which, if permitted to flourish, might develop to dangerous proportions.

"So you're goin' to take his part, too? It's a strange thing if I can't handle my hired help without advice from the house."

Mary flushed at the remark. Any open quarrel with her husband, especially before the children—for she still thought of the man and woman to her left and right as "the children" —was more painful to her than any submission could have been. It would be so much easier to change the subject, to follow the line of least resistance, and forget the incident as quickly as possible. That had been her constant policy after the first few years of their married life. At first there had been troubles and difficulties, but she had gradually adjusted herself to her niche, and their lives had run smoothly together because she never interrupted the current of his. But of late the conviction had been coming home to her that some time, somewhere, she must make a stand. It was all very well meekly to fall in line as long as only her own happiness was concerned, but if the future of her children should be at stake, or if the justice of their dealings with others should be the issue, then she would have to fight, and fight it out to a finish. And, quite unbidden, a strange surge of defiance welled in her when her husband so frankly told her to mind her own business.

"I was under the impression we were managing this farm together, you and I, John," she said, very calmly, but with a strange ring in her voice. "When we came West I understood it was to build *our* home. I didn't know it was just to be *your* home."

The look of surprise with which Harris greeter her words was absolutely genuine. A hot, stinging retort sprang to his lips, but by a sudden effort he suppressed it. His wife's challenge, quiet, unruffled, but with evidence of unbending character behind it, in some way conjured something out of the past, and he saw her again, the greying locks restored to their youthful glory and the careworn cheek abloom with the colour of young maidenhood as they had been in the gathering shadows that night when they swore to build their own home, and live their own lives, and love each other, always, only, for ever and ever. . . . And yet, to let her defiance go unchecked, to have his authority challenged before his own children —it would be the beginning of dissolution, the first crumblings of collapse.

"We will talk about that some other time, Mary," he said. "If Jim had answered my question fairly, as he had a right to, instead of beatin' around the bush, I might 've let him off. But when I wanted to know what kept him he simply parried me, makin' a fool of me and rubbin' it in with that infernal smile of his."

"So that's what started it!" exclaimed Beulah. "Well, I'll tell you what kept him, if he wouldn't. The cattle got into the oats through a break in the fence, and I couldn't get them out, and the dog went ki-yi-ing over the prairie after a rabbit, and just as I was beginning to —to—condense over it Jim came up and saved the situation. What if he did keep your old engine waiting? There are more important things than ploughing."

"Aha!" said Harris, knowingly. "Well, I guess it's just as well it happened as it did. Jim was gettin' altogether too good at runnin' at your heels."

"That's all the thanks he gets for working late and early, like no other hired man in the district. All right. You and Allan can milk the cows to-night, for I won't—see?"

Harris was accustomed to his daughter's frankness, and as a rule paid little regard to it. He was willing enough to be flayed, in moderation, by her keen tongue; in fact, he took a secret delight in her unrestrained sallies, but that was different from defiance. He could, and did, submit to any amount of cutting repartee,-and felt a sort of pride in her vigour and recklessness, but he had no notion of countenancing open mutiny, even from Beulah.

"We'll talk about that some other time, too," he said. "And you'll milk the cows to-night as usual."

Beulah opened her lips as though to answer, but closed them again, arose, and walked out of the kitchen. For her the controversy was over; the die was cast. Her nature admitted of any amount of disputation up to a certain point, but when the irresistible force crashed into the immovable object she wasted no wind on words. With her war was war.

Harris finished his meal with little relish. His daughter was very, very much to him, and an open rupture with her was among the last things to be imagined. . . . Still, she must learn that the liberty of speech he allowed her did not imply equal liberty of action. . . . His wife, too, had behaved most incredibly. After all, perhaps he had been hasty with Jim. No doubt he would meet the boy in Plainville or somewhere in the district before long, and he would then have a frank little talk with him. And he would say nothing more of the incident to his wife. He was beginning to feel almost amiable again when recollection of Beulah, and the regard which she was evidently culti- vating toward Travers, engulfed his returning spirits like a cold douche. It must not come to that, whatever happened.

"You better get over to Grant's, Allan, if you're goin'," he said as he left the table. "I've some shears to change that'll keep me busy until you get back."

An hour later Allan returned, accompanied

by George Grant, and operations in the field were resumed. Father and son were both anxious to make up for lost time, and they worked that night long after their usual hour for quitting. Just as the sun was setting George Grant left a last tank of water at the end of the field and started for home. As he passed the buildings he saw Beulah in the garden, and leaned over the fence for a short chat with her. The girl was thankful the gathering dusk hid the colour of her cheeks. George continued on his way, but still the steady panting of the engine, louder now, it seemed, than during the day, came pulsing down on the calm night air. The long twilight dragged on; the light faded out of the east and south, and at last shone like the spread of a crimson fan only in the north-west. It was quite dark when the two men, tired and dusty, came in at the close of their long day's labour.

The table was set for two. "We have had our supper," Mary explained. "We thought we wouldn't wait any longer."

"That's all right," said Harris, trying to be genial. But he found it harder than he had supposed. He was very tired, and somewhat embarrassed following the unpleasantness at noon. He had no thought of apologizing, either to wife or daughter; on the contrary, he intended to make it quite clear to them that they had been at fault in the matter, but he would take his time about reopening the subject. By waiting a day or two before reproving them he would show that he was acting in a judicial spirit, and without any influence of temper. Still . . . it was provoking that there should be nothing to talk about.

When supper was finished Allan went to the stables to give final attention to the horses—a duty that had always fallen to Jim—and Harris, after a few minutes' quiet rest in his chair, began to remove his boots.

"The cows are not milked, John," said his wife. She tried to speak in a matter-of-fact way, but the tremor in her voice betrayed the import of the simple statement.

Harris paused with a boot half unlaced. While his recollection of Beulah's defiance was clear enough, it had not occurred to him that the girl actually would stand by her guns. He had told her that she would milk the cows tonight as usual, and he had assumed, as a matter of course, that she would do so. He was not accustomed to being disobeyed.

"Where's Beulah?" he demanded.

"I guess she's in her room."

Harris laced up his boot. Then he started upstairs.

"Don't be too hard on her, John," urged his wife, with a little catch in her voice.

"I won't be too hard on anybody," he replied curtly. "It's a strange thing you

wouldn't see that she did as she was told. I
suppose I have to plug away in the field until
dark and then come in and do another half-
day's work because my women folk are too
lazy or stubborn to do it themselves."

If this outburst was intended to crush Mary
Harris it had a very different effect. She
seemed to straighten up under the attack; the
colour came back to her cheeks, and her eyes
were bright and defiant.

"John Harris," she said. "You know better
than to say that your women folk are either
lazy or stubborn, but there's a point where imposition, even the imposition of a husband,
has to stop, and you've reached that point.
You didn't have to stay in the field until dark.
There's another day coming, and the ploughing'll keep. It isn't like the harvest. It was
just your own contrariness that kept you
there. You fired the best man you ever had
to-day, in a fit of temper, and now you're trying to take it out on us."

Harris looked at her for a moment; then,
without speaking, he continued up the stairs.
The difficulties of his position were increasing;
it was something new to be assailed from the
bosom of his own family. He felt that he was
being very unfairly used, but he had no intention of shrinking from his duty as a husband
and father, even if its discharge should bring
pain to all of them.

He found Beulah in her room, ostensibly reading.

"Why are the cows not milked?" he demanded.

"I thought I made it clear to you at noon that they wouldn't be milked by me," she answered, "and there didn't seem to be anybody else hankering for the job."

"Beulah," he said, trying to speak calmly, "don't you think this nonsense has gone far enough?"

"Too far," she agreed. "But you started it—let's see you stop it."

"Beulah," he said, with rising anger, "I won't allow you to talk to me like that. Remember I'm your father, and you've a right to do as you're told. Haven't I given you everything—given you a home, and all that, and are you goin' to defy me in my own house?"

"I don't want to defy you," she answered, "but if you're going to let your temper run away with you, you can put on the brakes yourself. And as for all you've done for me—maybe I'm ungrateful, but it doesn't look half so big from my side of the fence."

"Well, what more do you want?" he demanded.

"For one thing, I wouldn't mind having a father."

"What do you mean? Ain't I your father?"

"No!" she cried. "No! No! There's no father here. You're just the boss—the foreman on the farm. You board with mother and me. We see you at meal-times. We wouldn't see you then if you didn't have to make use of us in that way. If you have a spare hour you go to town. You're always so busy, busy, with your little things, that you have no time for big things."

"I didn't know it was an offence to be busy," he answered. "It's work that makes money, and I notice you can spend your share. You're never so haughty about me workin' when you want a ten-dollar bill for somethin'. Work may be a disgrace all right from your point of view, but money isn't, and in this country you don't get much of one without the other."

"Now, Dad," she protested. "You're taking me up wrong. I don't think work is a disgrace, and I'm willing to work as hard as anyone, but I do think it's a shame that you should be thinking only of work, work, work, when you don't need to. I'd like to see you think about *living* instead of working. And we're not living—not really living, you know —we're just existing. Just making little twenty-four hour cycles that don't get us anywhere, except older. Don't you see what I mean? We're living all in the flesh, like an animal. When you feed the horses and put them under shelter you can't do anything more

for them. But when you feed and shelter
your daughter you have only half provided
for her, and it's the other half, the starving
half, that refuses to starve any longer."

"I'm not kickin' on religion, if that's what
you mean, Beulah," he said. "You get goin'
to church as often as you like, and——"

"Oh, it's not religion," she protested. "At
least, it's not just going to church, and things
like that, although I guess it is a more real religion, if we just understood. What are we
here for, anyway? Come now, you're a man
of sense and experience, and you must have
settled that question in your own mind long
ago. What's the answer?"

"Well, I'm here just now to tell you those
cows are to be milked before——"

"Yes, dodge it! You've dodged that question so long you daren't face it. But there
must be an answer somewhere, or there
wouldn't be the question. There's Riles, now;
he doesn't know there is such a question. He
takes it for granted we're here to grab money.
And then, there's Grants. They know there is
such a question, and I'm sure that to some extent they've answered it. You know, I like
them, but I never go into their house that I
don't feel out of place. I feel like they have
something that I haven't—something that
makes them very rich and shows me how very
poor I am. And it's embarrassing to feel poor
among rich folks. Why, to-night George

Grant stopped on his way home to say a word to me, and what do you suppose he said? Nothing about the weather, or the neighbours, or the crops. He asked me what I thought of the Venezuelan treaty. Of course I'd never heard of such a thing, but I said I hoped it would be for the best, or something like that, but I was ashamed—so ashamed he might have seen it in the dusk. You see, they're living—and we're existing."

If Beulah hoped by such argument to persuade her father, or even to influence him, she was doomed to disappointment. Harris listened to her patiently enough at first, but the conviction dawned upon him that she had been reading some silly nonsense that had temporarily distorted her young mind. Such foolishness, if allowed to take root, might have disastrous results. His daughter must learn to centre her mind on her work, and not be led away by whimsical notions that had no place in a busy life.

"You're talking a good deal of nonsense, Beulah," he said. "When you get older these questions won't worry you. In the meantime, your duty is to do as you're told. Right now that means milk the cows. I'll give you five minutes to get started."

Harris went to his room. A little later Beulah, with a light cloak about her shoulders and a suitcase in her hand, slipped quietly down the front stairs and out into the night.

CHAPTER IX

CRUMBLING CASTLES

A T the foot of the garden Beulah paused irresolute, the suit-case swinging gently in her hand. She had made no plans for the decisive step events of the day had forced upon her, but the step itself she felt to be inevitable. She was not in love with Jim Travers; she had turned the whole question over in her mind that afternoon, weighing it with judicial impartiality, supposing all manner of situations to try out her own emotions, and she had come to the conclusion that Travers was merely an incident in her life, a somewhat inspiring incident, perhaps, but an incident none the less. The real thing —the vital matter which demanded some exceptional protest—was the narrow and ever narrowing horizon of her father, a horizon bounded only by material gain. Against this narrowing band of outlook her vigorous spirit, with its dumb, insistent stretchings forth to the infinite, rebelled. It was not a matter of filial duty; it was not a matter of love; to her it was a matter of existence. She saw her ideals dimly enough at best, and she would burst every cord of affection and convention rather than allow them to be submerged in the grey, surrounding murk of materialism.

Perhaps it was custom and the subtle pullings of association that drew her feet down the path across the bench to the edge of the stream that gurgled gently in the still night. She stood on the gravel by the water's edge, packed firm by the wagon-wheels of twenty-five years, and watched her image as it swayed gently in the smoothly running current. There was no moon, but the stars shone down in their midnight brilliance, and the water lay white and glistening against the black vagueness of the bushy banks. She stooped and let it fondle her fingers. It was warm and smooth. . . . But it was shallow at the ford. . . . Farther up it was quite deep. . . . The stars blinked a strange challenge from the sky, as though to say, "Here is the tree of knowledge, if you dare to drink thereof."

At length she turned her back on the stream and retraced her steps up the path. The house loomed very sombre and still in the quiet night. A light shone dimly from her father's window. At intervals a deep, contented sighing came from the cows in the barn-yard. She took the path past the house and down to the corral, where she paused, her ear arrested by the steady drone of milking. A lantern sitting on the black earth, cast a little circle of light, and threw a docile cow in dreadful silhouette against the barn. And by that dim light Beulah discerned the bent form of her mother, milking.

"Mother, this is too much!" the girl exclaimed.

Her mother started and looked up. "You're leaving us, Beulah?" she asked. There was no reproach in her voice, nor even surprise, but a kind of quiet sorrow. "I couldn't let the poor brutes suffer," she explained.

"Yes, I'm leaving," said Beulah. "I can't stand it any longer."

The mother sighed. "I've seen it coming for some time," she said, at length. "I suppose it can't be helped."

"You're so passive," returned the girl, with a touch of impatience. "You make me want to fight. Of course it can be helped, but it can't be helped by always giving in."

"Your father has met one of his own mettle at last," said the mother, and the girl fancied she detected a note of pride, but whether of father, or daughter, or both, she could only guess. "Well, it's all very sad. Your father is a good man, Beulah. . . . I should send you back to your bed, but somehow I can't. I—I don't blame you, Beulah."

She had finished the last cow. Beulah helped with the pails of milk, and the two women went back to the house together. When

Mary had washed her hands she took her daughter's face between her palms and kissed her on the cheeks. Slowly Beulah's arms stole about her neck, and it took all the steel in her nature to prevent surrender.

"It's not you I'm going from," she managed to say. "You understand that, don't you? I'll write to you often, and we'll surely meet before long. . . . But I've just got to. There's no other way out."

"Stay till morning, Beulah. Your father may be disposed to give and take a little then, and you'll do the same, won't you? . . . Oh, my girl, don't break up our home like this!"

"You can't break up what you haven't got. Aside from you, why should I call this place home? I work here, and get my board and clothes. Well, I can work other places, and get my board and clothes. If I've got to be a cog in a money-making machine, I will at least choose the machine."

"What plans have you made? Where are you going?"

"Haven't made any plans, and don't know where I'm going. But I'm going. At present that's enough. The plans will come along as they're needed."

"Have you any money?" asked the mother, with a brisk effort at cheerfulness. She was already planning for her daughter in the new world she was about to enter.

"Enough to start me. That's all I need. I can earn more. It's not work I'm afraid of, although I suppose father won't be able to see it that way. He'll put all this down to laziness and obstinacy. It's neither. It's just a plain human craving to *live*."

"I sometimes wonder whether I'll be able to stand it through to the end," her mother whispered, somewhat fearfully, as though frightened by the admission. "I've—I've seen it coming with you, and I can't help feeling that perhaps this is only the beginning."

"Oh, mother, if you should!" cried the girl. "That would do it—that would open his eyes. He'd see then that there is something in the world besides wheat and cows, after all. You know, I think he's in a kind of trance. He's mesmerized by wheat. It was so necessary in those first years, when he was fighting against actual starvation, that it has become a kind of mania. Nothing short of some great shock will bring him out of it. If you would come—if you would only come too, things would be different."

"But I couldn't do that," said the mother, after a silence, and as though speaking with herself. "He's my husband, Beulah. You don't understand."

They talked then, in secret, sorrowful confidence, of many things, things for their ears only, and the grey was returning in the northern sky when the girl again left the house, and this time swung resolutely down the road that led to Plainville. Her heart was now at rest, even at peace. In the sacred communion of that last hour she had come to see something of her mother's problem and sacrifice; and although she was going out into the world alone, she felt that somewhere, some time, was a solution that would reunite the broken family and tune their varying chords in harmony. The North star shone very brightly amid the myriad finer points of light that filled the heavens. She raised her face to the cold rays. The stars had always a strange fascination for her. Their illimitable distances, their infinite number, their ordered procession—all spelled to her a Purpose—a Purpose that was bigger than wheat and land and money, a Purpose that was life, the life for which she groped vaguely but bravely in the darkness.

From an unhappy sleep in his room upstairs John Harris was awakened by the whine of the cream separator. A quiet smile stole across his strong, still handsome face. "Beulah has decided to be sensible," he whispered to himself.

In the morning the Harris household was astir early as usual. The farmer and his son gave their attention to the horses while Mary prepared breakfast, and it was not until they were seated at the table that Harris noticed his daughter's absence.

"Where's Beulah?" he demanded.

"I don't know," his wife replied.

"Ain't she up yet?"

"I don't know."

Harris rose from the table and went upstairs. He entered his daughter's room without knocking. The bed had not been slept in, and a strange apprehension suddenly tightened about his chest. He returned quickly to the kitchen.

"Mary," he said, "I want to know where Beulah is."

"I can't tell you where she is, John. She left here last night."

"Left here? Do you mean that she has run away?"

"Not just that, perhaps, but she has gone, and I'm not looking for her back for a while." The mother's voice was dry, and she talked in the restraint of subdued emotion.

"And you knew she was going?"

"I knew before she left. I didn't——"

"No. You didn't think it was worth mentioning to me. Just a matter we could talk about any time. I suppose you thought I wouldn't care."

"Well, you didn't seem to care very much, John. You gave your orders and went to bed. Beulah could obey or get out. You might have known she had enough of your own spirit to soon settle that question. She settled it just as you would have settled it if you had been in her place."

"Oh, of course, I'm to blame for the whole thing," said Harris, and his throat was thick as he spoke. His daughter was very dear to him, and that she would leave home had never entered his head. Why should she? Wasn't he a good father? Didn't he give her a good home, with plenty to eat and wear, and a little money to spend from time to time, and no questions asked? What more could a man do than that? Already his heart was crying out for his daughter—the cry of broken strings which never knew their strength until they broke. But to show any emotion, or to express regret for anything he had done, meant surrender, and if there was one thing John Harris could not do it was surrender. Not that he felt he had done anything wrong, or even imprudent; he was sincerely sorry for what had happened, but not for his part in it. And, lest gentleness should be mistaken for weakness, he clothed his real feelings in sharp words to his wife.

"Of course, you must take her part. I suppose you advised her to go. It was an awful thing for me to tell her she must do her work, but a small thing for her to run away. Well, I hope she likes it. If she thinks I'm going to hitch up a buggy and go chasing around the neighbourhood, begging her to come back, she's mistaken. She's gone of her own free will, and she can come back of the same, or not at all."

"I wouldn't look for her back too soon," remarked Allan. "Looks to me as though this thing had all been figured out ahead. Jim went yesterday morning; Beulah goes last night. Just a chance if they ain't married by this time."

"So that's it, is it?" exclaimed Harris, jumping up from his untouched breakfast. There was a fierce light in his eye and a determination in his face that boded ill to any who opposed him. He seized his wife roughly by the shoulder. "And you were a party to this, were you? You—you wouldn't even stop at that? Well, I'll stop it. I'll stop him, if I do it with a bullet. I'll show him whether any—any— *hired man*—can cross me in a matter of my own family."

His wife had risen, and was clinging to his wrists, half for protection, half in suppliance. "Now, John," she pleaded, "don't be rash. You don't know that Beulah's gone with Jim, and you haven't a word of proof of it."

"Proof! What more proof do I want? When did ever Beulah carry on like this before? Didn't she always do as she was told? And haven't they been thick as molasses this while back? Wasn't it over wasting time with

her that Jim got fired, and not a word of aꝺ-
mission of the real facts from him? What
more do you want than that? And on top of
it all you help her away, and keep it a secret
from me as long as you can. I daresay you
knew their plans from the first. You thought
I wouldn't be interested in that, either."

"I didn't know it," she protested, "and I
don't believe it. I don't believe either Beulah
or Jim had any such thought in their head.
But even if they did, Jim Travers is as decent
a young man as there is in Plainville district,
and you've nothing to be ashamed of except
your own temper, that drove them away in the
way they went."

"I won't listen to that kind of talk from you
any longer," said Harris sternly. "I'll chase
the young reprobates to earth, if it takes all
summer. And unless you can clear yourself of
being mixed up in this—well, there'll be something to settle on that score, too. Hitch up the
drivers, Allan, and be quick about it."

"You're not going to leave your ploughing,
are you?" asked his wife. The words sprang
to her lips without any misintent. It was such
an unusual thing for her husband, on any
account, to leave the farm work unfinished.
The practice on the Harris homestead was
work first, all other considerations second.

"That's enough of your sarcasm," he
snapped. "I would think when our name is

threatened with a disgrace like this you would be as anxious to defend it as I am. How is it you go back on me in a moment like this? You're not the woman you once were, Mary."

"And you're not the man you once were, John," she answered. "Oh, can't you see that we're just reaping what has been sown—the crop we're been raising through all these years? Beulah's very life has been crying out for action, for scope, for room, for something that would give her a reason for existence, that would put a purpose into her life, and we've not tried to answer that cry. I blame myself as much as you, John, perhaps more, because I should have read her heart—I should have seen the danger signals long ago. But I was so busy, I didn't think. That's the trouble, John, we've been so busy, both of us, we haven't taken time to keep up with her. The present generation is not the past; what was enough for you and me isn't enough for our children. It doesn't do any good to scold— scolding doesn't change conditions; but if we'd stopped and thought and studied over them we might have changed them—or cured them. We didn't, John; you were too busy with your wheat and your cattle, and I was too busy with my house-work, and what have we made of it? We've gathered some property together, and our cares have grown in proportion, but that which was more to us than all the property in the world we have lost—because we valued it less." The tears were slowly coursing down her cheeks, and her thin, work-worn arms were stealing about his neck. "Don't think, dear," she whispered, "that I'm indifferent, or that this hurts me less than you, or that I would shield myself from one iota of my just blame, but let us face the fact that it has been our mistake rather than Beulah's."

He removed her arms, not ungently. "I never thought it would come to this," he said. "I thought I humoured her every way I could. As for our hard work—well, work makes money, and I noticed Beulah could spend her share. There was no protesting about the work that earned the money when she wanted a new hat or a new dress, and she generally got what she wanted."

"You don't understand, John. It wasn't the work, it was the making a god of work, and giving it so much of our lives that there was none left for her. That's why she looked somewhere else—if she has looked somewhere else."

"Allan works as hard and harder than ever Beulah did, and Allan doesn't feel that way about it."

"That's true," she admitted, "but Allan's ambition is work. He works and is satisfied, but Beulah thinks, and is not satisfied. It's the difference in their nature, and we didn't take it into consideration." In every phrase she tried to link his blame with hers, that the burden might unite instead of separate them.

"If she'd thought a little more before this mad prank it would have been better for everybody," he said. "Well, she'll have plenty of time to think yet." He stepped to the kitchen door, and from the nail above took down the repeating-rifle.

"You're not going to take that!" she cried. "Don't take that, John. It can't possibly do any good, and it may do a lot of harm."

"I won't do anything foolish," he answered, "but I'll take it along, just the same."

Allan, with the drivers harnessed to the top buggy, was now at the door. Without saying good-bye to his wife Harris joined him, and the two set off on their search. Almost at the gate they met George Grant, who had come over to haul water for another day's ploughing. He stopped in some surprise at the turn-out.

"I guess we won't be ploughing to-day," said Harris. He hesitated before George's questioning look, and a certain sense of family shame came upon him. But it was evident that he could hardly search for Beulah without mentioning her departure, and he might as well make a clean breast of the affair.

"Nothing wrong at home, I hope, Mr. Harris?" said the young neighbour, noting his troubled appearance. "Nobody sick, or anything?"

"Yes, there is something wrong," said Harris, trying vainly to conceal the bitterness in his voice. "Beulah's left us."

"Who, Beulah? I can hardly believe that, Mr. Harris. It was only last night I was talking with her."

"Well, she's gone. Left through the night. We—well, I'll tell you, George—we had a little disagreement, but I'd no notion she'd take it so much to heart. Of course you know about the trouble with Jim yesterday. Taking everything together—there won't be no ploughing to-day." Harris had said more than he meant; he could feel the colour mounting into his hair, and the bad English of his last words betrayed a subtle recklessness rather than carelessness of speech.

"Don't you believe a word of it," said George. "I know Jim, and I know Beulah, and if anybody else hinted what you've said you'd want to use that rifle on them. Like enough Beulah's staying somewhere around the neighbourhood, and she'll be back when she has time to think it over."

"That proves you *don't* know Beulah," said Allan. "As for Jim, I was never able to get below that smile, and I saw more of him than you did, George."

"Well, I hope you find a way out," said

George, sincerely. "It would have been like her to come over to our place, but she isn't there. Maybe you'll find her at Morrison's."

"That's possible," said Harris. "We'll go over there, anyway."

But Morrisons knew no more of Beulah's whereabouts than did George, and inquiry at other homes in the neighbourhood was equally futile. Harris shrank from carrying his search into the town, as he dreaded the publicity that would be attached to it. He was a subscriber, somewhat in arrears, to the local paper, and by calling on the editor and squaring up for a year in advance he could probably make himself solid in that quarter, but the gossip of the villagers could not be silenced by any such simple method. But as the day wore on and the search continued fruitless he finally found himself in Plainville. If Beulah and Jim were really married the Presbyterian minister would be likely to know something of the matter, and the Rev. Andrew Guthrie was a man of sense and discernment. Harris had frequently gone to hear him preach before the labours of the farm had grown to their present magnitude, and he even yet contributed five dollars a year to the stipend.

Mr. Guthrie received his guest cordially, albeit with some wonderment as to which member of the family might be sick, but delicacy forbade a direct question. Now, in agricultural communities it is something of an offence to approach any matter of importance by frontal attack. There must be the due amount of verbal skirmishing, reconnoitering, and out-flanking before the main purpose is revealed. Consequently, Harris, for all his torture of suspense, spent some minutes in a discussion of the weather, the crops, and the prospect of a labour shortage in harvest.

"They'll be all well at home, I hope?" said Mr. Guthrie at length, feeling that the custom of the community had been sufficiently honoured.

"Yes, all that's there," said Harris.

"All that's there? I didn't know any of your folks were away. Perhaps Mrs. Harris is down East? I'm sure a summer amid the orchards of her old home would be a delight to her, and, of course, Mr. Harris, you are able to gratify yourself in these little matters now. Things are not what they were in the early days, Jack, when I preached in Tom Morrison's log-house, and you led the bass at the services. I'll warrant that voice of yours could sing yet if you gave it a chance."

Harris received these remarks with a mixture of feelings. The minister's reference to his financial standing carried with it a certain gratification, but it consorted poorly with his recent conversations with his wife and with his present mission.

"And Beulah?" continued the minister, conscious that his first shot had gone wild. "She's a fine young woman now. I see her in church occasionally. In fact, I was speaking with Mrs. Burton, the choir leader, a day or so ago, and Beulah's name was mentioned between us."

"It was about Beulah I came to see you," said Harris, with averted eyes. Then in a few words he gave his version of what he knew and what he suspected.

"I fear I can add nothing to your information," said Mr. Guthrie. "They haven't been here, and, as you say, if Beulah contemplated marriage I think she would have called on me. Travers, too, I knew a little, and thought him a decent chap. But we must find the girl and talk this over quietly with her. Is there any place in town she would be likely to go to? What about Mrs. Goode's boarding-house? I will just call up on the telephone. I can make inquiry without the necessity of any explanations."

Inquiry at the house of Mrs. Goode brought a strong ray of light out of the darkness. Beulah had been there during the morning, and had explained that she was leaving on the west-bound train, which even now was thrumming at the station. On learning this, without a word, Harris sprang into the buggy, while Allan brought a sharp cut of the whip across the spirited horses. They reached the railway station half a minute too late; the train was already pulling out, and as Harris's eyes followed it in anger and vexation they plainly saw Jim Travers swing lithely on to the rear platform.

With an oath the farmer reached for his rifle, but Allan wrenched it from his hands before any onlookers noted the action. "Don't be a fool," he whispered, and started the horses homeward.

CHAPTER X

FOR the first time in his life Harris surrendered his purpose to the judgment of his son, and as they drove homeward along the dusty trail in the heat of the day the consciousness came home to him that Allan was right. To have used his gun would, of course, have been madness; he had never seriously intended doing anything so rash, although for one impetuous moment his passion had made him irresponsible. And, as he thought it all over, he concluded that nothing was to be gained by pursuit of the runaways. There was only one west-bound train in the day; he could not give chase until the morrow, and they would be able to lead him by twenty-four hours as long as he cared to keep up the pursuit. True, he might telegraph ahead to the police, but that meant publicity, and would probably be ineffectual in the end. She had gone of her own free will, and although his heart hurt even under his anger, now that she had gone she might stay. She had left a good home, a fond father, and a share in the family estate for a—hired man—

[152]

and she might now make the best of her bargain. Harris assured himself, with absolute
sincerity, that he had done his duty in the
matter, and that in exchange for all his kindness his daughter had treated him very badly
indeed.

During the drive homeward his thoughts
persistently turned to the share his wife had
had in Beulah's departure, and his feeling toward Mary grew more and more hostile. Not
that he altogether disbelieved her when she
professed ignorance of the young couple's intention; he could not go so far as to think that
she had lied to him, but he was inwardly convinced that she had at least an inkling of their
plans, and that, so far from attempting to dissuade them, she was really in sympathy with
their wild escapade. Harris was very fond of
his wife, who had shared with him all the
hardships of pioneer life, and who, he admitted, had been a faithful and devoted help-
meet, and her desertion of him in the present
crisis was therefore all the less to be excused
or condoned. He resolved, however, that there
should be no open breach between them; he
would neither scold nor question her, but
would impress her with his displeasure by
adopting a cold, matter-of-fact, speak-when-
you're-spoken-to attitude toward her.

Under the circumstances it was not remarkable that Harris's work began to loom larger

than ever in his life. The space left vacant by his daughter he filled with extra energy driving the great ploughs through the mellow summer-fallow. A new tank-man was engaged, and the rumble of the engine was heard up and down the fields from early morning until dark. From his wife he held aloof, speaking with strained courtesy when speech was necessary. She, in turn, schooled for years in self-effacement, hid her sorrow in her heart, and went about her work with a resignation which he mistook for cheerfulness, and which confirmed him in his opinion that she knew more of Beulah's intentions than she had cared to admit. Only with Allan his relations remained unchanged; indeed, the attachment between the two grew deeper than ever. The young man avoided any reference to Beulah; what he felt in his own heart he kept to himself, but the father shrewdly guessed that he laid the whole blame on Travers.

So the summer wore on; the black bosom of the fallow field widened day by day, and the smell of growing wheat filled the dew-laden evening air. The picnic season, the time of athletic competitions, baseball matches, and rural sociability, rolled by, but Harris scarcely knew of its passing. He had long ago ceased to take any personal interest in the frivolities of the neighbourhood; he saw in picnics and baseball games only an unprofitable misuse of time, and when he thought of them at all it was to congratulate himself that Allan was not led away by any such foolishness. Finding no great happiness in his own home, he had fallen into the way of walking over to Riles's on Sunday afternoons, and the two spent many hours in discussion of their proposed land-seeking expedition.

Meanwhile Mary plodded along with her housework, toiling doggedly from five in the morning until half-past nine or ten at night. Beulah's departure had left all the labours of the home upon her hands; her husband had made no suggestion of securing help, and she had not asked any. The new man made no offer to milk any of the cows; a dozen hours in the field was day enough for him, and whatever time was over he spent smoking cigarettes in the shelter of the barn. Allan occasionally did help with the milking, and more frequently with turning the separator, but it was so late when he stopped his work in the field she was sorry for him, and tried to have the milk cleared away before he arrived on the scene. One or two postcards she had had from Beulah, but they brought no great information. They came in the open mail; her husband was welcome to read them if he chose, but as he had sought his own company exclusively since Beulah's departure she made no attempt to force them upon him.

THE HOMESTEADERS

At last one morning came a letter, a big fat letter, left in by a neighbour passing by, as the custom was for any settler going to town to bring out the mail for those who lived along his route. She tore the envelope open nervously and devoured its contents with hungry eyes.

"MY DEAR MOTHER,

"Here I am, in the shadow of the Rockies. That may sound poetical, but it's a literal fact. It is still early in the evening, but the sun has disappeared behind the great masses to the west, and the valley which my window overlooks is filling up with blackness. The Arthurses are pure gold, and I have told them everything. They don't blame anyone, not even father. How is he? Slaving as usual, I suppose.

"Well, I must tell you about my trip. When I left the house that night I had no idea where I was going, but the simplest thing seemed to be to go first to Plainville. The North Star led that way, and it seemed a good guide to follow. As I walked the lights came out in the Arctic sky—a great bow of them, swelling and fading in their delicate tints. I watched them and plodded along, trying not to think very much about anything.

"You've no idea how heavy that suit-case got, but I took my time, as there was nothing to gain by reaching town before daylight.

THE HOMESTEADERS

When I got there it struck me it might be a good plan to have some breakfast, so I walked round to Goode's boarding-house. Mrs. Goode was bustling about, and received me with open arms. 'Well, my Land! if it ain't Beunah Harris!' she exclaimed—she always called me Beunah—'Goodness, child, what are you doing about this early in the morning? But there, I needn't ask, knowin' what a worker your father is. I'll be bound he drove you in before sunrise to lose no time with his ploughin'. Well, that's what makes the mare go. I wish my man had some of it—he's snorin' up on the second floor at this minute like to lift the shingles. I often say to myself, "For the little he does and the lot he eats the Lord knows what keeps him so thin."' (It's a grievance of Mrs. Goode's that her husband won't fatten up; she thinks it's a reflection on her cooking.) 'And with your suit-case! You'll be taking the train? West, is it, or East? But you'll be hungry, child. Take off your things there while I see to my buns—I always give the boarders hot buns for break-fast——' you know how she rattles on. But she's a good soul, if a bit conceited over her cooking, and wouldn't take a cent for my keep either. Of course she didn't wait for me to answer her questions, and she really suggested the plan which I took. After breakfast I went over to the station, and asked what the fare was to Arthurs' station; I found I had enough money for the trip, and I bought a ticket without further ado.

"I won't try to tell you all about my trip—it would take a book. But what a country it is! Of course I had learned in school that there was about two feet of map between the Red River and the Rockies, but there's only one way to know how big it is, and that's to travel it. If you've got any imagination at all a trip over these enormous prairies must set it stirring. For the most part there's no settlement; not a house, nor stack, nor any sign of life. Pretty much like Manitoba was, I guess, when you first saw it, but bigger, and grander, and more suggestive of the future. You see, Manitoba has made good, for all the doubters, and this bigger West will do the same, on a bigger scale. As we rolled along through that unbroken prairie, with here and there a great herd of horses or cattle in the distance, I felt at last that I was really beginning to live. Not that I was doing anything grander than running away from home, but still that feeling came over me—the feeling that here was a country where things were going to happen, and that I was going to play some part in their happening.

"Well, if I ramble on like this it'll be a real book after all. Calgary is the big cow-town of the West, just beginning to aspire to higher—

THE HOMESTEADERS

or lower (there's a real question there)—civilization, and mixing schaps and silks on its streets in a strange struggle between the past and the future. But my stay there was short, as I was able to catch my branch train with little delay, and that night saw me at Arthurs' nearest station. The homestead rush is on here in earnest; the trains are crowded, mostly with Americans, and the hotels are simply spilling over. They're a motley crowd, these homesteaders. Down with us, you know, the settlers were looking for homes, and a chance to make a living, but up here they're out for money—the long green, they call it. Their idea is to prove up and sell their lands, when they will either buy more or leave the country. But the great point is that they are after money rather than homes. They belong to a class which has been rushing for a generation ahead of a wave of high land values—I heard a man say that in the train, and I made a note of it—they're rovers by birth and training, with no great home instinct. To them one place is as good as another—provided always there's money to be made there—and one flag is almost as good as another. Of course this will right itself in time; the first flood of landseekers are soil-miners, but the second are home-builders—the man said that too; you see I'm picking things up; I want to know about something besides the weather—and when that second flood comes this country won't know itself.

"But to come back to the hotel; that's what I did when I had taken a good walk about the little town, and admired myself almost homesick looking at fine horses tied to hitching-posts and fine men swaggering about in the abandon of cow-boy costumes. One thing I have learned already, and the discovery shocked me a little at first; the cow-boy considers himself better clay than the farmer—the 'sod-buster' he calls him—and treats him with good-humoured contempt. I wanted to ask someone about Arthurs, and I didn't like to inquire in the hotel. There was a lot of drinking going on there. But near the door were two young men talking, and I overheard one of them mention Arthurs' name. Pulling myself together, I asked him if he could tell me where Arthurs lived.

" 'Yes, miss,' he answered, lifting a big hat and showing when he spoke a clean set of teeth. 'It's twenty-five miles up the river. Were you expecting him to meet you?'

"I explained that I had intended to drop in on them by surprise, but I had had no idea they lived so far from town.

" 'Oh, that's not far,' he said. 'Can you ride?'

"Everybody here rides horseback. It's the standard means of locomotion. And the women ride astride. I was a bit shocked at first, but you soon get used to it. But twenty-five miles is different from a romp round the pasture-field, so I said I was afraid not.

" 'Arthurs is coming down with the buck-board,' remarked the other man. 'I passed him on the trail as I came in.'

"Sure enough, a little later Arthurs himself drew up at the hotel. I wouldn't have known him, but one of the young men pointed him out, and it would have done you good to see how he received me. 'And you are Jack and Mary's daughter,' he said, taking both my hands in his, and holding me at arm's length for a moment. Then, before I knew it, he had drawn me up and kissed me. But I didn't care. All of a sudden it seemed to me that I had found a real father. It seems hard to say it, but that is how I felt.

"Well, he just couldn't keep away from me all evening. He showered me with questions about you and father, which I answered as well as I could, but I soon found I couldn't keep my secret, so I just up and told him all. He was very grave, but not cross. 'You need time to think things over, and to get a right perspective,' he said, 'and our home will be yours until you do.'

"We drove home the next day, up a wonder-ful river valley, deep into the heart of the foot-hills, with the blue mountains always beckoning and receding before us. Mrs. Arthurs was as surprised and delighted as he had been, and I won't try to tell you all the things she said to me. She cried a little, too, and I'm afraid I came near helping her a bit. You know the Arthurs lost their little girl before they left Manitoba, and they have had no other children. They both seemed just hungry.

"There's nothing so very fine about their home, except the spirit that's inside it. I can't describe it, but it's there—a certain leisurely way of doing things, a sense that they have made work their servant instead of their master. And still they're certainly not lazy, and they've accomplished more than we have. When they left Manitoba in the early days, discouraged with successive frosts, they came right out here into the foothills with their few head of stock. Now their cattle are numbered in thousands, and they have about a township of land. And still they seem to live for the pure happiness they find in life, and only to think of their property as a secondary consideration.

"Now I really must close. Mrs. Arthurs sends a note, and I'm quite sure it's an invitation. Oh, mother, what could be lovelier! Now don't say you can't. Father has plenty of money; let him hire a housekeeper for a while. The change will do him good.

THE HOMESTEADERS

"Love to you, dearest, and to Allan, if he still thinks of me.

"BEULAH.

"P.S.—I forgot to mention that Jim Travers left Plainville on the same train as I did. He could hardly believe his eyes when he saw me there. I told him I was going West on a visit, but I don't know how much he guessed. Said he was going West himself to take up land, but he wanted to call on some friends first, and he got off a few stations from Plainville. Between you and me, I believe he changed his plan so that the incident—our being on the train together, you know—could not be misunderstood if the neighbours got to know of it. It would be just like Jim to do that."

With Beulah's letter was a short but earnest note from Lilian Arthurs, assuring the mother of her daughter's welfare, and pressing an invitation to spend the autumn in the glorious scenery and weather of the foothill country. Mary Harris read both letters over again, with frequent rubbing of her glasses. Love for her daughter, desire to see her old friend once more, and growing dissatisfaction with conditions at home, all combined to give weight to the invitation so earnestly extended. "If I only could!" she said to herself. "If I only could! But it would cost so much."

The dinner was late that day, and Harris was in worse humour than usual. He had just broken a plough-beam, which meant an afternoon's delay and some dollars of expense. When he had started his meal his wife laid the full envelope before him. "A letter from Beulah," she said.

Without a word he rose from the table, took the letter in his hand, and thrust it into the kitchen range. A blue flame slowly cut round the envelope; the pages began to curl like dry leaves in autumn, and presently the withered ghost of the missive shrank away in the dull glare of the coal fire behind.

CHAPTER XI

THE PRICE OF "SUCCESS"

AT last the ploughing was finished, and, although the rich smell of wheat in the milk filled the air, it still would be almost a month before the ripening crops were ready for the binder. Harris felt that he could now allow himself a breathing spell, and that the opportunity to investigate the rich lands of the Farther West was at hand. Many nights, while Mary milked the cows, he had walked over to Riles', and the two had discussed their forthcoming venture until they had grown almost enthusiastic over it. Riles, it must be said, was the leading spirit in the movement; although already possessed of sufficient land and means to keep him in comfort through his advancing years, the possibility of greater wealth, and particularly of wealth to be had without corresponding effort, was a lure altogether irresistible. And Harris fell in with the plan readily enough. A quarter of a century having elapsed since his former homesteading, he was now eligible again to file on free Government land; Allan could do the same, and, by also taking advantage of the purchase of script, it was possible to still further increase their holdings. In addition to all this, Riles had unfolded a scheme for staking two or three others on free homestead land: it would be necessary, of course, to provide them with "grub" and a small wage during the three years required to prove up, but in consideration of these benefactions the titles to the land, when secured, were to be promptly transferred to Riles and Harris. This was strictly against the law, but the two pioneers felt no sense of crime or shame for their plans, but rather congratulated themselves upon their cunning though by no means original scheme to evade the regulations.

Harris found the task of disclosing his intentions to his wife more unpleasant than he would have supposed, and it took him some days to make up his mind to broach the subject. He felt that he was doing what was for the best, and that his business judgment in the matter could hardly be challenged; and yet he had an uncomfortable feeling that his wife would not fall in with his plans. That, of course, would not be allowed to affect his plans; since Beulah's departure nothing but the most formal conversation had taken place in their household; yet it would certainly be easier for him if Mary should give her encouragement to his undertaking. He felt that he was entitled to this, for was it not for her that he was making the sacrifice? Was not all he had hers? And were not all his labours directed toward increasing her reserve against the rainy day? And yet instinctively he felt that she would oppose him.

It was the evening of a long day in July when, very much to Mary's surprise, her husband took the handle of the cream separator from her. To the sad-hearted woman it seemed that the breach was at length beginning to heal, and that happiness would shortly return to their hearthside. Below the din of the separator she actually found herself humming an old love-song of the 'eighties.

But her happiness was of short duration. When the milk had been run through, and the noise of the whirling bowl no longer prevented conversation, Harris immediately got down to business.

"Allan and me will be leavin' for the West in a day or two," he said. "I suppose you can get along all right for a few weeks until harvest. Bill (the hired man) will be here."

In an instant she saw the motive behind his apparent kindness, and the hopes she had just entertained only deepened the flood of resentment which swept over them. But she answered quietly and without apparent emotion: "That's unfortunate, as I was planning for a little trip myself."

"You!" he exclaimed. "You plannin' a

trip! Where in the world do you want to go?"
Such a thing as Mary going on a trip, and,
above all, unaccompanied by himself, was un-
heard of and unthinkable.

"Yes, I thought I would take a little trip,"
she continued. "I've been working here pretty
hard for something over twenty-five years, and
you may say I've never been off the place. A
bit of a holiday shouldn't do me any harm."

"Where do you think of goin'?" he demanded, a sudden suspicion arising in his
mind. "Goin' to visit Jim and Beulah?"

"I think you might at least be fair to Beulah," she retorted. "If you had read her letter, instead of putting it in the stove, you
would have known better."

"I ain't interested in anythin' Beulah may
have to say, and any other letters that fall into
my hands will go in the same direction. And
what's more, she's not goin' to have a visit
from any member of this family at the present
time. I'm goin' out West to take up land, and
Allan's goin' with me. It ain't fair or reason-
able for you to try to upset our plans by a
notion of this kind."

"It isn't a notion, John, it's a resolve. If
you are bound to take up more land, with more
work and more worry, why go ahead, but remember it's your own undertaking. I helped
to make one home in the wilderness, and one
home's enough for me."

"Don't be unreasonable," he answered. "There's a great opportunity right now to get land for nothin' that in a few years will be worth as much or more than this here. I'm ready to go through the hardship and the work for the sake of what it will do for us. We can be independently rich in five years, if we just stand together."

"Independent of what?" she asked.

"Why, independent of—of everything. Nothin' more to worry about and plenty laid up for old age. Ain't that worth a sacrifice?"

"John," she said, turning and raising her eyes to his face. "Answer me a straight question. What was the happiest time in your life? Wasn't it when we lived in the one-roomed sod shanty, with scarcely a cent to bless ourselves? We worked hard then, too, but we had time for long walks together across the prairies—time to sit in the dusk by the water and plan our lives together. We have done well; we have land, horses, machinery, money. But have we the happiness we knew when we had none of these? On the contrary, are you not worried morning, noon, and night over your work and your property? Don't you complain about the kind of help the farmers have to hire nowadays, and the wages they have to pay? And if you get more land won't all your troubles be increased in proportion? John, sit down and think this thing over. We don't need more property; what we need is a chance to enjoy the property we already have. The one thing we haven't got, the one thing it seems we can't get, is time. Time to think, time to read, time for walks on the prairie, time for sunsets, and skies, and—and kindness, and all the things that make life real. We have the chance to choose now between life and land; won't you think it all over again and let us seek that which is really worth while?"

"Now I know where Beulah got her nonsense," he retorted. "All this talk about real life is very fine, but you don't get much life, real or any other kind, unless you have the cash to pay down for it. You can't buy beefsteaks with long walks over the prairie, nor clothe yourself and family with sunsets. For my part I want some real success. We've done pretty well here, as you say, but it's only a beginnin' to what we can do, if we set about it, and don't wait until the cheap land is all gone. I don't see why you should go back on me at this time o' life, Mary. We've stood together for a long while, and I kinda figured I could count on you."

"So you can, John; so you can to the very last, for anything that is for your own good, but when you set your heart on something that means more trouble and hardship and won't add one iota to your happiness, I think it is my duty to persuade you if I can. We've been drifting apart lately; why not let us both go back to the beginning and start over again, and by kindness, and fairness, and liberality, and—and sympathy, try to recover something of what we have lost?"

"I have always thought I had been liberal enough," he said. "Didn't I build you a good house and buy furniture for it, and do I stint you in what you spend, either on the table or yourself? More than that, didn't I put the title to the homestead in your name? And ain't I ready to do the same with the new homestead, if that's the sticker?"

"I never thought of such a thing," she protested. "And you shouldn't claim too much credit for putting the homestead quarter in my name. You know when you bought the first railroad land you were none too sure how things would come out, and you thought it might be a wise precaution to have the old farm stand in your wife's name."

"That's all the thanks I get," he said bitterly. "Well, I'll take the new one in my own name, but I'll take it just the same. If you don't want to share in it you won't have to. But for the present it's your duty to stay here and run things till we get back."

"What are you going to do after you get your new farm? You can't work two farms a thousand miles apart, can you?"

"Oh, I guess that won't worry us long. The

Americans are comin' in now with lots o' good money. I was figurin' up that this place, as a goin' concern, ought to bring about forty thousand dollars, and I'll bet I could sell it inside of a week."

"Sell it?" she exclaimed. "You don't mean that you intend to sell this farm?"

"Why not? If somebody else wants it worse'n we do, and has the money to pay for it, why shouldn't I sell it?"

The tears stood in her eyes as she answered: "In all these years while we have been building up this home I never once thought of it as something to sell. It was too near for that— a part of ourselves, of our very life. It seemed more like—like one of the children, than a mere possession. And now you would sell it, just as you might sell a load of wheat or a fat steer. Is this place—this home where we have grown old and grey—nothing to you? Have you no sentiment that will save it from the highest bidder?"

"Sentiment is a poor affair in business," he answered. "Property was made t' sell; money was made t' buy it with. The successful man is the one who has his price for everythin', and knows how t' get it. As for growin' old and grey on this farm, why, that's a grudge I have against it, though I don't think I'm very grey and I don't feel very old. And if I get my price, why shouldn't I sell?"

"Very well," she answered. "I've nothing more to say. Sell it if you must, but remember one thing—I won't be here to see it pass into the hands of strangers." She straightened herself up, and there was a fire in her eye that reminded him of the day when she had elected to share with him the hardships of the wilderness, and in spite of himself some of his old pride in her returned. "I leave to-morrow for a visit, and I may be gone some time. You reminded me of your liberality a few minutes ago; prove it now by writing me a cheque for my expenses. Remember I will expect to travel like the wife of a prosperous farmer, a man whose holdings are worth forty thousand dollars cash."

"So that's your decision, is it? You set me at defiance; you try t' wreck my plans by your own stubbornness. You break up my family piece by piece, until all I have left is Allan. Thank God, the boy, at least, is sound. Well, you shall have your cheque, and I'll make it a big one that it may carry you the farther."

Even in the teeth of his bitterness the mention of Allan's name strained the mother's heart beyond her power of resistance, and she turned with outstretched arms towards her husband. For a moment he wavered, the flame of love, still smouldering in his breast, leaping up before the breath of her response. But it was for a moment only. Weakness would have meant surrender, and surrender was the one thing of which Harris was incapable. He had laid out his course with a clear conscience; he was sincerely working for the greatest good to his family, and if his wife was determined to stand in her own light it was his duty to pursue the course in defiance of her. So he checked the impulse to take her in his arms, and walked stolidly to his desk in the parlour.

He returned shortly and placed a cheque in her hands. She looked at it through misty eyes, and read that it was for two hundred dollars. It represented a two-hundredth part of their joint earnings, and yet he thought he was dealing liberally with her; he half expected, in fact, that his magnanimity would break her down where his firmness had failed. But she only whispered a faint "Thank you," and slowly folded the paper in her fingers. He waited for a minute, suspecting that she was overcome, but as she said nothing more he at length turned and left the house, saying gruffly as he went out, "When that's done I'll send you more if you write for it."

It was now ten at night, and almost dark, but Harris's footsteps instinctively turned down the road toward Riles'. Riles' reputation in the community was that of a hard-working, money-grubbing farmer, with a big bony body, and a little shrivelled soul, if indeed the latter had not entirely dried up into ashes. A few years ago Harris had held his neighbour in rather low regard, but of late he had been more and more impressed with Riles' ability to make his farm pay, which was as great as or greater than his own, and what he had once thought to be hardness and lack of humanity he now recognized as simply the capacity to take a common-sense, business view of conditions.

At the gate he met Allan, returning from spending a social hour with the grant boys.

"Where going, Dad?" the younger man demanded.

"Oh, I thought I'd take a walk over t' Riles'. There's a lot o' things t' talk about."

"What's the matter, Dad?" The strained composure of his father's voice had not escaped him.

"Nothin' .... I might's well tell you now; you'll know it in a little while anyway. . . . Your mother is goin' away—on a visit."

"Like Beulah's visit, I suppose. So it's come to this. I've seen it for some time, Dad, and you must 've seen it too. But you're not really goin' to let her go? Come back to the house with me—surely you two can get together on this thing, if you try."

"I have tried," said Harris, "and it's no use. She's got those notions like Beulah—quittin' work, and twilights and sunsets and all that kind o' thing. There's no use talkin' with her;

reason don't count for anything. I gave her a good pocketful o' money, and told her to write for more when she needed it. She'll get over her notions pretty soon when she gets among strangers. Go in and have a talk with her, boy; there's no use you bein' at outs with her, too. As for me, I can't do anything more."

"I suppose you know best," he answered, "but it seems—hang it, it's against all reason that you two—that this should happen."

"Of course it is. That's what I said a minute ago. But reason don't count just now. But you have your talk with her, and give her any help you can if she wants t' get away at once."

Allan found his mother in her room, packing a trunk and gently weeping into it. He laid his hand upon her, and presently he found her work-worn frame resting in his strong arms.

"You're not going to leave us, mother, are you?" he said. "You wouldn't do that?"

"Not if it could be helped, Allan. But there is no help. Your father has set his heart on more land, and more work, and giving up this home, and I might as well go first as last. More and more he is giving his love to work instead of to his family. I bear him no ill-will —nothing, nothing but love, if he could only come out of this trance of his and see things in their true light. But as time goes on he gets

[176]

only deeper in. Perhaps when I am away for a while he'll come to himself. That's our only hope."

The boy stood helpless in this confliction. He had always thought of difficulties arising between people, between neighbours, friends, or members of a family, because one party was right and the other wrong. It was his first experience of those far more tragic quarrels where both parties are right, or seem to be right. He knew something of the depth of the nature of his parents, and he knew that beneath an undemonstrative exterior they cherished in secret a love proportionate to the strength of their characters. But the long course down which they had walked together seemed now to be separating, through neither will nor power of their own; it was as though straight parallel lines suddenly turned apart, and neither lost its straightness in the turning.

So he comforted his mother with such words as he could. Loyalty to his father forbade laying any of the blame on those shoulders, and to blame his mother was unthinkable; so with unconscious wisdom he spoke not of blame at all. Presently it occurred to him to think of his mother's departure as temporary only, and with joy he found that she readily accepted the notion.

"Of course, while we are away, why shouldn't you have a visit?" he said. "Here you have been chained down to this farm ever since I can remember, and before. We can easy enough arrange about the cows; and Bill can board with one o' the neighbours, or batch, and you can just have a good trip and a good rest, and nobody needs it more. And then, when I get settled on my own homestead, you'll come and keep house for me, won't you?"

"You're sure you'll want me?" she asked, greatly comforted by his mood. "Perhaps you'll be getting your own housekeeper, too."

"Not while I can have you," he answered. "You'll promise, won't you? Nothing that has happened, or can happen, will keep you from making my home yours, will it? And when Dad gets settled again, and gets all these worries off his mind, then things'll be different, and you'll come, even if he is there?"

"Yes, I'll come, even if he is there, if you ask me," she promised.

Harris did not come back that night. A light rain came up, and he accepted the excuse to sleep at Riles'. The truth was, he feared for his resolution if it should be attacked by both his wife and son. Surrender now would be mere weakness, and weakness was disgrace, and yet he feared for himself if put to the test again. So he stayed at Riles', and the two farmers spent much of the night over their plans. It had been decided that they were to leave within the next couple of days, but Harris broke the news that his wife was going on a visit, and that arrangements would have to be made for the care of the farm. He carefully concealed the fact that Mary was leaving against his will, or as the result of any difference. Such an admission would have damaged him in the estimation of Riles, who would have put it down to weakness. In Riles' code no insubordination should be tolerated from man or beast, but least of all from a wife. He would have found ready means to suppress any such foolishness.

Riles took the suggestion of a few days' delay with poor grace.

"Yes, an' while you're chasing up an' down fer a housekeeper the Yankees get all the homesteads. They're comin' in right now by the trainload, grabbin' up everythin' in sight. We'll monkey round here till the summer's over, an' then go out an' get a sand farm, or something like. Couldn't your wife do her visitin' no other time?"

"I'll tell you, Riles," said Harris, who had no desire to pursue a topic which might lead him into deep water, "you go ahead out and get the lay of the land, and I'll follow you within a week. I'll do that, for sure, and I'll stand part of your expenses for going ahead, seein' you will be kind o' representin' me."

The last touch was a stroke of diplomacy.

The suggestion that Harris should pay part of his expenses swept away Riles' bad humour, and he agreed to go on the date originally planned, and get what he called "a bede on the easy money," while Harris completed his arrangements at home.

He was to get "a bede on the easy money" in a mann'er which Harris little suspected.

When Harris returned home the next forenoon he found that Mary had already left for Plainville. He sat down and tried to think, but the house was very quiet, and the silence oppressed him. . . . He looked at his watch, and concluded he had still time to reach Plainville before the train would leave. But that would mean surrender, and surrender meant weakness.

CHAPTER XII

R ILES found the journey westward a tire-some affair. His was a soul devoid of enthusiasm over Nature's wealth or magnitude, and the view of the endless prairie excited in him no emotion other than a certain vague covetousness. It was his first long rail journey in over twenty years, but his thoughts were on the cost of travel rather than on the wonderful strides which had been made in its comfort and convenience. Riles indulged in no such luxuries as sleeping-car berths or meals served in the diner, and two nights in a crowded day-coach, with such hasty meals as could be bought for a quarter at wayside stations, made the journey a somewhat exhausting one. Back in the observation car, sleek commercial travellers, well groomed and well dressed and enveloped in comfortable self-satisfaction, gravely discussed politics, business or real estate, or exchanged the latest tit-bits of wit accumulated in their travels. Riles probably could have bought and paid for the worldly possessions of the whole group, and have still a comfortable balance in the bank.

But a sleeper berth cost the price of two bushels of wheat, and even in a good year Riles' crop seldom exceeded ten thousand bushels.

As fate would have it, Riles selected as the base of his homestead operations the very foot-hill town to which Beulah Harris had come a few weeks before. He sought out the cheapest hotel, and having thrown his few belongings on the bed, betook himself to the bar-room, which seemed the chief centre of activity, not only of the hotel itself, but of the little town. Men were lined three deep against the capacious bar, shouting, swearing, and singing, and spending their money with an abandon not to be found in millionaires. Riles was no great student of human nature; he had a keener eye for a horse than a fellow-man, but the motley crowd interested and, in a certain way, amused him. Land-seekers, some in overalls and flannel shirts, some in ready-mades with dirty celluloid collars and cheap, gaudy ties—big, powerful men with the muscles and manners of the horse—and others, lighter of frame, who apparently made an easier and a better living by the employment of their brains; cowboys in schaps and sun-burn and silk handkerchiefs; ranchers, stately English and French stock, gentlemen still five thousand miles from the place of their breeding; lumbermen and river-drivers, iron bodies set with quick, combative intellects; guides, locaters, freighters, land dealers, gamblers, sharks, and hangers-on wove back and forth plying the shuttle from which the fabric of a new nation must be wrought.

Riles debated with himself whether the occasion justified the expenditure of ten cents for a drink when a hand was placed on his shoulder, and a voice said, "Have one with me, neighbour." He found himself addressed by a man of about his own age, shorter and somewhat lighter of frame and with a growing hint of corpulence. The stranger wore a good pepper-and-salt suit, and the stone on his finger danced like real diamond.

"Don't mind if I do, since y' mention it," said Riles, with an attempted smile which his bad eye rendered futile. One of the bartenders put something in his glass which cut all the way down, but Riles speedily forgot it in a more exciting incident. The man in the pepper-and-salt suit had laid half a dollar on the bar, *and no change came back*. Riles congratulated himself on his own narrow escape.

"You'll be looking for land?" inquired the stranger, when both were breathing easily again.

"Well, maybe I am, and maybe I ain't," said Riles guardedly. He had heard something of the ways of confidence men, and was determined not to be taken for an easy mark.

"A man of some judgment, I see," said his new acquaintance, quite unabashed. "Well, I don't blame you for keeping your own counsel. The rush of people and money into the West has brought all kinds of floaters in its train. Why"—with growing confidence—"the other night——"

What happened the other night remained untold, for at that moment came a clattering of horse's hoofs on the wooden walk at the door, and a moment later a gaily arrayed cowboy rode right into the room, his horse prancing and bodying from side to side to clear the crowd away, then facing up to the bar as though it were his manger. Riles expected trouble, and was surprised when the feat evoked a cheer from the bystanders.

"That's Horseback George," said the man in the pepper-and-salt. "They say he sleeps on his horse. Rides right into a bar as a matter of course, and maybe shoots a few bottles off the shelves as a demonstration before he goes out. But he always settles, and nobody mind his little peculiarities."

Horseback George treated himself twice, proffering each glass to his horse before touching it himself, and stroking with one hand the animal's ears as he raised the liquor to his lips. Then he threw a bill at the bar-tender and, with a wild whoop, slapped the horse's legs with his hat, and dashed at a gallop out of the bar-room and away down the trail.

The stranger was about to resume his conversation when a big fellow near by shouted in a loud, raucous voice, "Come, pard, set 'er up. Who's drinkin with me?"

No one answered, and the big man looked about the crowd with a deepening scowl.

"So you're not drinkin'?" he said. "Fill two glasses, pard, and set 'em right there." He turned his back to the bar, resting his elbows on it, and surveyed the crowd contemptuously, meanwhile chewing a mouthful of tobacco with a rapid, swinging motion of the jaw.

"Guess you fellows don't know who *I* am," he said. "I——"

"No, and don't give a damn," said a lumberjack near by.

"Well, you will before you're through. You're goin' t' drink with me, an' you'll drink with both hands on the glass. Come up an' take your med'cine." As he spoke his hand rested on his hip-pocket.

The head bar-tender poked him in the ribs. "No gun play here," he said. "You're not in Montana now."

"I guess I know where I am," he retorted. "An' what d'ye think I pack a gun for? T' tell the time by? This (not printable) is goin' t' drink with me, or I'll fix him so's you c'n see through him both ways." With the word he whipped out a revolver and fired into the floor at the lumber-jack's feet, while a considerable part of the crowd scurried for the door.

"Put up your gun, you (equally unprintable)," shouted the lumber-jack, throwing his hat on the floor, "and I'll crack your slats quicker'n you can count 'em."

"It's all right, Pete," said the bar-tender, addressing the lumber-jack. "You can lick him hands down, but that won't pay the bills if you get in the road of a bullet. Now you," turning to the other, "stow that artillery, an' stow it quick, or I'll call the Mounted Police."

For answer the stranger took a handful of tobacco from his mouth, and with a swing of his arm plastered it over the mirror behind the bar. "That for the Mounted Police," he said. "Now there's goin' t' be some drinkin' or some shootin', an' maybe a little o' both." He ploughed the floor with another bullet, and the crowd again visibly thinned away. Riles had backed into a corner; the man in the pepper-and-salt suit had disappeared.

Having no weapon, the lumber-jack kept his distance, but if epithets could kill his bullying provoker would have been carried out a corpse. The man with the revolver, on the other hand, seemed taking his time, playing with his victim, like a wild beast sure of his prey.

Suddenly there was another stir about the door, and a young fellow in scarlet tunic and yellow-striped riding-pants walked briskly in. His lithe figure, his clean boyish face, his military alertness, were in striking contrast to the ambling, carelessly-dressed crowd. He had taken in the situation at a glance, and walked, neither faster nor slower, direct to the desperado. The latter found himself confronted by an unexpected dilemma. If he took his gun off the lumber-jack to cover the policeman he knew perfectly well that the promised slat-cracking process would begin immediately. If the policeman had only stood at the door and ordered him to put up his gun, or parleyed, or thought of his skin as a policeman should, he would have had time to plan his campaign. But this boy in scarlet was a revelation of something new in policemen. It was only eight steps from the door to where the outlaw stood, and those eight steps at parade pace occupied about three seconds. The gentleman from Montana was quick enough with his gun, but not particularly nimble in intellect, and he never faced a situation quite like this before. What was this policeman going to do, anyway? Would he never stop and deliver his ultimatum? He had not even drawn his gun!

By this time the policeman was beside him. He did not seize him, nor shout at him, nor menace him in any way, yet somewhere in his manner and bearing was a sense of irresistible power.

"Perhaps you don't know that it's against

the law to flourish a revolver in this country,"
he said. "Better let me keep it for you until
you are leaving town."

"Against the law!" said the ruffian, now recovering himself. "That's a good one. Why,
ever'thin' I've done for twenty years has been
against the law. I cracked up the law for
chicken-grit years ago."

"Not the Canadian law," said the Mounted
Policeman. "You'll only offend against it
once, and it won't be the law that gets
cracked."

"Thas' so?" sneered the other. "Then
what'll happen?"

"I'll arrest you."

"You? I could eat you in three bites. I
can lick you with one hand."

"How many like me do you think you could
lick?" asked the policeman, with imperturbable composure.

The man from Montana had removed his
eye from the lumber-jack, who was now danc-
ing about in menacing attitudes.

"Forget it, Pete," ordered the policeman.
"Now, how many like me can you lick?"

"About six," said the other, speaking with
much deliberation.

"All right," said Sergeant Grey. "Then my
chief would send seven. Now, will you come
with me or wait for the seven? By the way,"
he continued, "the lock-up is a sort of beastly

place to stow a man, especially when he's visiting the country for the first time. I think I'll let you sleep here, on your promise to appear at court at ten to-morrow morning. Let me help you to your room. But first, I'll have to trouble you for your gun."

"What if I clear out through the night?"

"You won't—not very far." There was a metallic ring in the last words that penetrated the shell of the man who had made a business of breaking law for twenty years, and he calmly handed over his revolver.

"Search me if I know why I do it," he said, turning to the bar-tender. "I could eat that kid in three bites."

"Yes," said the man behind. "But you couldn't digest the whole British Empire, and that's what you've got to do if you start nibbling on any part of it. Besides, he mightn't make as easy chewin' as you think. You'd find him more brisket than sirloin when you get your teeth into him. I've seen him throw an' handcuff a bigger man than you right in this room, an' never turn a hair in doin' it. An' take it from me, stranger, what he says about sendin' seven if the job's too big for six is gospel, an' the quicker you get that in your block the safer your hide'll be in Canada."

Sharp at ten the next morning the man who made a business of breaking the law appeared before the magistrate, paid a fine of fifty dollars, and surrendered his weapon to the King's officers for good. When he returned to the hotel and demanded his bill for the night's lodging he was surprised to learn he had none.

"Sergeant Grey settled for you," said the clerk with a faint smile. "Said you were his guest last night."

It was the first time in a long experience that he had found that law could be rigorous and yet absolutely just. It upset his whole crude philosophy of his relation to society and the State, and stretched before him the straight and easy road to citizenship.

To return to the scene of the night before. When the bar-room had settled down to normal, and no one showed a disposition to do any general buying, Riles betook himself to his room. He had just got into bed when a knock came at the door.

"Who's there?" he demanded.

"Gen'l'man to see Mr. Riles," said the porter.

"Well, shoot 'im in. The door ain't locked," said Riles, in considerable wonderment as to who his visitor might be.

The door opened, and a well-dressed man of average height, with carefully combed hair and clean-shaven face, save for a light moustache, stood revealed in the uncertain glow of the match with which Riles was endeavouring to find his lamp. His visitor was a man of twenty-eight or thirty years, with clear eyes and well-cut face, and yet with some subtle quality in his expression that implied that under his fair exterior lay a deep cunning, and that he was a man not to be trusted in matters where his own interests might be at stake.

"Hello, Hiram," he said quietly. "You didn't figure on seeing me here, did you?"

At first glance Riles did not recognize him, and he raised the oil lamp to turn the light better on the stranger's face.

"Well, if it ain't Gardiner!" he exclaimed. "Where in Sam Hill did you come from?"

"It's a big country, Hiram," he said with a touch of bitterness, "but not big enough for a fellow to lose himself in." He sat down on the side of the bed and lit a cigar, tendering another to Riles, and the two men puffed in silence for a few minutes.

"Yes, I've hit a lot of trail since I saw you last," he continued, "and when you're in the shadow of the Rockies you're a long piece from Plainville. How's the old burg? Dead as ever?"

"About the same," said Riles. "You don't seem t' be wastin' no love on it."

"Nothing to speak of," said the other, slowly flicking the ash from his cigar. "Nothing to speak of. You know I got a raw deal there, Hiram, and it ain't likely I'd get enthusiastic over it."

[191]

"Well, when a fellow gets up against the law an' has t' clear out," said Riles, with great candour, "that's his funeral. As for me, I ain't got nothin' agen Plainville. You made a little money there yourself, didn't you?"

The younger man leaned back and slowly puffed circles of fragrant smoke at the ceiling, while Riles surveyed him from the head of the bed. He had been a business man in Plainville, but had become involved in a theft case, and had managed to escape from the town simply because a fellow-man whom he had wronged did not trouble to press the matter against him. Riles' acquaintance with him had not been close; except in a business way they had moved in other circles, and he was surprised and a little puzzled that Gardiner should find him out on the first night of his presence in the New West.

Gardiner showed no disposition to reopen the conversation about Plainville, so at last Riles asked, "How d'you know I was here?"

"Saw your scrawl on the register," he said, "and I've seen it too often on wheat tickets to forget it. Thought I'd look you up. Maybe can be of some service to you here. What are you chasing—more land?"

"Well, I won't say that, exactly, but I kind o' thought I'd come out and look over some of this stuff the Gover'ment's givin' away, before the furriners gets it all. Guess if there's anythin' free goin' us men that pioneered one province should get it on the next."

"You don't learn anything, Riles, do you? You don't know anything more about making money than you did twenty years ago."

"Well, maybe I don't, and maybe I do, but I can pay my way, an' I can go back t' Plainville when I like, too."

"Don't get hot," said Gardiner, with unshaken composure. "I'm just trying to put you wise to yourself. Don't make any difference to me if you spend your whole life sodbusting; it's your life—spend it any way you like. But it's only men who don't know any better that go on to the land nowadays. It's a lot easier to make a living out of farmers than out of farming."

"Well, p'r'aps so, but that's more in your line. I never——"

"That's just what I say—you never learn. Now look at me. I ain't wearing my last suit, nor spending my last dollar, either, and I haven't done what you'd call a day's work since I came West. There's other things so much easier to do."

"Meanin'?——"

"Oh, lots of things. Remittance men, for instance. These woods are full of them. Chaps that never could track straight in the old ruts, and were sent out here where there aren't any ruts at all. They're not a bad bunch; brought up like gentlemen, most of 'em; play the piano and talk in three or four languages, and all that kind of stuff, but they're simply dangerous with money. So when it comes to hand, in the public interest they have to be separated from it."

"Sounds interestin'," said Riles.

" 'Tis, too, especially when one of 'em don't take to the treatment and lays for you with a gun. But my hair's all there. That's what comes of wearing a tall hat."

"Tell me," said Riles, his face lit up with interest, "how d'ye do it?"

" 'Twouldn't do you any good," said Gardiner. "You've steered too many plough-handles to be very nimble with your fingers. But there's often other game to be picked up, if a man knows where to look for it."

"Well, I wisht I knew," Riles confessed. "Not anythin' crooked, y' know, but something like—well, something like you're doin'. I've worked hard for ev'ry nickel I ever made, an' I reckon if there's easy money goin' I've a right t' get some of it."

"Now you're beginning to wake up. Though, mind you, some of it isn't as easy as it looks. You've got to know your business, just like farming or anything else. But you can generally land something to live on, even if it ain't a big stake. Take me now, for instance. I ain't doing anything that a preacher mightn't do. Happened to fall in with a fellow owns a ranch up the river here. Cleaned him empty one night at cards—stood him up for his last cent, and he kind o' took a notion to me. Well, he's the son of a duke or an earl, or some such thing, and not long ago the Governor goes and dies on him, leaving him a few castles and bric-à-brac like that and some wagon-loads of money. So he had to go home for the time being, and as he wanted someone to run his ranch, who should he think of but me. Suppose he thought if I happened to bet it at poker some night I wouldn't lose it, and that's some consideration. He's got a thousand acres or so of land up there, with a dozen cayuses on it, and he gives me twenty-five pounds a month, with board and lodging and open credit at the Trading Company, to see that it doesn't walk away in his absence. Besides that, I hire a man to do the work, and charge his wages up in the expenses. Got a good man, too—one of those fellows who don't know any better than work for a living. By the way, perhaps you know him—comes from Plainville part—Travers his name is?"

"Sure," said Riles. "He worked for Harris, until they had a row and he lit out. It kind o' balled Harris up, too, although he'd never admit it. If he'd Travers there it'd be easier for him t' get away now."

"Where's Harris going?"

"He ain't goin'; he's comin'. Comin' out here in a few days after me. I'm his kind o' advance guard, spyin' out the land."

"You don't say? Well, see and make him come through with the expenses. If I was travelling for Jack Harris I wouldn't be sleeping in a hen-coop like this. He's worth yards of money, ain't he?"

"Oh, some, I guess, but perhaps not so much more'n his neighbours."

"Nothing personal, Riles. You've got to get over that narrowness if you're going to get into the bigger game I've been telling you about. I don't care how much you're worth —how much is Harris bringing with him?"

"Couple of hundred dollars, likely."

"I wouldn't show my hand for that. How much can he raise?"

"Well, supposin' he sold the old farm——"

"Now don't do any reckless supposing. Will he sell the farm?"

"Sure, he'll sell it if he sees something better."

"How much can he get for it?"

"Thirty or forty thousand dollars."

"That's more like a stake. Hiram, it's up to you and me to show him something better —and to show it to him when he's alone. . . . You're tired to-night. Sleep it out, and we'll drive over to the ranch to-morrow together. We ought to pick something better than a homestead out of this."

CHAPTER XIII

NOTWITHSTANDING the exhaustion occasioned by his journey Riles was early about. The hotel bed was strange to him, and the noises that floated up from the bar-room interrupted his slumbers. At least, he told himself it was the noises, but the fact is a great new thought had been sown in his brain, and had started the cells whirling in dizzy speculation. The unexpected meeting with Gardiner, the latter's evident prosperity, and his frank contempt for men who made their living by labour, had left a deep impression upon Riles. He had no idea by what means Gardiner proposed that they should possess themselves of Harris's money, and he felt some doubt about any such attempt being rewarded with success. Nevertheless, Gardiner seemed to think the matter a simple one enough, and Gardiner's good clothes and good cigars were evidence of his ability to carry his plans into effect.

The streets had not yet assumed their morning activity when Riles emerged from the hotel, but the unclouded Alberta sunshine was bathing every atom of out-of-doors in a warmth and brilliance that might have found, and in very truth did find, a keen response in the inanimate objects of its affection. The jubilant laugh of running mountain water rippled through the quiet air, fragrant with the perfume of balm-of-Gilead and balsam; to the eastward the sunshine poured into broad valleys of undulating, sweeping plain, and in the west the great mountains, clad in their eternal robes of white, loomed silent and impressive in their majesty. Even Riles stopped to look at them, and they stirred in him an emotion that was not altogether profane—a faint, undefined consciousness of the puniness of man and the might of his Creator. No one can live for long in the presence of the mountains without that consciousness, and it is a great day for the mountain-dweller when he learns to distinguish between the puniness of man, the animal, and the infinity of man, the thinking soul.

Riles breakfasted as soon as the dining-room was opened, eating his meal hurriedly, as he always did, albeit the French-fried potatoes, to which he was unaccustomed, could be poised on his knife only with considerable effort. Then he sat down in an arm-chair on the shady side of the hotel to wait for Gardiner. He had suddenly lost his interest in the free lands which had been the purpose of his journey.

His wait was longer than he had expected, and he broke it several times by strolls about the little town. In size it was much the same as Plainville, but that was the chief point of resemblance. True, it had its typical stores, selling everything from silks to coal oil; its blacksmiths' shops, ringing with the hammer of the busy smith on ploughshare or horseshoe; its implement agencies, with rows of gaudily-painted wagons, mowers, and binders obstructing the thoroughfare, and the hempen smell of new binder twine floating from the hot recess of their iron-covered storehouses; ·a couple of banks, occupying the best corners, and barber shops and pool-rooms in apparent excess of the needs of the population. All these he might have found in Plainville, but there were here in addition half-a-dozen real estate offices, with a score or more curbstone dealers, locaters, commission-splitters, and go-betweens, and the number and size of the livery stables gave some clue to the amount of prospecting going on from this base of supplies. The streets were lined with traffic. Riles estimated that in two hours as many teams passed him as might be seen in Plainville in a week; long rows of box-cars were unloading on the side tracks; farmers' effects and household goods of every description were piled in great heaps about the railway yards; while horses, cattle, pigs, and poultry contributed to the dust and din of the settlers' operations. Great wagons of lumber were being loaded at the lumber yards, and an unbroken procession of wagons and farm machinery of every description was wending its way slowly into the distance where lay hope of home or fortune for the new settler.

It was almost noon when Gardiner appeared ᴖn the scene. "You don't hurt you'self in the mornin's," was Riles' greeting.

"Don't need to," he answered cheerily. "Besides, I'd a long session after I left you last night. No, no particulars at present. I told you you had spoiled your hands for that kind of work. How d'ye like this air? Isn't that something worth breathing?"

"Good enough," said Riles, "but I didn't come out here for air."

"No, you came for land. I'm surprised you're not out bouncing over the prairie in a buckboard long before this."

Riles shot a quick glance at Gardiner. But he was puffing a cigar and drinking in the warm sunshine with obvious satisfaction.

"So I might o' been, but I thought we kind o' made a date last night, didn't we?"

"Did we? Oh yes; now I remember. But I thought perhaps you'd feel different about it in the morning. A man generally does. I won't hold you to anything you said last night, Riles."

Riles could not recall that he had said anything that committed him in any way, but
Gardiner's tone implied that plainly enough.

"I ain't changed my mind," he said, "but I
don't know 's I said anything bindin', did I?
I thought we was goin' t' drive out t' your
place t'-day an' talk things over."

"Well, I just didn't want you to lose any
time over me if you thought things wouldn't
work out," said Gardiner. "It takes more
nerve, you know, than hoeing potatoes. But
you're welcome to the hospitality of the ranch,
in any case. I came in on horseback, so we'll
get a team at one of the stables and drive out."

In a short time they were on their way. The
road skirted the river, threading its way
through the narrow belt of cotton-woods and
evergreens that found footing in the moist soil
of the valley. Here and there, through an
opening in the trees, or across a broad wedge
of prairie, could be seen the mountains, now
bathed in a faint purple, silently receding before them. A soft breeze, neither hot nor cold,
but moist and fresh from the great table-lands
of snow, pressed gently about the travellers,
but their thoughts were of neither the scenery
nor the weather.

"It's all right, Riles," Gardiner was saying.
"If you're prepared to stay with the deal we
can pull it through—no doubt about that.
That is, if Harris will sell his farm and come

out here with the cash in his jeans. If he won't do that, you better get busy on your homestead proposition right away."

"He'll do it all right, if he sees somethin' worth while. But Harris 's no spring chicken, an' you'll have t' show him somethin' t' his likin' before he loosens up."

"I don't care whether he loosens up or not," said Gardiner. "All I care is that he brings the money, and brings it in bills. No cheques, mind you. Get him out here with the cash on him, and I'll do the loosening up, if it comes to that."

Riles was somewhat alarmed at the sinister turn of the conversation. He had no compunction about getting the better of his old neighbour, the man who had entrusted him with the discharge of their joint mission, but he had considerable respect for the force, if not the principle, of the law.

"You don't mean that you'd do anythin'—anythin' that wasn't right?" he said. "I wouldn't want t' get mixed up in no scrape, y' know."

"You mean that you think more of your skin than you do of Harris's coin. Well, there's no accounting for tastes. But as for doing anything wrong—you ought to know me better than that. It will all be clean and above board, and no violence if it can be helped, but if Harris is unfortunate nobody's to blame for that. Of course, if you're afraid to take a sportsman's chance for a half of forty thousand dollars, call the deal off. I've got lots of other fish to fry."

"You don't understand," said Riles. "I ain't a'scared, but I don't want t' do nothin' that'll get us into trouble. Harris is an old neighbour o' mine, an'——"

"I understand perfectly. You wouldn't mind a piece of Harris's money served on a platter and wrapped in tissue paper, but you want somebody else to take the chances. Now, there won't be any chances to speak of, but what there are you take your share. If that's a bargain it's a bargain, and if it isn't we'll talk about the weather. What d'you say?"

"It's a bargain," said Riles, "provided your plan'll work out."

"It's got to work out. It's like going up in a balloon—if it doesn't work out it's all off with the engineer. You got to take the chance, Hiram, and then make good on the chance."

Riles chewed vigorously at his tobacco. "Explain how you're goin' to pull it off," he said, "an' then I'll tell you yes or no."

"Not on your life," said Gardiner. "I don't show my hand until I know who's sitting across."

There was silence for half a mile, while Riles turned the matter over in his mind. He was naturally a coward, but he was equally a money-grabber, and it was one instinct against the other. Avarice won it, and at length he extended his hand to Gardiner. "I'm in on anythin' you're in on," he said.

"That sounds like it," said Gardiner, with enthusiasm. "Now the whole thing's simple as A B C, and not half as dangerous as running a traction engine or breaking a broncho. It all rests on getting him out here with the money, and that's where you come in. I don't mind telling you if it wasn't for the help you can give there I'd handle the job myself, and save dividing the proceeds."

"Yes, that's the point, all right," said Riles, somewhat dubiously. "How're we goin' t' get him out here with all that money?"

"Think, Riles," said Gardiner, puffing complacently at a fresh cigar. "Think hard."

Riles wrinkled his forehead and spat copiously at the front hub, but the inspiration would not come. "I give it up," he said at last. "You'll have t' plan it, an' I'll carry it out."

"That's what comes of hard work, Hiram; you lose all your imagination. Right now you haven't any more imagination than a cabbage. Now, I could suggest a dozen schemes to suit the purpose if I had to, but one will do. Suppose this:

"These mountains up here are full of coal —more coal than can be burnt in a million years. It's a bad road in, but once you get there you'll see it lying in seams, ten, fifteen, twenty feet thick, and stretching right through the rocks as far as you like to follow it. That coal's going to make a bunch of millionaires some day, but not until you can get at it with something bigger than a cayuse. But railroads come fast in this country, and there's no saying how soon a man might cash in if he invested just now."

"You ain't goin' t' wait till a railroad comes, are you? We'll like enough be dead by that time."

"Hiram, I told you you had no imagination. Wait a moment. Now, suppose that some strange eccentric chap owns one of these coal limits. He lives up in the mountains, a kind of hermit, but we fall in with him and offer him forty thousand dollars for his limit, worth, say, half a million, or more if you feel like it. He says, 'All right, but mind I want the money in bills, and you'll have to bring it out to me here.' Now can you think of anything?"

"Harris don't know nothin' about coal," protested Riles. "He wouldn't bite at anythin' like that."

"Your faith has been neglected as well as your imagination. You've got to paint it to him so's to get him interested. That's all. Our business is to get Harris, with the money in his wallet, started up into those mountains. It's mighty lonely up there, with timber wolves, grizzly bears, precipices, snow-slides, and trails that lead to nowhere, and if Harris is unfortunate—well, he's unfortunate."

The plan gradually penetrated Riles' slow-working mind. At first it numbed him a little, and his face was a strange colour as he turned to his companion, and said, in a low voice, "Ain't it risky? What if the police catch on?"

"They won't. They're all right for cleaning up a rough-house, but don't cut any figure in fine art work like we'll put over. I tell you, Riles, it's absolutely safe. Of course, ordinary precautions must be taken, same as you would with a vicious horse or any other risk you might run. The main thing is to see that he has the money in bills; anything else would be risky and lead to trouble. Then this fellow that's supposed to own the mine must be kept in the background. We——"

"But who *does* own the mine?"

Gardiner made a gesture of exasperation. "You don't get me, Hiram. Nobody owns the mine. That part of it's all a myth—a fairy tale manufactured because we need it. But Harris mustn't find that out—not, at any rate, until it's too late. Then if anything ever does leak out, suspicion will be directed toward some mysterious mine-owner, and the police will be wearing out shoe-leather hunting the cracks in the foothills while you and I are taking in the sights of Honolulu or South America. We'll quietly make an appointment for Harris to meet the mine-owner somewhere up in the hills. We'll direct him where to go, and leave it at that. Of course we won't go with him; we'll have other business about that time."

Riles looked at Gardiner with frank admiration. It seemed so simple now, and in his growing enthusiasm he felt that he would have little difficulty in persuading Harris to raise all the cash possible and bring it with him. And it seemed so safe. As Gardiner said, the mountains were full of danger, and if something should happen to Harris—well, he would be unfortunate; but lots of other people had been unfortunate, too.

Gardiner turned his team down a side road, forded the river, climbed a steep, slippery bank, and drew up beside a cluster of ranch buildings sheltered with cotton-woods and spruces. The old, long log-house, reminiscent of the days when the West was a land and a law unto itself, might have stirred the heart of poet or artist; the hard-beaten soil of the corral hinted still of the brave days of the open range and cattle beyond the counting. As the team, in their long, steady trot, swung up beside the stables, an alert young fellow came quickly out and busied himself with the unhitching.

"Guess you ought to know our visitor, Jim, shouldn't you?" said Gardiner. "Another Manitoban chasing the free land."

Travers at once recognized Riles and extended his hand. "Well, Mr. Riles, we weren't looking for you here, although I suppose I shouldn't be surprised, for there was some talk of your coming West before I left Plainville. What do you think of it? And did you see the mountains this morning? Worth the trip themselves, aren't they?"

"Look pretty good, all right, Jim," said Riles, with an attempt at affability, "but I reckon you wouldn't grow much wheat on 'em, an' scenery's not very fillin'. How you makin' it go you'self?"

"Nothing but luck since I landed," said Jim. "Got a good homestead and a good job right away. You must let me take you out to my farm before you go back. How's everybody? Harrises well, I hope?"

"Guess they're well enough, but gettin' kind o' scattered for a family group. Beulah lit out when you did—but I guess I can't give you no information about that."

The smile did not depart from Travers' face, but if Riles had known him as well as he should he would have seen the sudden smouldering light in the eye. But the young man answered quietly, "I saw Beulah the day I left Plainville, and I understood she was going West on a visit. She isn't back yet?"

"Innocent, ain't chuh?" said Riles, in a manner intended to be playful. "It's all right; I don't blame you. Beulah's a good girl, if a bit high falutin, an' a few years' roughin' it on the homestead'll take that out of her."

But Jim had dropped the harness and stood squarely facing Riles. The smile still lingered on his lips, but even the heavy-witted farmer saw that he had been playing with fire. Riles was much the larger man of the two, but he was no one to court combat unless the odds were overwhelmingly in his favour. He carried a scar across his eye as a constant reminder of his folly in having once before invited trouble from a younger man.

"What do you mean?" demanded Travers. "Put it in English."

But Gardiner interposed. "Don't be too sensitive, Jim," he said. "Riles has forgotten his parlour manners, but he doesn't mean any harm. You weren't insinuating anything, were you, Hiram?"

"Course not," said Riles, glad of an opportunity to get out of the difficulty without a direct apology. "No offence intended, Jim. Beulah's all right, an' you're all right, an' that's what I always said."

Travers was not in the least deceived as to Riles' high-mindedness, but he realized that the man was the guest of his employer, and he decided not to press the point. Gardiner and Riles went to the house, and Jim presently saddled his own horse and rode out on the prairie. He had already lunched, and it was Gardiner's custom to cook for himself when at home.

Inside, the two men were soon seated at a meal which Gardiner hastily but deftly prepared. They ate from plates of white enamelled ware, on a board table covered with oilcloth, but the food was appetizing, and the manner of serving it much more to Riles' liking than that to which he had been subjected for some days. The meat was fresh and tasty; and the bread and butter were all that could be desired, and the strong, hot tea, without milk but thick with sugar, completed a meal that was in every way satisfactory. Riles' eyes, when not on his plate, were busy taking in the surroundings. The log walls were hung with mementoes, some of earlier days and some of other lands, and throughout the big room was a strange mixture of elegance and plainness. At one end were rows of shelves, with more books than Riles had ever seen, and above stood a small piece of statuary worth the price of many bushels of wheat.

Gardiner noted the interest of his guest, and smiled quietly to himself. He supposed that Riles had the usual notions about the Far West—a notion that here he was on the outer-

most rim of the finer civilization of even the
Middle West. But he knew also that this plain
log building contained furnishings and decora-
tions altogether beyond anything that Riles
had ever seen or heard of—things, indeed, so
far removed from the life of the hard-working
farmer that they might have come from another world than his own. When the meal
was finished Gardiner swept the soiled dishes
into a big galvanized iron tub, there to await
attentions from Jim at a convenient season,
and invited Riles to look about the house.

They entered another room, immediately
to the north of the large apartment which
served all general housekeeping purposes. The
floor was of plain boards, smooth with the rid-
ing-boots of many years, and in the centre lay
the skin of a great bear. An old-fashioned
carved table, of some size, and three leather
chairs, were the principal furniture. Two
swords hung diagonally across the far wall,
and above them was an old flag, discoloured
with sun and rain. Ancient firearms decorated
the walls, and odd pieces of strange clothing
hung about in profusion.

"This is His Nibs' drawing-room," said
Gardiner. "This junk you see about you has
been gathered from the corners of the earth
during the last few centuries. In there"—indicating another room through a door to the
left—"is his bedroom—a regular museum of

stuff running to no end of money, if you went to buy it. He has a couple of pictures worth more than a quarter-section of land, and that mat you see through the door—a prayer-rug he calls it, though he don't use it much for that—is worth over five hundred dollars."

Gardiner enjoyed the look of amazement that slowly spread over Riles' face. "He's been stuffin' you," said Riles at length, thinking of his own extravagance when he paid ninety cents a yard for a carpet for their front room at home. "He's been stuffin' you sure. There ain't no mats worth any money like that."

"It's gospel," said Gardiner. "Why, man, he has a set of chess worth more than the best team on your farm, and that statue affair up there—you simply couldn't buy it. The place is just bristling with valuables of one kind and another."

But Riles appeared suddenly agitated. He seized Gardiner by the arm, saying, "If this stuff's worth 's much as you figure, why don't we make a clean-up here, when the duke, or whatever he is, is away? That'd be safer, wouldn't it?"

"No, it wouldn't. It'd be easy enough to get away with the stuff, but how'd you turn it into money? The police would get you sure on a game like that. Of course, if you should decide to go in for culture, without the 'agri' ahead, you might like to have the prayer-mat for your own knees. No, you can't put over anything like that. And now we better be getting down to business."

Gardiner drew a couple of chairs up to the carved table, opened a drawer, and produced writing materials. "We can't get a letter away to Harris any too soon. Nothing like making hay while the sun shines, you know, and if he gets out here before we put our plan up to him, it would be natural enough for him to want to see the mine-owner himself. So hitch yourself to that pen there, and let us see what kind of a hand you are at fiction."

Riles would rather have done a day's work in the field than write a letter, but Gardiner insisted it must be done by him. Much of the afternoon was spent in the struggle, and Gardiner's fertile imagination hād to be appealed to at several ,critical points. But at last the letter was completed. It ran as follows:

"john Harris esq
　　　"planvil man
"sir i take up my pen to let you no that i am all well hoppin this will find you the same well this is a grate contry their is sure a big out ov doors well mr Harris i think i see somthing here a hole lot better than 3 years on a homstead homsteads is all rite for men that Hasunt got any mony but a man with sum mony can do better i wisht i Had sold my plase before i left i could ov done well here their is lots ov chantez

to make big mony their is a man here owns a cole mine he is what they call Xsentrik He is a Hermitt and lives in the Hills His mine is wurth 500000$ but He dont no it He will take 80000$ for it and we can sell it rite away for perhaps 500000$ i think we should take this up it is a grate chants if you will sell your plase rite away and bring all the mony you can then i will sell mine for the balluns be sure and bring all the mony you can if you dont like the cole mine there is lots of other chantez they will make you rich and bring the mony in bills not chex becaws He wont take chex becaws He is Xsentrik their is a man here sais His frend in new york would pay 500000$ for the cole mine if he was here and He is sending Him word so Hurry and let us get holt ov it furst then we'll sell it to Him and make a killing dont fale

"your obedyunt servunt
"HIRAM RILES."

Gardiner read the letter carefully, suppressing his amusement over Riles' wrestlings with the language, and finally gave his approval.

"Now, you must make a copy of it," he said. "It's only business to have a copy. That was a fine touch of yours about going back to sell your own farm. I believe you have some imagination after all, if it only had a chance to sprout."

Riles protested about the labour of making

a copy, but Gardiner insisted, and at last the work was completed. The sound of galloping hoofs was heard outside, and a cowboy from a neighbouring ranch called at the door to ask if there was anything wanted from town. "Here's your chance to mail your letter," Gardiner called to Riles with unnecessary loudness. "Mr. Riles dropped in here to write a letter," he explained to the rider.

Having with much difficulty folded his epistle until it could be crumpled into an envelope, Riles sealed, stamped, and addressed it, and a moment later the dust was rising down the trail as the cowboy bore the fatal missive to town. The die was cast; the match had been set to the tinder, and the fire must now burn through to a finish, let it scorch whom it would.

Gardiner took up the copy, folded it carefully, and put it in his pocket-book. "Now, Mr. Riles," he said, "we're in for this thing, and there's no backing out. At least you're in for it. You have sent a letter, in your handwriting, such as it is, to Harris, and I have a copy of it, in your handwriting, in my pocket. If this thing ever gets out these letters will make good evidence."

CHAPTER XIV

THE GAMBLERS

HARRIS found some difficulty in providing that affairs of the farm would proceed satisfactorily during his absence, but at last they were arranged, if not exactly to his liking, at least in a manner that promised no serious loss. It was most unfortunate that Mary, in a moment of headstrong passion quite without precedent in his experience of her, had determined upon a visit just at the time when she was particularly needed at home. If Harris had been quite fair he would have remembered that there had been no time in the last twenty-five years when she had not been needed at home, and the present occasion was perhaps no less opportune for her visit than many others. But he felt a deep grievance over his wife's conduct, and while he missed her sorely he was determined that no act of his should shorten her visit or imply that the business of the farm was in any way suffering from her absence. He had managed their affairs successfully in the past; he would continue to manage them successfully in the future; and he only hoped that time would impress upon her the fact that he was doing everything for the best. He assured himself that he was actuated only by a desire for the highest good for his family, even while their disobedience and ingratitude rendered his task unnecessarily difficult.

The hired man, in consideration of having no field work to do, finally consented to milk the cows and deliver the milk daily to Mrs. Riles, who would convert it into butter—for a consideration of so much per pound. To his good neighbours, the Grants, Harris turned for assurance that should he and Allan be delayed on their trip, or should the harvest come in earlier than expected, ample steps would be taken to garner it.

So, with these arrangements complete, the farmer and his son drove into Plainville one fine bright morning at the end of July, ready for their first long trip into the New West. Indeed, it was Allan's first long journey anywhere; an excursion to Winnipeg at the time of the summer exhibition had been the limit of his experience of travel, and the hard work of the farm had not yet extinguished the young man's desire for novelty and excitement. He looked forward to their expedition with a feeling akin to enthusiasm, and he secretly cherished the hope that their travels might bring them again into the company of his mother and sister, for whom, with the slacken-

[217]

15

ing of labour, he now felt an increasing loneliness.

Harris got off at the railway station to buy the tickets; Allan went to the post office on the odd chance of any letters awaiting delivery, and the hired man turned the horses homeward. The station agent was threading his way through his car report, and remained provokingly unconscious of Harris's presence at the ticket window. The farmer took no pains to conceal his impatience, coughing and shuffling obviously, but it was not until the last box-car had been duly recorded that the agent deigned to recognize his existence.

"Nothing for you from——," he said, mentioning the mail order house from which Harris made most of his purchases.

"Well, I didn't expect anythin'," retorted the farmer, "although you're just as likely to have it when I don't as when I do. How much is a ticket to Calgary?"

"You got the land fever, too?" the agent asked, as he consulted his tariffs. "Riles went up the other day. You'll be making a clean-up on the cheap land, I suppose. But I tell you, Harris, if I'd a farm like yours you couldn't pry me off it with a pinch-bar. No more worries for little Willie, and I'd leave the free land to those that haven't got any—like myself."

"Worry!" snorted Harris. "What do you worry about? You get your pay, whether it freezes or hails or shrivels up with one of these Dakota scorchers."

The agent thought of the piles of reports on his table, but as he thumped the stamp on the tickets he answered, "Oh, I worry over the Monroe doctrine." He left the farmer counting his change, and turned to his reports. "Another money-grubber gone crazy with the heat," he muttered. "If I'd his wad wouldn't I burn this wire with one hot, short sentence!"

Harris met his son on the platform. "What d'ye think, Dad? A letter from Riles." He drew the crumpled missive from its envelope. "Looks like a laundry ticket," he said, "but I figured it out, and he wants you to sell the farm and buy a coal mine."

Harris read the letter through, not without some difficulty. At first he was inclined to laugh, but the earnestness of Riles impressed him through the makeshift English.

"What d'ye think of it, Dad?" said the younger man, at length. "Of course we don't know anything about coal, but then——"

"It must look good to Riles or he wouldn't want to put any money in it," commented Harris, after a few minutes' reflection. "Riles is pretty cautious. He's got money in the bank drawin' three per cent.; he's afraid to lend it out among the farmers. And he ain't easy talked into a new scheme, either."

"D'ye suppose we could sell the farm?" The

idea of a big, profitable speculation suddenly appealed to Allan with much greater force than the prospect of three years on a homestead. He knew that vast sums of money had been made, and made quickly, in the Far West, but he had never before thought of himself or his father sharing in this sudden wealth. They had worked hard for their money, and took it as a matter of course that they should continue to work hard for it. But the vision of quick riches, the prospect of realizing it in his own person, the dizzy thought that Fortune, which had seemed to move in a circle quite apart from his existence, might actually now be within a hand's reach—these intoxicated him with a sudden hope which burst the old bounds of his imagination and set up new and wilder ambitions.

"D'ye suppose we could sell the farm?" he repeated. It began to seem that the short-cut to wealth hinged on the possibility of selling the farm.

"I guess we could sell it, all right," said Harris. "Maybe not for that much cash, but we can get cash on the agreement, if we need it." He, too, found the inborn gaming instinct which cries out for money without labour welling within him and surging up against his long-established, sober judgment. But he was not a man to act precipitately, or risk all on a single throw unless he were very, very sure of the result.

"Of course, maybe it's all right," he continued. "But it's a good thing to buy your buggy before you throw away your cart. If this thing's as good as Riles says, it will keep until we can see it for ourselves. If it don't, somethin' else'll turn up."

"Yes," said Allan, "but if we find it's all right when we get there, and we've only a few measly hundred dollars along, we'll want to kick ourselves all the way home. Lots of fellows are making big money just because they had some capital to work with, and why shouldn't we do it, too? Couldn't you fix it some way to get the money without coming back, if everything looks all right? That'd save time, and expense too."

"There's something in that. There's time to see Bradshaw yet before the train comes. We'll kind o' leave it standin' in his hands."

They made a hurried call on Bradshaw, the lawyer, and asked him to be on the look-out for a buyer for the farm.

"Mind, I'm not actu'lly puttin' it up for sale," Harris cautioned him, "but I want you to keep your eye open for a buyer. Forty thousand dollars takes the whole thing as a goin' concern, an' the more cash the better. Get a line on a buyer if you can, and if I send you word to sell, see, you sell, and if I don't send you word, don't do anythin'. You understand?"

"I think I understand you perfectly," said the lawyer, who was also a dealer in real estate. Indeed, since the activity in farm lands had commenced he might be said to be a real estate dealer who was also a lawyer. "Not many buyers have that much ready cash, Mr. Harris, but it could no doubt be arranged to sell your agreement, or raise a mortgage on the property, that would give you the whole amount in your hand." Bradshaw, along with his other pursuits, was agent for a mortgage company, and always valued two commissions higher than one.

The lawyer wrote something on a sheet of paper. "This is a power of attorney, which will enable me to complete the documents without the delay of sending them to you, if you should decide to sell," he explained. Harris signed the paper, and Allan witnessed it.

With this understanding the journey westward was undertaken, and completed without event of importance. As his daughter had done a few weeks before, and his wife still later, Harris spent a few hours in the young city just beginning to stir itself on the sleepy, sunny slopes where the prairies ran into the foothills, stretching one last long tongue far up the valley of the Bow and lapping at the feet of the eternal snows. His original plan had been to spend a day or two in Calgary, "sizing up" the land situation for himself before joining Riles,

but the possibilities of the coal mine speculation had grown upon him with every mile of
the journey. He had only to use his ears to
hear of so many men, apparently no more
capable men than he and Allan, who had grown
suddenly rich from fortunate investments. It
was a case of recognizing the opportunity when
it presented itself, and having the nerve to
seize it without hesitation. He found himself
now in a country and an atmosphere where
"playing safe" was somewhat to a man's dis-
credit—where the successful man was the man
who dared to throw discretion to the winds
and take the chance. And because money, not
earned in the country, was pouring in from
outside, and by its own buoyancy raising the
price of land and labour, the chance, even the
foolish chance, was likely to turn out to advantage and justify the daring of the specu-
lator rather than the discretion of the careful
buyer. Harris had, all his life, lived in an atmosphere of conservatism, where saving a
penny was greater merit than making two, but
he was amazed to find how quickly the
gambling spirit of the new land seized upon
him. Unlike Riles, he was a man who responded to his environment; in a community
of hard-working, money-saving farmers he
worked hardest and saved most; but in a community of reckless, unlicensed speculation he
had the qualities which would soon make of

him the greatest gambler of them all. He was astonished and somewhat frightened by this hitherto unrevealed side of his own character. His long-dormant imagination began to revive; with imagination came hope and optimism; and hope and optimism, unchecked, soon breed recklessness. He saw the evidence of prosperity on every side—not the prosperity that hedges itself about with socialisms and affected dignity, but the prosperity that stays on the job in its shirt-sleeves. He saw men who were doing big things—building railways, opening up wildernesses, farming or carrying on business transactions on a scale of which he had never dreamed—and he began to see that the only reason these men could do these things was that they dared to do them. Well, he too—he and Allan—would dare some things. . . . He paid a dollar for their lunch without a grumble, and again they took the train.

Riles met them on the station platform. He had met every train for a week, as it had been agreed that it would be better that the Harisses should not visit Gardiner's ranch until plans were more fully developed. Jim was still there, and Gardiner insisted that Jim should not meet Harris at present. He allowed Riles to think that he feared trouble if former employer and employee should meet; as a matter of fact, he feared that if their coal mine proposition should reach the ears of Travers the young man would attempt to dissuade Harris from having anything to do with it, or at least would urge a fuller investigation than might be desirable. Besides, he meant to make of Travers an unwitting party to the affair.

Riles, in overalls and shirt-sleeves, leaned against the iron rail at the back of the station platform, his big hands stuffed in the bulging band of his trousers, and his under-jaw busy with an ample ration of tobacco. He watched the passengers alighting from the train with little interest; he had no particular expectations of meeting Harris on this occasion, and, if the truth be told, he had little desire to meet him. Riles had no pangs of conscience over his part in the plot against his old neighbour, but he had an uneasy feeling of cowardice. When suddenly his eye fell on Harris and his big, strapping son, his first impulse was to slip away in the crowd before they should notice him. But it was only for a moment; the next, Harris was calling, " 'Lo, Hiram," and the two were shaking hands as old friends met in a far country.

"Didja get my letter?" asked Riles, ignoring the commonplaces with which it was their custom to introduce any important topic. "Didja sell the farm?"

"I got the letter, Hiram, but I didn't sell the farm. Thought we'd just have a look over this coal mine before goin' into the business altogether."

"H-s-h. Throttle your voice down. This place is full of men on the look-out for somethin' like that, an' you can't keep it too dark until it's all settled."

"Well, ain't we going to put up somewhere?" said Allan, breaking the silence that followed Riles' warning. "There ought to be an Alberta hotel here, somewhere. I saw one in every town for the last two hundred miles."

"I got that beat," said Riles, with a snicker. "Boardin' on a lord, or duke, or somethin'."

"Don't say?"

"Yeh. You mind Gard'ner? Him 'at lit out from Plainville after that stealin' affair?"

"The one you got credit for bein' mixed up in?" said Allan, with disconcerting frankness. "A lame kind of a lord he'd make. What about him?"

"Well, he struck a soft thing out here, fo' sure. This lord I'm tellin' you about's gone off home over some bloomin' estate or other, an' Gard'ner's runnin' his ranch—his 'bloody-well rawnch' he calls it. Gets a good fat wad for ridin' round, an' hires a man to do the work. But it was Gard'ner put me on t' this coal mine deal."

"Let's get settled first, and we'll talk about Gardiner and the mine afterwards," said Harris, and they joined the throng that was now wending its way to the hotels.

"How's your thirst, Hiram?" inquired Harris, after he had registered.

"Pretty sticky," confessed Riles. "But they soak you a quarter to wash it out here."

"Well, I got a quarter."

"A quarter apiece, I mean."

"Well, I got a quarter apiece," said Harris. "Come on."

Riles followed, astonishment over Harris's sudden liberality, and misgiving as to how he himself could avoid a similar expenditure, struggling for uppermost place in his mind.

"Pretty strong stuff they have here," he said, after Harris and Allan had "set 'er up" in turn. "Keel you over if you don't watch it."

"Does taste kind o' snakey," said Harris. "Guess that's enough for this time. Now come upstairs and tell us all about this deal you have on."

When the travellers had thrown off their coats and vests, and all were seated in the little bedroom, Riles cleared his throat.

"Well, there ain't much t' tell yuh, more'n I said in m' letter," he started. "As I said, it's Gard'ner you'll have t' thank for this thing, good or bad. I ain't a coal miner, an' I told him that, an' I told him you wasn't neither, but he says that don't make no difference. He says there's all kinds o' money in it, an' I reckon that's what we came out here for, ain't it?"

"Yes, provided the thing's sound," said Harris. "Anyone can see with half an eye that there's easier ways of makin' money than bustin' up this prairie sod for it. But you and me've worked hard for what we've got, Hiram, and we want t' go mighty careful about spendin' it."

"I suppose you've sent home word to sell your farm, have you?" put in Allan. "You'll be chipping in at the same time?"

"Oh, yes, I'll be chippin' in. Of course. But I didn't just say to sell the farm yet. I'll have t' get back an' straighten things up some first. You see, I thought you'd get my letter before you left, an' you could kind o' make your deal then, an' your payment would hold the bargain bound until I could sell mine, y' see, Harris?" Riles was beginning to address himself mainly to the older man.

"Don't take me up wrong," said Allan. "I'm in on this along with Dad, if he's in; an' if he's out, I'm out. But I was just kind o' curious about it."

"It's all right, it's all right," assured Riles, with great magnanimity. Inwardly he was cursing Gardiner for having left this task to him. He was suspicious of a trap in the simplest question, and feared that any minute he might find himself floundering in a mesh of contradictions.

"Where is this coal mine, and who's got it?" said Harris.

"I ain't saw it myself," admitted Riles. "They're awful p'tic'lar about lettin' people see it," he continued, with a sudden flash of inspiration. "It's so valu'ble, y' know."

" 'Fraid somebody'll bring it home in their pocket, I suppose," said Allan.

Riles pretended to laugh heartily.

"But where is it?" insisted Harris. "Is there a railroad near, or how do you get at it?"

"It's up in the mountains, an' that's all I can tell you; but it's all right, an' there's a pile o' money in it. I guess I better bring Gard'ner down in the morning, an' he'll explain all about it. Y' see, he knows the fellow 'at owns it, an' I don't, an' he'll be able to tell you. That is, if you're goin' in on it. Gard'ner won't say much unless he knows you're goin' in on it."

"Well, he'll have to say a good deal before he knows," said Harris. "I ain't buyin' a pig in a poke. He's got t' show me, and then if it's all right, why, it's all right."

"Oh, it's all right," said Riles, although inwardly he felt little enthusiasm over the attitude of either father or son. He was annoyed that Allan should be present. On the whole, it would be better to leave the rest of the explaining to Gardiner.

"What d'ye think of it, Dad?" said Allan, when Riles was gone.

"Maybe all right," said Harris. "Wouldn't

be surprised but it is. At the same time, I ain't goin' to put a cent in it till I'm dead sure. And anyway, there's no use lettin' Riles think we're keen on it."

"That's what I think. You think Gardiner's all square in it?"

"I don't know. Likely he's getting a fat commission from somewhere, but that's fair enough, if he makes the deal. But he won't see any o' our money till I have the opinion of the best lawyer in town. That's all we can say till we see it."

"That seems safe," Allan agreed. "Just the same, I think there's lots more chances to use our money to advantage here than down in Manitoba, don't you?"

"Yes, I think there is. You see, this is a new country, and everythin's on the jump. Think how much we could 'a' made in Manitoba in the early days if we had the money and knew where t' put it. Well, out here they've got the benefit of our experience, an' they'll do as much here in five years as we did in twenty-five. We had t' make the money t' develop our country—had t' make it right at home on our farms, an' that's slow. But here the money's rollin' in from outside."

"What d'ye say if we sell the old farm anyway, an' then if this mine business don't look good, we'll plunk it into farm land?"

"Might do worse," his father agreed. "We'll have a look round for a day or two, anyway."

The next morning they began a round of the real estate offices. Great activity prevailed everywhere, and dealers seemed to have hardly time to give them attention. In one little box of a place they mentioned that they might be on the market for say a couple of thousand acres.

"Think I can fix you up all right," said the proprietor; "and there's one sure thing, you can't put your money anywhere where it's safer or 'll grow faster. Why——"

At that moment a man in a pepper-and-salt suit went by the door.

" 'Scuse me a minute," said the dealer, rushing to the door and sending a shrill whistle down the street. The man in the pepper-and-salt turned, and the dealer beckoned him into the little office.

"You know that five-thousand-acre block you bought last week," he said in a low voice, but loud enough to be heard by the Harrises. "Bought it at six dollars, didn't you? Well, I can give you seven to-day, for a quick sale."

"Couldn't think of it, my dear fellow," protested the lucky buyer. "I simply couldn't think of it."

"Couldn't think of making five thousand dollars in a week? It don't look too bad to a working man like me."

"But it's nowhere near the value of the land. Why, they're selling stuff in Illinois to-day that ain't to be compared with it at a hundred and fifty dollars an acre. It's only a question of time until this is as much. You've got better land here, and better climate, and you're a thousand miles nearer the Pacific Ocean, that's going to carry the commerce of the future. Seven dollars? It's an insult to Canada to mention such a price."

"Well, say," continued the real estate man, in a still more confidential tone, "I was allowing myself a little margin on the deal, even at seven dollars. But I had a man in here a few minutes ago that'll buy that block at eight-fifty. I'll pay you eight dollars net to put it through."

"Sorry, but he'll have to get down deeper than that if he wants it. Tell him I might consider ten dollars, but mind, I ain't making any promise." And the man in the pepper-and-salt suit continued his course down the street, just the same as if he were not making five thousand dollars a week.

"Big capitalist from New York, that fellow," explained the dealer. "Simply coining money up here, and always salting it into more land."

The incident left a deep impression on the Harrises. They did not know, of course, that the man in the pepper-and-salt suit always went by the door when likely-looking strangers were in, and that he always refused a profit of ten thousand dollars as a matter of little consequence—except for its influence on the unsuspecting party of the third part.

CHAPTER XV

THE LURE OF EASY MONEY

IN the afternoon Gardiner and Riles drove into town and met the Harrises in the waiting-room of the hotel. Gardiner's greeting was friendly, but not over-familiar, as became a man who had recently suffered some reflection on his character. He shook Harris and Allan by the hand, inquired after the cattle and the crops, but discreetly avoided family matters, having learned from Riles that all had not been going smoothly in their domestic affairs. Gardiner knew a little room at the back of the bar, to which he escorted his guests. Having ordered a bottle and glasses on the table, he turned the key in the door.

"You can't be too careful," he explained. "You know, the walls have ears, and if it gets out that this coal mine can be picked up at the price we have on it, it will be taken before night. I understand your money is not here yet, Mr. Harris?"

"No. Not started, I guess. The fact is, I haven't sold the farm."

"Well, I don't want to hurry you, but we've got to act quickly, or not at all. Of course, we don't figure on taking any chances. Our idea is to turn the property over at once, at a good profit. That's the way you feel about it too, isn't it?"

"I'm not a coal miner."

"Exactly. Neither are the men who own most of the mines of this country. There comes a time, Mr. Harris, when we realize that we don't have to get down with pick and shovel to make ourselves some money—in fact, the man with pick and shovel hasn't time to make any real money. I am glad you feel like I do about it, for I have already taken the liberty of putting the proposition up to a New York syndicate."

"You mean if *we* don't come through, they will?"

"No, I mean that we'll come through—and they'll come after us. My idea is not to take any chances, but to sell the property, or as good as sell it, before we buy it. So I sent a Government report on it to this syndicate, as I heard they were looking out for coal lands in the West, and I just took the liberty of offering it to them for a cool quarter of a million, and gave them until to-night to accept or refuse, by wire. I'm a little anxious for an answer, although if they don't take it others will. You see, the old fellow that owns it simply hasn't any idea what it's worth. He has lived in the hills until he looks like one of 'em, and a satchelful of money in real bills will simply dazzle him. A cheque wouldn't serve the purpose; he'd be suspicious of it, and he'd come down to investigate, and someone would be sure to crimp our deal."

"But what is your plan for the deal, Mr. Gardiner?" asked Harris. "We can't go into the mountains with a load of bills and buy a mine like a man might buy a steer. There'll have to be papers, titles, and such things, I suppose, to make it right with us and with the Government."

"Of course," Gardiner agreed. "We will take the money with us, but we won't give it to him until we get the papers. We'll just let him see it—nibble it a little, if you like—and then we'll lead him into town with it, like you lead a horse with oats. The sight of so much money will keep him coming our way when nothing else would. And we'll slip him a hundred or two, and get a little receipt for it, just to prevent him changing his mind if he should be so disposed."

"And suppose I don't like the look of the mine when I see it?"

"Then you bring your money back down with you and put it into farm lands, or anything else that takes your fancy. After you look it over, if you don't want to go in on it, Mr. Harris, perhaps Riles and I can raise enough ourselves to swing the deal, but you see we thought of you from the first, and we will stay with our original plan until you have a chance to decide one way or another."

"Well, that sounds fair," said Allan, and his father nodded. "But we haven't sold the farm, and until we do I guess there isn't much money in sight."

"Bradshaw'll sell the farm quick enough if I send him word," his father assured him. "He may not get it all in money, but he'll get a good part of it, and he has ways o' raisin' the balance so long's the security is good. I've half a mind t' wire him t' close 'er out."

At this moment there came a knock on the door, and a boy presented a telegram for Gardiner. He opened it, read it, and emitted a whoop like a wild Indian. "They're coming through," he shouted, "coming through! How does half of two hundred and fifty thousand dollars look to you, Mr. Harris?"

Harris reached out eagerly for the telegram, while Allan, his arm thrown over his father's shoulder, read it in boyish excitement:

"If investigation confirms Government reports we will pay two hundred fifty thousand. Our representative leaves at once for personal interview."

The name at the end of the telegram was unknown to either Harris or his son, but Gardiner assured them it was one to conjure with in the financial world. Riles' excitement was scarcely less than Allan's. Gardiner choked a flood of questions on his lips with a quick imperative glance. Even Riles did not know that the telegram had been written a few doors down the street by a stoutish man in a pepper-and-salt suit.

"I'll take a chance," said Harris, at last. "I'll take a chance."

"Chance nothing!" interjected Gardiner, with momentary abruptness. "It was a chance a minute ago; it's a certainty now. It's the cinch of a lifetime."

"Where's some paper?" asked Allan. "Let's get a telegram away right off."

Gardiner produced a notebook and, at Harris's dictation, drafted a telegram to Bradshaw, directing him to dispose of the farm at once along the lines of the instructions already given him. He was to cash the agreement and wire the proceeds to Harris.

Then followed long anxious days. Fortune seemed to hang on Bradshaw's success in making an immediate sale of the farm. It was a large order, and yet Harris felt confident a buyer would be found. The price asked was not unreasonable, especially when it was remembered that the crop would go to the purchaser, and was now almost ready for the binder. Bradshaw was in constant touch with well-to-do farmers from the South who were on the look-out for land, and his own banking facilities would enable him to forward the cash as soon as a sale was assured, without waiting for actual payment by the purchaser. So Harris was confident in the midst of his anxiety.

A gentleman's agreement had been made with Gardiner and Riles that not a word was to be said concerning their investment until it was a completed fact. Gardiner dropped in occasionally to learn if any word had come from Plainville, but it was not until the afternoon of the fourth day that the fateful yellow envelope was handed in at the hotel. As it happened, Gardiner and Riles were present at the moment. They slipped into the back room and waited in a fever of expectation for Harris to announce the contents.

Harris and Allan read the message twice before speaking; then Allan repeated-it aloud:

"Twenty thousand dollars proceeds sale goes forward by wire your bank. Correspondence follows. Will explain failure to get price asked. "BRADSHAW."

Harris was torn between emotions, and his face worked with unwonted nervousness as he struggled with them. That Bradshaw should have sold the farm for half the price he had stipulated seemed incredible. It was robbery; it was a breach of trust of the most despicable nature. On the other hand, if the amount available would enable them to buy the mine, the huge profit assured from that investment would much more than offset the loss on the farm. Gardiner and Riles, too, were visibly downcast when they heard the amount, but Gardiner promptly grappled with the situation.

"It's less than we figured on," he said, "but perhaps we can get through still. The thing to do is to get out to the mine at once with this money. It will be sufficient to prove the genuineness of our intentions, and induce him into town. Then Riles can put up some and I can put up some, and that, with the twenty thousand, should hold the deal until Riles can realize on his farm. Within a very short time we can turn the whole thing over to the New Yorkers, and take in the profits."

"Say, Gardiner," said Allan, speaking as one who had been struck by a new and important thought. "Where do you come in on this deal? Is your old gink up in the hills coming through for half?"

"Not a cent," said Gardiner. "As for where I come in, well, dealing with old friends like Riles and the Harrises, I considered that a secondary matter. I fancy that when they feel the profits in their pockets they will be disposed to be not only fair, but generous, and, of course, if I put up part of the money I will expect my share of profit. But I'm not asking for any assurance; I'm just going to leave that to you."

"Well, that's decent, anyway," Harris agreed. "I haven't as much money as I expected, but if we can pull it through it may be all right yet. Of course, you remember that I haven't promised to put up a dollar unless I like the looks of the mine when I see it?" Harris still had qualms of hesitation about entering into a transaction so much out of his beaten path, and he took occasion from time to time to make sure that an avenue of retreat was still open.

"That's the understanding, exactly," Gardiner assured him. "You're the man with the money, and if you don't like it, don't pay."

Harris at once visited the bank, and returned shortly with the information that the amount, less a somewhat startling percentage for transmission and exchange, was already deposited to his credit.

"Then let us lose no more time," said Gardiner, with enthusiasm. "You will need a team and rig, and you better pack a couple of blankets and some grub. Make the stableman throw in a couple of saddles; you may have to ride the last part of the trip. Riles and I will make it the whole way on horseback." Gardiner then remembered that it would be necessary for him to go back to the ranch and change horses, but he described in detail the road they should take, and assured them they could not miss it. It was the main road up the river valley—up, and up—and if they drove hard they would reach that night a spot where an old, deserted cabin stood back in a clump of poplars. It would be a good place to spend the night, and Riles and Gardiner would meet them there, if, indeed, they did not overtake them on the road. Neither Harris nor Allan had any fear of a strange trail; they had been bred to a sense of direction and location all their lives, and were confident they would find no difficulty in reaching the rendezvous.

"Better make your own arrangements about the horses," Gardiner whispered as they left the room. "We can't be too careful to keep our business secret."

As they stood for a moment in the waiting-room it occurred to Allan that some shooting might be found in the mountains. "You haven't got a gun you could lend me, I suppose?" he said to Gardiner.

"What do you want a gun for?" Gardiner demanded brusquely.

"Might get a shot at a partridge, or something. No harm in having one along, is there?"

"Oh, no, but I don't expect you'll see anything to justify the trouble. Anyway, I haven't got one."

"There's a shot-gun here," said the hotel clerk, who had overheard the last remarks, "if that would suit you. A Cholly who was taking a short course in poker put it up a few days ago as a stand-off on his eat score. There's ten bones against it; if it's worth that to you, take it."

He handed the gun over the counter, and Allan examined it with interest. He recognized an English weapon of a value out of all proportion to the price asked.

"I'll take it," he said, and paid down the money. There was a momentary darkening of Gardiner's face which nobody noticed.

The little party then moved out to the street. Gardiner had regained his smooth manner, and gave some final directions about the road.

"Oh, we'll find it all right," said Allan, in high spirits, "and we'll beat you to the shanty unless you've some faster nags at home than any I see you driving. So long."

"So long," called Gardiner. "So long, and good luck."

"So long, an' good luck," repeated Riles. He was trying to play the game, but, as Gardiner often reminded him, he had no imagination. It would have been quite impossible for Riles, on his own initiative, to have thought of wishing the Harrises "good luck" on the journey they were about to commence. . . . They were interesting types of villains—one, gentlemanly, suave, deep, and resourceful; the other, coarse, shallow, slow-witted, and brutal. The offence of one against society was wholly intellectual; of the other, almost wholly physical. Gardiner fully appreciated the difference, and in his heart he felt a contempt and loathing toward Riles which he concealed only as a matter of policy. And he had worked out in his mind a little plan by which Riles, when his usefulness was ended, should be shuffled off without any share in the booty. At present he tolerated him because of necessity. There was work before them for which Riles was peculiarly qualified.

The Harrises went at once to a livery stable, where they arranged for a team and outfit. They then bought some cartridges for the gun, and a small handbag in which to carry the money.

When Harris presented himself at the bank wicket and asked for the full amount to his credit in cash, the sallow-faced teller turned a trifle paler still and slipped into the manager's office. A moment later the manager himself appeared before them.

"That's a pretty heavy order on a country bank, Mr. Harris. Of course we could give it to you in exchange, but to pay twenty thousand dollars or thereabouts in bills will drain us to almost our last dollar. Can't you use a marked cheque, or a draft on a Calgary bank?"

"Well, no," Harris said; "I'm afraid we can't."

"A marked cheque is as good as bills," the

banker argued, "and much easier to carry, not to speak of being safer," he added, as an afterthought. "Travelling with that amount of money on you is a sort of defiance of natural law, especially with the country full of strangers, as it is at present." The banker looked from the powerful frame of the farmer to·the equally powerful frame of the farmer's son, and his eye fell on the gun which the latter carried under his arm. "But, I guess," he continued with a laugh, "there isn't much danger on that score."

"Nothin' t' speak of," said Harris. "And while I don't want t' break your bank, I do want t' get that money, and t' get it in bills, or part of it in gold an' silver would do. The fact is, I don't mind tellin' you I've a deal on, an' I've undertaken t' put up this money in cash —to-night."

The banker ruminated for a few minutes. Experience had told him that with a certain class of men money in bills was more valuable than money in a cheque or draft. The very bulk of the currency seemed to impress them. He had seen an old-timer refuse a twelve-hundred-dollar marked cheque for his property, and yet surrender greedily at the sight of a thousand one-dollar bills piled on a table before him. This was a trait of human nature found in many persons unaccustomed to the handling of considerable sums of money, and sharp traders considered it good business to take advantage of it. The banker thought he understood why Harris wanted all the money in bills, although the sum was larger than he had ever seen handled in that way before.

A young man emerged from somewhere and locked the front door of the bank.

"It's closing time now," said the teller, addressing the manager. "We have enough cash on hand to pay this gentleman, and we can wire for more bills, which will reach us in time for to-morrow's business."

"Pay it, then," said the manager. "Mr. Harris has a right to his money in that form if he wants it. But," he added, turning to Harris, "I'd advise you to keep both eyes on it until your transaction is completed."

The counting of the money was a bigger task than either Harris or Allan had thought, but at last it was completed, and they were ready for the road. The banker looked after their buggy as it faded out of sight up the river road.

"Hang me if I like that!" he said to himself.

The long drive up the valley in the warm August afternoon was an experience for the soul of painter or poet. Even John and Allan Harris, schooled as they were in the religion of material things, felt something within them responding to the air, and the sunlight, and the dark green banks of trees, and the sound of rushing water, and the purple-blue mountains heaving and receding before them. The sweat trickled in narrow tongues down the backs of their horses, reminding them that the ascent was much steeper than it appeared. As they topped each new ridge they looked expectantly forward to a greater revelation of the mountains, but this was constantly denied by ever-recurring successions of ridges still ahead. The long, smooth swell of the plain gradually gave way to the more abrupt formations of the foothills, and here and there in their rounded domes protruded great warts of green-grey rock where the winds of ages had whipped the sand down into the valleys. Little clusters of green poplars, like vast goatees, nestled on the northern chin of the hills across the valley, where the Chinook had failed to spread its balmy winter-blight among them; here and there were glimpses of thousands of cattle feeding on the brown ranges. The sun, like a bubble of molten gold blown from the bowl of heaven, hung very close in a steel-bright, cloudless sky. Lower it fell, and lower, until a fang of rock two miles high pierced its under-edge, and sent a flood of fire pouring in a thin, bright border along the crest of the Rockies. The travellers stopped their horses on a ridge to watch the marvellous transformation; light before them, light behind them, at their feet the shadows creeping up the mountain sides, and the valley beneath transformed as by some fairy wand into a sea of amber.

Allan breathed deeply of the high, clear air, and in his eye was something which revealed that the light without had some way struck to new life the slumbering light within. He had no words of expression—no means of conveying his emotion; but he thought of his mother and Beulah—Beulah, who had so often protested against the substitution of existence for life. He had never had much patience with her queer notions, but now, in this moment when he knew that in some strange way he had invaded the borderland of the Infinite, Beulah stood up before his eyes—Beulah, his sister, resolute, defiant, reaching out, demanding life, life! He turned to his father, but was silenced by the sight of a line of moisture crawling slowly down the weather-beaten cheek. John Harris was driving again the pioneer trail from Emerson; at his side was Mary, young, beautiful, and trusting, and before them lay life. . . . And they had not found that life. . . . He made a dry sound in his throat, and the horses moved on.

Darkness settled about them. One or two stars came out. The poplars took on the colour of the spruce; the river fretted more noisily in its rocky channel. A thin ribbon of cloud lay across the mountains, and a breeze of wonderful mellowness came down through the passes.

At length, just as they were thinking of pitching camp for the night, Allan espied a deserted cabin in a cluster of trees by the side of the road. They turned into the wood and unhitched the horses.

The building was some old prospector's shack, long unoccupied save for occasional hunter or rancher, and the multitude of gophers that had burrowed under its rotting sills. The glass was gone from a single window looking out upon the road; the door had fallen from its hinges; the floor had been broken down in spots by the hoofs of wandering cattle. A match revealed a lantern hanging on the wall, and a few cooking utensils, safe from all marauders under the unwritten law of the new land.

The two men first made their horses comfortable, and then cooked some supper on a little fire at the door of the shack. Harris was tired, so they cleared a space in the corner farthest from the door, and spread their blankets there. Harris lay down to rest, the precious bag of money by his side.

"You might as well drop off for a nap," Allan suggested. "They must have been delayed, and may not make it to-night at all. We're here for the night, and you may as well rest if you can. I won't turn in myself until you waken."

"I believe I'll do as you say," his father agreed. "Keep a keen ear an' don't leave the building without wakin' me."

Allan looked out at different times for Gardiner and Riles, but there seemed no sound in all the world save the rushing of water. A cold draught crept along the floor. . . . He fancied his father had fallen into a nap. . . . The night chill deepened, and at length Allan hung a blanket as best he could across the open door. His gun gave him a sense of companionship, and he took it in his hands and sat down beside his father. . . . It was very lean and graceful in his fingers.

While the banker worked in his garden in the long August evening the thought of the two men with a bag full of money kept recurring and recurring in his mind, and smothering the natural pride he felt in his abounding cabbages. True, it was no business of his, but still he could not feel entirely at ease. As he bent over his hoe he heard hoofs clatter in the street, and, looking up, saw the erect form of Sergeant Grey on his well-groomed Government horse. At a signal from the banker the policeman drew up beside the fence.

They talked in low voices for ten minutes. "It may be a wild-goose chase," said the sergeant at last, "but it's worth a try." Half an hour later his horse was swinging in his long, steady stride up the road by the winding river.

CHAPTER XVI

GARDINER and Riles rode only a short distance out of town, then turned their horses into the deep bush, and waited. The afternoon wore on heavily, and the goad of suspense hounded them sorely, but there was nothing to do but wait. It would be a fool's trip, as Gardiner said, to go hunting unless they were assured of game.

But at last the Harrises' team and buggy rattled by. When it had secured a good lead the two horsemen emerged from their covering and took a cross road to Gardiner's ranch.

"We better eat," said Gardiner, and busied himself with starting a fire. "Of course, the cook's out. Fishing, I guess," he continued, as he noticed that Travers' fishing rod was gone from the wall. "Perhaps it's just as well. He might be asking questions."

Riles ate his meal in haste and silence. He was taciturn, moody, and excitable, and made no response to Gardiner's attempts to open conversation upon trivial subjects.

"Upon my soul," said Gardiner at last, "you don't seem any more than enthusiastic. One would think you were going to a funeral, instead of a—a division of profits."

"Perhaps I am," said Riles sourly. "We'll know better when we get back."

"Well, if you feel that way about it, you better stay at home," said Gardiner, with pointed candidness. "If ten thousand dollars is no good to you perhaps I can use your share in my own business."

"That wouldn't let me out," protested Riles. "You've got me mixed up in it now, and if things go wrong I'm in for it, but if things go right you're willin' t' take all the money."

"Things won't go wrong," Gardiner assured him. "They can't. Everything is planned to a fraction, but if we see there's going to be a hitch—why, the owner of the mine'll fail to turn up, and we'll all come back to town, and no one a bit the wiser."

Gardiner arose and took a bottle from a cupboard. He poured a big glass and set it before Riles. "Drink that, and the world will look more to your liking," he said.

Riles responded to the liquor, and presently the two were in animated discussion of their plans. Riles was eager to know the details, of which he had been kept in complete ignorance, but Gardiner would disclose nothing until they were on the road. "Jim may come in any minute," he explained, "and Jim might hear enough to make him curious. And it's just a little too soon to excite his curiosity.

"That reminds me," Gardiner continued. "Jim has a very neat little revolver here somewhere. I think I'll borrow it. We might see some game, as Allan says."

A search disclosed revolver and cartridges in Travers' trunk. Gardiner loaded the weapon and put it in his pocket.

"What about me?" demanded Riles. "Ain't I t' have no gun?"

"Better without it," said Gardiner. "It might go off. If we really see any game, and there's a chance of a second shot, I'll lend you this one."

The sun was dipping almost to the mountains when they set out on a cross-trail through the valley. Down by the river, well screened with cotton-woods, Travers fished in a pool close by the ford. He heard voices, and, looking up quickly, saw Riles and Gardiner riding slowly down the road. At first he thought Gardiner had seen him, but in a moment he revised that opinion. The two rode close by, and stopped their horses to drink with their forefeet in the river. Jim was going to call to them when he heard his own name mentioned. He was no eavesdropper, but he obeyed the impulse to listen and keep out of sight.

"Travers doesn't suspect a thing," Gardiner was saying. "It's just as well. He figures on making old Harris his father-in-law some day, and he might do something foolish if he caught on. If the old man loses all his money he won't be so desirable from a son-in-law's point of view. . . . Well, we'll see how he stands the night in the old shanty up the river road. Strange things have happened there before now, let me tell you, Riles."

If Jim had been prompted by curiosity at first a very different emotion laid hold of him as he caught the gist of Gardiner's remarks. He had no delusions about the principles of either Gardiner or Riles. His relations with his present employer had been pleasant but by no means confidential, as he had never sought nor valued Gardiner's friendship. He was convinced that Gardiner was kind in a general way to those with whom he came in contact, because kindness cost nothing and might upon occasion be exceedingly profitable. Riles, on the other hand, was coarse and unkind simply because his nature rose to no higher plane. Gardiner was clever enough to conceive almost any depth of villainy, and Riles was brutal enough to carry out the muscular part of the plot. Travers had not known Harris to be in the district, but he had suspected for some days that Gardiner and Riles were hatching mischief in their long absences together. The information that Harris was going up the river to-night, apparently with a large sum of money, and the fact that these two men also were going up the river, gave to Travers' nimble mind framework on which to hang almost any kind of plot.

He leaned forward in the trees, but at that moment Riles clutched Gardiner's arm and said something in a low voice. The two men rode through the river, and their words were drowned in the lisp of the water.

The smile did not leave Travers' lips as he wound up his reel and stole swiftly along a cattle-track up from the river, but a sudden light gleamed in his eyes and his muscles hardened with excited tension. He knew the shanty to which Gardiner referred, as they had once been there together, and he resolved that if there were going to be any "doings" in that locality to-night he would furnish a share of the excitement. Unfortunately, the ford was on a cross-road little used, and it was two miles back to the ranch. Had he been raised on the ranges he would not have been caught so far from his horse, but a Manitoban sometimes uses his legs to walk with, while his brother in Alberta finds them useful only for wearing schaps and straddling a saddle. By the time Travers reached the ranch buildings, caught and saddled his horse, made a fruitless search for his revolver, substituted a rifle which lay at hand, and at length found himself upon the trail, darkness was setting in, and Gardiner and Riles had many miles' start of him.

When the two plotters stopped to let their horses drink at the ford Gardiner suddenly broke off from their conversation to make a few remarks about Travers and Harris. Riles had listened indifferently until his eye caught sight of Travers, half concealed among the cotton-woods that fringed the stream. He clutched Gardiner's arm.

"S-s-sh," he cautioned. "Jim's just behind the bank. I'm sure I saw him, an' he heard you, too."

"Good," said Gardiner, quite undisturbed. "Now we can go on." They reined up their horses and plunged into the swiftly-running water. "You see," said Gardiner, as the horses took the opposite bank with great strides, their wet hoofs slipping on the round boulders that fringed the stream,—"You see, I knew Jim was there all the time. Those remarks were intended for his benefit."

Riles parted with a great chew of tobacco. "You beat me," he said, wiping his lips with the back of his hand. "You plumb beat me."

Gardiner enjoyed the note of admiration in his companion's voice. He enjoyed also the knowledge that Riles was utterly at sea; that he had no more idea than the horse he rode what lay before them that night.

"It's all quite simple," said Gardiner, after a pause. "Jim will hurry back to the ranch, saddle his horse, and follow us. By the way,

I didn't tell him I borrowed his revolver. That may delay him some. But he should arrive at the shack in time to be taking a few stealthy observations just about the moment the Harrises are hunting for their money bag. I hope Allan doesn't use that shot-gun on him. A shot-gun makes an awful hole in a man, Riles."

Riles experienced an uncanny feeling up his spine.

"Well," continued Gardiner, "I promised to lay the whole plan before you, when we were safe on the road with no possibility of any strange ears cocked for what a man might happen to say. . . . Look at that sunset, Riles; isn't that magnificent!"

"Good enough, I suppose," said Riles, "but I hope we didn't come out here to see the sunset. How about this plan of yours?"

"Riles," admonished Gardiner, "you've no more soul than a toadstool. You haven't any imagination. I wonder you have faith enough to wind your watch. Now if you could paint a picture like that it would make you more money than you ever saw—including what you're going to see to-night.

"But to get down to the scheme. It's all easy sailing now. The big thing was to get them on the road with the coin. That's what I needed you for, Riles. And you didn't do too bad. I had to prod you along a bit, but you'll thank me for it when it's all over."

"Yes, but it's them that's got it, not us," commented Riles.

"Sure, but it'll be different in the mornin'. Riles, you *are* a gloomy devil. Here you have ten thousand dollars right in your mit and you're as happy as a man with a boil. Now this is how it will work out, to a T. The two Harrises will get up to the shanty about dark. They'll pitch camp there and begin to wonder when we'll be along. Well, we won't be along until it's good and dark, even if we have to kill time on the road. If Travers catches up on us we'll just let him make one of the party, which will be sort of embarrassing for Jim. But he won't catch up. Well, when it's good and dark —there'll be no moon till after midnight— and they're both sleepy with their long drive in the high altitude, we will arrive near by. You will go up to the door and take a look on the quiet. I will go up to the window and do the same. There's no glass in the window, and there's no door on either, as I remember. We'll size up things inside, particularly the location of the coin. Then you show yourself. Tell 'em I have the owner of the mine out there in the trees, but the old fellow won't come in until he has a talk with them. Tell 'em they better not show the money until they chat with him a few minutes. Likely they'll fall for that, as they don't seem to have the slightest suspicion. But if they balk at leaving the money let them bring it along. Once out in the dark the rest will be easy. But I figure they'll leave the money in the shack—it's just for a few minutes, you know—and they'll reason that it's safe enough with no one but ourselves within miles. Well, you lead them off down through the bush. As soon as you do that I'll slip in through the window, gather up the long green and cache it somewhere in the scrub. You won't be able to find me at first, but when you do I'll say that the old fellow wanted to go up to the shack himself to meet them, and I let him go. Then we'll all go back to the shack, and find both the money and the old man—the mine-owner, you know —missing. Then we'll start a hue and cry and all hit into the bush. You and I will gather up the spoil and make a quiet get-away for the night. Of course we'll have to turn up in the morning to avert suspicion, but we can tell them we got on the robber's trail and followed it until we lost ourselves in the bush. In the meantime the Harrises will be tearing around in great excitement, and they're almost sure to run on to Travers. Harris recently fired Travers, and Allan had a fight with him, if you told me right, so it's not likely they'll listen to any explanations. They'll turn him over to the police, and as it's the business of the police to get convictions, they'll have to frame up a case against him or be made to look stupid—and that's the last thing a police-man likes. Then you and I will quietly divide the proceeds of our investment, and you can go back to your farm, if you like, and live to a ripe old age and get a write-up in the local paper when you shuffle off. As for me—I'm not that type, Riles, and I'll likely find some other way to spend my profits."

"It looks easy," Riles admitted. "But what about Jim? He'll tell what he heard you say at the ford."

"Let him. Nobody'll believe it. Remember that when he tells that he'll be under arrest, and when a man's under arrest his word is always discounted. To be arrested means to be half convicted. It takes two good wit-nesses to offset the moral effect of arrest, and Travers will have no witnesses.

"It's all quite easy," Gardiner continued. "And if it should fail there are a dozen other ways just as easy. But we won't let it fail. We mustn't let it fail, on your account."

"On my account? What more account mine than yours?"

"Well, you see, Harris, no doubt, has your letter stowed away somewhere, and it would make bad evidence for you. I don't think it mentions me at all. Besides, I know a way through a pass in these mountains, and if it doesn't turn out right—why, I'm glad I know the way. You see, I've nothing to lose, and nobody to worry over me. But it's different with you, Hiram. You have a wife and a fine farm down in Manitoba, and it would be inconvenient for you to slip away without notice. So I say that on your account we mustn't let it fail."

"You didn't say nothin' about that before, I notice," said Riles.

"You mustn't expect me to do your private thinking as well as that of the firm," Gardiner retorted. "You had the facts—why didn't you patch them together for yourself? You're in a mess now if things don't go right. But, as I said, I'm going to stick with you and see that they do go right."

They rode along in silence in the gathering darkness. Had they been able to read each other's minds they would have been astonished at the coincidence of thought. Gardiner was planning to make away with the money when he got out of the building. Why should he divide with Riles—Riles, who would only hoard it up, and who had plenty of money already? Not at all. Riles might sue him for his share, if he wanted to—and could find him, to serve notice! On the other hand, Riles' slow wits had quickened to the point of perceiving that there lay before him a chance of making twenty thousand dollars instead of ten thousand, if he only had the nerve to strike at the strategic moment. When he got the Harrises out of the shack, by hook or crook he would leave them and follow Gardiner. He was much more than Gardiner's match in strength and he had little fear of the revolver, provided he could take his adversary unawares. If the worst came to the worst, and he could not give the Harrises the slip, he would take them with him, and they would all come upon Gardiner red-handed with the loot. Then he would explain to Harris how he had discovered Gardiner's plot and frustrated it. . . . The idea grew upon Riles, and he rode along in a frame of mind bordering upon cheerfulness.

It was now quite dark, and the horses picked their steps carefully along the hillside trails. At last Gardiner drew up and pointed to a heavy clump of trees. A faint glimmer of light shone through it.

"That's the shack," he whispered. "They have a lantern there. We better get off the road and tether our horses in this coulee. Don't go too close; their horses may call to ours, and they will come out to meet us."

They turned down a narrow ravine with scarce room to walk single file between the branching trees. The stream was almost dry, and the horses' hoofs clanked alarmingly along the bed of the creek. They tied them where the woods closed all about them, and there seemed no chance of discovery.

"Quietly, now," said Gardiner, as they stole

toward the old building. "Things seem to be working out as we planned, but we must make sure of every detail, so that we can change the attack if necessary."

The two men stole up the rough road leading to the hut. Riles felt his heart thumping, and his lungs seemed half choked for air, but Gardiner lost none of his composure, and would have lit a cigarette had he not feared the light would betray them. The glow of the lantern came from the building, shining in a long, fading wedge from the sashless window, but seemed strangely obscure about the door. As they approached this mystery was revealed; a blanket was seen to hang over the doorway.

"That's a good sign," whispered Gardiner. "One, or both of them, are sleeping. That's why they feel the cold. If they had stayed awake they would have built a fire and perhaps walked about outside. This mountain air gets a man that isn't used to it. I'll bet you could go to sleep yourself this minute, Riles, if you weren't so scared."

"I ain't scared, damn you," said Riles, though the words trembled in his teeth. "If it comes to a show-down we'll see who's scared."

"That's good," said Gardiner. "That's the way to talk. If you just keep that up for a few minutes it'll all be over."

They paused for a moment to listen. The

night was moonless and starry, except where a bank of clouds came drifting up from the south-west. A moist breeze, smelling of soft, mountain snow, gently stirred the trees about them. But from the shanty no sound could be discerned. They approached nearer, and still nearer.

"Now, you go to the door, and I'll take the window," Gardiner ordered. "Shove the blanket aside a little and size up the situation before you speak. We must make sure they're there, and there alone."

Gardiner waited until he saw Riles fumbling carefully with the blanket that hung in the doorway. Then he darted quickly to the window.

CHAPTER XVII

THE FIGHT IN THE FOOTHILLS

WHILE Allan sat in the little cabin he gradually became oppressed with a sense of great loneliness. From time to time he looked at the face of his sleeping father, and suddenly the knowledge struck him like a knife that it was the face of an old man. He had never thought of him as an old man before, but as he lay on the rough floor, sleeping soundly after his long drive, there was something in the form that told of advancing years, and Allan could see plainly the deepening furrows in his strong, still handsome face. As he looked a vast tenderness mingled with his loneliness; he would have stooped and caressed him had he not feared to disturb his slumbers. Allan's love for his father was that of man to man rather than son to parent; it was the only deep passion of his young life, and it ran with a fulness that could not be checked. Of his mother he thought with kindliness, tinged with regret that all had not of late been quite as it should be in their domestic circle; toward his sister he felt a vague longing and uneasiness,

[265]

18

and a new feeling which had taken root that afternoon that perhaps after all she was right in seeking to live her life as she would; but it was to his father that his great emotion turned.

He looked upon the sleeping man now, with the wealth of a lifetime's labour at his side, and the bond of trust and confidence between them seemed so tight it brought the moisture to his eyes. He thought of the past years; of their labour on the farm together—hard labour, but always relieved by their comradeship and mutual ambitions. A hundred half-forgotten incidents came to mind, in all of which his father was companion and chum rather than parent and corrector. And after all, hadn't it been worth while? Had not they, in their way, really given expression to their lives as best they could in the black, earth-smelling furrows, in the scent of tallowy, straw-aromaed steam from their engine, or the wet night-perfume of ripening wheat? How those old smells beat up from the mysterious chambers of memory and intoxicated his nostrils with fondness and a great sense of having, in some few hallowed moments, dove-tailed his own career into the greater purpose of creation! Allan did not analyze these thoughts and memories, or try to fit them into words, but they brought to him a consciousness of having lived—of having known some experiences that were not altogether material and temporal.

And then his memory carried him still further back—back to the days when he was a little child, and in the mirror of the darkness he could see his own small figure trudging. in the track of the plough and hanging to the rein-ends that dropped from the knot on his father's ample back. Back to the old sod shanty, with its sweet smell of comfort when the snow beat against the little window and the wind roared in the rattling stove-pipe, and his mother sat by the fire and plied her flying needles. What wonderful times they were, and what wonderful dreams in the little, thoughtful child-mind just catching the first glimmerings of life! Could it be this old cabin, these rotting logs, this earthy floor, that were stirring memory cells asleep for twenty years? He would not allow his mind to be drawn into speculation—the thing was the remembrance, now, when it was offered him. Old lullabies stole into his brain; a deep peace compassed him, and consciousness faded thinner and thinner into the sea of the infinite. . . .

Allan sat up in a sudden, cold chill of terror. Had he been asleep? What cold breath of dread had crossed his path? He was no coward; the sense of fear was almost unknown to him, but now it enveloped him, stifled him, set his teeth chattering and his limbs quaking. He had heard nothing, seen nothing. The gun was in his hands as it had lain when last he remembered it; his father slept by his side, and near the wall lay the precious satchel. And yet he shook in absolute, unreasoning, unfounded terror. His eyes wandered from the lantern to the door—to the blanket hanging limply in the door; and there they stared and stayed as though held in the spell of a serpent. Subconsciously, certainly without any direction of will of his own, he raised the shot-gun to his shoulder and kept it trained on the sagging blanket. . . . The blanket seemed to move! It swayed at first as though a light breeze had touched it, and yet not as though a breeze had touched it. The impulse seemed too far up—about the height of a man's shoulder. The blood had gone from Allan's face; he was as one in a trance, obeying some iron law outside the realm of the will and the reason. He cocked his gun and tightened his finger on the trigger, and watched. . . . And then, so plain that it must have been real, he saw stealthy fingers feeling their way about the blanket.

Then Allan fired.

In an instant he was wide awake, and wondering terribly what had happened. The explosion blew out the lantern, and the building was in utter darkness. His father was clambering to his feet with "Allan, what is it? What is it, Allan?" The blanket had been torn from its hangings as by a heavy weight, and something was writhing in it in the doorway. Allan sprang up and would have rushed upon it, but in the darkness he collided with another man. His fingers found his adversary's arm and ran up it to his throat, but before they could fasten in a fatal grip there was another flash of light, and a hot pang stabbed him in the breast. There was a strange gurgling in his lungs, a choking in his throat, a spinning dizziness in his head, as he staggered over the mass in the doorway and fell into the night.

Gardiner had reached the window just in time to see Allan's gun trained on the doorway. For an instant he stood dumfounded; there was something uncanny in the sight of the young man sitting there in silent, absolute readiness for the attack. He drew back to warn Riles, but he was too late. At that moment the gun spoke; there was the sound of a heavy body falling, and stifled noises bore ample evidence of the accuracy of Allan's aim. But even in that moment of uncertainty Gardiner had not lost thought of their purpose, and his quick eye took in the sleeping form of John Harris and the location of the leather bag beside the wall. Without an instant's hesitation he vaulted through the window and, revolver in hand, began to steal his way softly toward the treasure.

He had not taken three steps when Allan

plunged full force into him. He staggered with the shock, but recovered himself only to find the young farmer's strong fingers clutching for his throat. It had been no part of Gardiner's plan that there should be bloodshed in the carrying out of the robbery, but he was a man of quick decision, who accepted conditions as he found them. . . . A slight pressure on the trigger, and Allan fell, coughing, through the door.

Gardiner retained his sense of location, and slipped silently to the wall. Harris was rushing about the rotten floor in the darkness, crying, "What is it, Allan? For God's sake, what has happened? Are you shot?" and for his own noise he could not hear Gardiner's stealthy movements. Gardiner's hand fell on a log of the wall, and his keen fingers traced their way along it. Five steps, he judged, and the bag would be at his feet. At the fifth step his toe touched an object on the floor; he leaned over and raised the booty in his hand.

By this time his eyes had responded to the intense darkness, and he could discern a square of greyer gloom where the window admitted the night. He moved rapidly and silently toward it, but almost with the last step his foot slipped through a broken spot on the floor, and he staggered and fell. The revolver was thrown from his grasp, but he was able to pitch the bag through the window as he crashed to the floor.

The sound arrested Harris, and before Gardiner could extricate himself the farmer was upon him. At first he seemed to think it was Allan, and felt about in the darkness without attempting to defend himself. This gave Gardiner an opportunity; he was able to clasp his arms about Harris's shins, and, with a quick turn of the body, cast his adversary headlong to the floor. At the same moment he freed himself from his entanglement and made another dash for the window.

But Harris, still numbed from his heavy sleep, now realized that some kind of tragedy had occurred, and guessed enough to believe that Allan was a victim. From his prostrate position, with one powerful leg he interrupted Gardiner's flight, and the next moment the two men were rolling on the floor in each other's arms. Harris was much the stronger man of the two, but Gardiner was active and had some skill in wrestling. Besides, Harris had been taken wholly by surprise, and had no idea who his antagonist was, while Gardiner had full knowledge of all the circumstances, and the struggle was less uneven than might have been supposed. Inwardly cursing the luck that had thrown the revolver from his hand, Gardiner sought in the darkness for his adversary's throat, nose, or eyes. Harris, seizing the younger man by the waist, lifted him bodily from the floor and crashed him down again upon it, but the next instant Gardiner had one of his hands in both of his, and, bringing his knee down with great force on Harris's elbow, compelled him, at the risk of a broken arm, to turn face downwards on the floor. Gardiner again wrenched violently to break free, but Harris's grip was too much for him, so with the quickness and fury of a tiger he threw himself upon the farmer's back and wrapped his free arm about his throat. With his air partially cut off Harris released the grip of his other hand, and Gardiner instantly took advantage of this move to bring both arms to bear on Harris's throat. Things began to go badly with the farmer; face downwards on the floor, he was unable to shake his adversary off, and was losing strength rapidly with his choking. Gardiner no longer sought an opportunity to break away; his blood was up and he was in the fight to the finish, ruled at last by his heart instead of his head. Had he been content merely to retain his present advantage, unconsciousness would soon have overcome his victim, but he tried to improve his grip, and the attempt proved disastrous. His thumb, seeking better vantage, fell into Harris's gasping mouth. Harris was no more depraved than most of mankind, but when fighting for life, and choking to death in the hands of an unknown enemy, he was ready to seize any advantage, and with a great effort he brought his jaws together upon the intruder.

With a yell of pain Gardiner sprang to his feet, jerking the farmer into a half-sitting posture as he did so, and Harris, with a great gasp for air, relinquished his sudden and unexpected advantage. But Gardiner's head was again in command; he rushed through the door, half falling over the obstruction as he went, and in an instant was lost in the gloom of the night.

For some minutes Harris lay on the floor, recovering his breath. As the oxygen welled back into his lungs he began to realize that, save for his choking, he was unhurt. With returning strength his thought reverted to Allan, and, calling the boy's name, he sprang to his feet. The first thing was to get a light. He found matches in his pocket, struck one, and peered eagerly into the gloom as its flickering flame beat back the darkness. A blanket, rolled and stained, lay in the doorway, and within it was a figure that might once have been a man. Harris's heart almost stopped at the sight: "Allan," he gasped, "my boy, Allan!" He tiptoed across the crumbling floor toward it, holding the match before him. A man's boot and part of a trouser leg protruded from the mass. He held the match downward, leaning over them. They were not Allan's.

"Thank God," he murmured, swelling with a great hope, "thank God for that."

He struck another match and found the lantern. When he had lighted it he surveyed the little building, and saw Allan's gun lying at the end farthest from the door. Not until that moment did he think of the money. Allan had been uppermost in his mind, and when he thought of Allan money was no consideration. But now a great wave of understanding rushed in upon him. Yes, the bag was gone. They had been attacked by robbers. Knowledge of their expedition had in some way got to evil ears, and while he slept Allan had been set upon. The boy had emptied his gun—the huddled mass in the doorway told that tale plainly enough—but other robbers had seized the cash and Allan had pursued them empty-handed. They had fired at him as he rushed from the building—that was the flash he saw a few reconds after the first loud report. He was not quite clear as to his own share in the fight, but he saw the general plan of it plainly enough. He began to wonder what had happened to Gardiner and Riles. Had they been shot down as they wound through the woods? This was evidently the work of a gang prepared to stop at nothing. Harris never for a moment suspected his old neighbour of treachery. He was himself a hard, grasping, money-seeking man, but he had a code of honour none the less, and within its limitations none was more honourable than he. To have done what Riles had done would have been quite impossible for John Harris, and because it was impossible for him its possibility for Riles never suggested itself.

Harris had not yet fully realized the loss of his money. It was overshadowed by the more tragic events of which one evidence lay before him. His anxiety for Allan loomed larger in his mind, although he had little doubt the boy would take proper care of himself, and, even if unarmed, would come back with the money and perhaps with a prisoner. The fact that Allan had not taken his gun was reassuring; if there had been any great danger he would not have left it behind. But he must get out now and aid in the search.

As he reached this decision his eye caught a gleam of something shining on the floor. He walked to it and found a revolver, fully loaded except for one chamber, which had been discharged. "This is evidence," said he—"important evidence." Harris had all the Old Ontario contempt for this kind of weapon, and knew comparatively little about it, but he concluded from its appearance that it was almost new. As he examined it his eye fell on the initials, "J. T.," cut in the grip.

"J. T.," he said to himself. "J. T. Those initials seem familiar. I'll just leave this thing where I found it, until the police see it."

Replacing the weapon on the floor, he stole

out of the cabin, avoiding the silent obstruction in the doorway. Outside he stood for a moment undecided. The circle of light from his lantern might beacon Allan back to the shanty, but it would also prove a signal to the robbers, if they were still in the vicinity. The night was now very dark, clouds having obscured the stars, and an occasional big drop of rain spat about him. The roar of water came up from the valleys, but above or through that roar suddenly he fancied he heard a sound from the bushes near at hand. He held his breath and listened intently. He half wished he had brought the revolver with him. Yes, there it was again—a human sound, beyond question, half groan, half gurgle. He turned in the direction from which it came and stole quietly forward. Half-a-dozen yards from the building the light revealed, first a shadow, and then a figure lying on the ground. With some trepidation Harris approached. The man's arms had been extended when he fell, and his coat was thrown over his head. Harris stooped and drew it down over the shoulders exposing the face.

It was Allan.

The first shock of the revelation almost stopped the heart of the old farmer, and he sat back as one dazed, unable to accept the testimony of his own eyes. Then came a panic of uncertainty, and he fell upon the boy, groping wildly for his heart, and at last pressing upon it in an agony of fear. . . . Yes, the beat was there, faint and uneven, but unmistakable. With a sudden surge of returning hope he brought his ear down to the open mouth, fringed with light red foam, and could hear the air labouring in the ravaged lungs. Then came that human sound, half gurgle, half groan; but to Harris, in the reaction from his first paralyzing fear, it was as very music from heaven. His boy still lived, and still should live.

Tenderly he turned the body to a more comfortable position, laying his folded coat beneath the head for a pillow. He loosened the shirt about the neck, and far down the heaving chest saw the sodden red that marked his wound. Rain fell in scattered drops, and he brought another blanket from the cabin, caring little now for the silent form in the doorway in the sudden shadow of his greater tragedy. He spread the blanket over the wounded boy, and sat down by his side, caressing his temples with his big fingers, and wondering what to do next.

As he sat the helplessness of his position grew upon him. He was deep in the foothills, many miles, as far as he knew, from the home of any settler. In daylight he could, no doubt, find his way back to town, but daylight might be too late. He did not know whether Allan was dying on his hands at that moment. Certainly to attempt to move him in the buggy would be dangerous in the extreme.

And as he sat he thought of the missing money, the fruit of his life's labour, snatched from him in a moment in the darkness. The loss did not hurt him as deeply as he might have thought; he was numbed by the greater blow that hung over him. If Allan would only live! . . . The boy had been his constant companion since babyhood. All his hopes, all his ambitions, which had found their expression in his years of feverish toil, had been wrapped about Allan. He had no one else. . . . His better self revolted at that thought. "You have a wife and daughter," it said, "ready to share your life as soon as you are ready to share theirs." He forced his mind from that phase of his position, but it reverted to it again and again. He could not wander in memory up the path of his boy's life without meeting his boy's mother. And all the pain and unhappiness of the later years—how it cut like an evil bank of fog across the once bright course of their career! But he had suffered for their sakes, holding fast to his own course because he knew it to be best. . . . Best? And it had brought him to this? . . . The question would not down. Rather than relax an iota from his own purposes he had broken up his family; he had crushed them under the wheels of his inflexible will, and now that same will had driven his son to destruction and himself to ruin.

It is not easy for a man who has laid out a career and followed it with all the energy of a virile nature, recasting his gods from time to time to conform with the evolution of his ideals, but recasting always in the mould of his own will rather than any vessel of creed or persuasion—it is not easy for such a man to stop at fifty and say, "I was wrong." It requires a break in his process of evolution, a shock sufficiently powerful to pulverize his gods before his face, to drive home the truth that they were not gods at all but merely idols of his own creation. In Harris's later life two idols had grown up to the exclusion of all others; they were the wealth which he had builded with his hands and the boy Allan about whom he wrapped all the affection of his nature; and they had crumbled to dust even while he worshipped.

He found a flask thrown from some camper's pack, and filled it with water at the mountain stream that rushed by a few rods below the cabin. He placed the liquid to the boy's lips and fancied that some drops found entrance. He had staunched the wound as best he could with fragments torn from the lining of his coat, and he sat down again to watch. Until morning he could do nothing more. Then some camper, lumberman, or surveyor might happen along the road. If not, he would have to move Allan at all risks.

It took time for him to realize the utterness with which his plans had collapsed. As the night wore on he was able to weigh his disaster in a more balanced mind, but its magnitude grew in the weighing. From prosperous ambition he had been swept in an hour to penniless ruin. His destruction was almost complete. The old farm, the scene of his labours—his and Mary's—was gone. If Allan should die there remained nothing more.

Suddenly he fancied he heard the sound of horses' hoofs in the clay road along the hillside, now softened with the light rain. The sound ceased as suddenly as it began, and it occurred to him that it might be one of the robbers returning. The lantern was burning low, but as a precaution he now turned it quite out. There were some cartridges in Allan's pocket; he felt for them and decided to bring the gun out of the cabin. But before he could put this decision into effect he observed the form of a man moving silently but briskly toward the cabin. He held his breath and remained obscured in the bushes. Dimly he discerned the form stop at the door and peer into the darkness.

There was no doubt in the mind of Harris as to the evil intent of the visitor. He had come on horseback near the building, and had then dismounted and stole up to it on foot. That in itself was sufficiently incriminating. One who was riding through the mountains on a legitimate errand, and who knew nothing of the night's affray, would take no such precautions. Unarmed as he was, Harris resolved that the robber, probably the murderer of his son, should not on any account escape him. With the blanket which he had brought to cover Allan was a bag in which they had carried oats for their horses; this he found in the darkness, and stole after his victim. He overtook him standing at the door, in apparent hesitancy whether to enter the building. Without an instant's warning Harris threw the bag about his head, and with a quick twist of his powerful wrist had his prisoner securely gagged. Throwing him violently to the ground, he tied the sack in a hard knot, and, despite all struggles, dragged him back to where Allan lay. Here he relighted the lantern, and, cutting part of the blanket into strips with his pocket-knife, securely tied his captive hand and foot. At first the prisoner tried to talk, but he could not speak intelligibly through the closely-drawn sack, and presently he gave up and lay in silence in the wet grass.

And again the leaden night wore on, broken only by occasional gurglings in the throat of Allan, or futile struggles by the prisoner. Harris felt little curiosity concerning the identity of the man in gags before him, or the victim of Allan's gun in the doorway. They were absolute strangers to him, and he even feared that if he should look into the face of the one that still lived his anger over the assault upon Allan would burst all bounds and he would kill his victim on the spot. He was slowly forced to the conclusion that Riles and Gardiner had also met with foul play, and that no help was now to be expected from that quarter. The light rain had drifted past, and bright stars gleamed through great rents in the shattered clouds. The gibbous moon, too, looked down, and its cold light intensified the shadows. The night grew colder, and Harris spread his own outer garments upon his son, and at last lay down with Allan in his arms that he might communicate heat from his body to the struggling frame so sorely robbed of blood. And even in his distress and his terrific fear for Allan there came some reminiscence of old delight at the feel of the boy's limbs against his, and fleet-footed memory ran back again to the childhood of Allan. But on its way it met the childhood of Beulah, and conjured up the mother-face leaning in tenderness over the sick-beds of infancy. And John Harris buried his face in the heaving chest of his child and wept in his grief and loneliness.

Just as the first bars of grey in the eastern sky proclaimed approaching dawn, the sound of horse's hoofs came distinctly up the valley. Harris drew himself into a sitting posture, and listened. Allan was still breathing, and apparently with less effort than earlier in the night. The sound of the horse came nearer and nearer. At last it was in the road just below, and a moment later would have passed by had not Harris called out. His voice sounded strange and distant in his own ears, and cost him an unwonted effort.

Sergeant Grey instantly swung his horse from the road and, dismounting, proceeded in the direction of the voice.

Harris told his story with such coherence as he could. He and his son had come up into the hills to arrange for the purchase of a property which they had become interested in through a third party, Gardiner. They carried with them a large sum of money as proof of the sincerity of their intentions. At this little cabin they were to be joined by Gardiner and by another, named Riles, who also was taking an interest in the property. As they waited in the cabin, and as he, Harris, slept after his long drive, they were suddenly set upon by outlaws. Allan shot one down—the body still lay in the doorway—but was himself badly wounded, and had not spoken since. Harris had encountered another, but after a severe fight the robber had escaped. The little black bag in which the money was carried was gone with all its contents. Although he had waited all night in great anxiety, Gardiner and Riles had failed to appear, and it could only be supposed that they too had met with foul play. But some hours after the assault one of the party had returned, dismounted from his horse at some distance, and stolen softly up to the shanty. Harris had followed him, and, taking him by surprise, had been able to make him prisoner.

Sergeant Grey looked from Harris to Allan, and then to the prisoner, who seemed to lie in a semi-conscious condition amid his bonds and gags.

"You were foolish to come into the hills with so much money alone," he said. "I would have been at your service for the asking, and this would not have happened. But now that it has happened, the first thing is to provide for the wounded man, and the next is to place this suspect in custody. And you will need some toning up yourself after your night's experience. Then we will have a full investigation. I know a rancher's house a few miles down the valley where you and your son will have the best attention."

The mounted policeman made a brief examination of Allan, as best he could in the grey dawn, for the lantern now had no oil. "He has not bled very much," he said. "He has a strong frame and ought to have a fighting chance. I will just have a look at the scene of the crime, and then we will move him."

He made a hurried survey of the cabin, merely satisfying himself that the man in the doorway was quite dead, and then, with Harris's assistance, quickly found the horses and harnessed them to the buggy. He also found another horse near the roadway, saddled and bridled. "We will make the prisoner ride his own horse," he said, "while you take your son in the buggy."

They placed the wounded and still unconscious Allan in the buggy as gently as they could, and then Grey gave his attention to the prisoner. Having searched his clothing for weapons, he cut away the bonds that securely held his arms and feet, and released the sack from his half-choked throat. The man writhed and gasped for fresh air, and the policeman drew the sack away and revealed the face of Jim Travers.

CHAPTER XVIII

CONVERGING TRAILS

BEULAH Harris raised her arms above her head and drank in the fresh mountain air that flooded through the open window. A smoky red, with brighter shafts of yellow behind, streamed up from the eastern sky and sent a glow of burnt-orange colour through her bedroom. The girl stretched her spread fingers to the limit of their reach, and with extended toes sought the iron bars at the foot of the bed, filling her lungs with the fresh foothill ozone. Then she dropped her hands, palm upward, with the backs of her finger-tips resting on her eyes, and felt that it was good to be alive.

They had been great times—wonderful times—these weeks spent in the freedom and harmony of the Arthurses' household. Mr. and Mrs. Arthurs—Uncle Fred and Aunt Lilian, as she now called them—had opened their hearts and their home to Beulah from the first. Indeed, the girl was often conscious of their gaze upon her, and at times she would look up quickly and surprise a strange, wistful look of yearning in their eyes—a look that they tried very hard to hide from her. They wanted to leave her free to live her own life—to shape her career, for a time at least, wholly in accordance with her impulses.

And such a life as she had lived! Arthurs had at once placed a horse at her disposal, and with a fierce delight at the leap she was taking through conventions she swung her right leg over the saddle and sat to place like any man. Although born and raised on a farm, horse-back riding was to her something of a novelty, and the assumption of the masculine position was a positive epoch in her career. How the people of Plainville would have been scandalized if they could have witnessed her shocking familiarity with a horse! She thought of an English girl who had been cut by the good society of Plainville because she dared to ride like a biped instead of a mermaid. And she laughed in a wild exultant freedom, while the wind whipped her hair about her shoulders, and she felt her mount firm beneath her as they cantered across the brown foothills.

Such hills they were! In her native plains they would have been mountains of themselves, wonders of Nature to point out to strangers and to hold in a kind of awe across the country-side, but here they were foothills, mere fragments dropped from the trowel of the Builder as He reared the majestic Rockies behind. And though she often in the early morn-

ing, or at sunset, or when the moon was full
and white, feasted her eyes and her soul on the
cold splendour of the mighty range, it was to
the warm brown foothills, with their stubbling
of little trees and their solemn warts of grey-
green rock, that her heart turned with something of human affection. At first Uncle Fred,
or Aunt Lilian, or, a little later, one of the two
cowboys rode with her on her expeditions, but
her prairie sense of direction quickly adapted
itself to her new surroundings, and she soon
learned to keep a keen eye for the precipitous
cut-banks that drop sheer from a level plain
and lie as unsuspected in the saffron sunlight
as a coyote among the ripened willows. There
were quicksands, too—spots where the water
sprang from the hillside in a crystal stream
and in a few yards soaked into the kneady
earth as in a sponge—but all these places were
fenced; even in Alberta, where cattle grow like
rabbits on the range, the paving of sink-holes
with beef steers is an expensive expedient. So
Beulah quickly got her foothill sense, and in a
week was riding, care-free and exultant, across
the ranges as her heart listed or her horse preferred.

One morning, just as the first grey of dawn
mottled the darkness of her chamber, Beulah
heard her door open, and through the uncertain light she discerned Arthurs gently entering with a rifle in his hand. She sat up, alert,

but not afraid; the tingling health in her veins left no place for fear and suffered no foolishness on the part of her nervous system.

"What is it, Uncle Fred?" she whispered.

"H-s-h," he cautioned. "You know we have been losing calves with the timber wolves? Well, there are two of the murderers just across from the corral. I thought you might want to see them."

In an instant her feet were on the floor, and, hand in hand, she and Arthurs stole to the window. At first her eyes could distinguish nothing in the darkness, but by following Arthurs' index finger she at last located two gaunt, shaggy creatures a little way up the hillside beyond the corral, and a couple of hundred yards from the house.

"However did you know they were there?" she whispered. "You must have cat's eyes. I could hardly see them when you pointed them out."

"Not cat's eyes, Beulah," he answered. "Just rancher's eyes. I heard the horses snorting, and I fancied there were visitors. Now, will you take first shot?"

"Oh, that would be a shame. They would get away, and besides, I might kill a horse."

"Well, won't press it this time," said Arthurs, "because I have a little personal score to settle with these fellows. I guess I have about five hundred dollars invested in each of them."

THE HOMESTEADERS

The wolves were moving leisurely about on the hillside, showing no disposition to run away, but apparently afraid to approach closer to the ranch buildings. Arthurs leaned his rifle across the window sill and took steady aim, while the girl held her breath with excitement. Then there was a quick flash, that shut the scene momentarily from their eyes; the next moment they saw one of the wolves leap into the air and fall, a sprawling mass, upon the ground, while the other darted with the speed of a greyhound toward the neighbouring bushes. Arthurs followed him with a bullet, but even so fine a marksman could have found him only by chance in that uncertain light.

"Well, I guess there's a widow in Wolfville this morning," said Arthurs, as he leisurely threw the discharged cartridge from the barrel. "My apologies, Miss Beulah, for this somewhat unconventional call and the interruption of your beauty sleep."

But Beulah was standing, wrapped in admiration. "Oh, Uncle Fred," she exclaimed. "You're just wonderful. If I could only shoot like that!"

"It's all a matter of training," he told her. "Of course, you must have good eyes and steady nerves, but you have those already. The rifle is yours whenever you want it, and all the ammunition you can carry. There's just one stipulation—for the first week shoot only at foothills, and, remember, aim low."

So Beulah became a rifle enthusiast, and it astonished her how rapidly she improved in marksmanship. With a little instruction from Arthurs and the cowboys in the matter of sighting and holding her weapon, she developed quickly from a stage of dangerous uncertainty in her gunnery to one of almost expert accuracy. Then she made of the rifle a companion on her horseback excursions, to the destruction of gophers, rabbits, and even a badger and a coyote. It was a brave day when she rode into the corral with a coyote strung across her saddle.

The river near by teemed with trout, and the girl soon caught the fascination of the angler. Mrs. Arthurs had a pair of high rubber boots, which she used when she herself went whipping the blue water, and, anchored in these as far out as she dared go into the gravel-bottomed stream, the girl laced the cold current back and forth. And the wild exultation of her first bite! The fish darted up and down stream, pulling out line faster than she could reel it in, and Beulah, in her excitement, waded deeper into the stream as she followed the quivering line. But mountain streams are treacherous; one step too far plunged her into twenty feet of water, and the next moment she was spinning round and round in the current. She had learned to swim a few strokes in the creek on her father's farm, and her meagre skill now stood her in good stead, for she was able to keep afloat until the current threw her against a gravel bar that jutted into the river. She dragged herself ashore, very wet, and of a sudden, very frightened, and sat down on the warm stones. It was here that she recorded another resolution; she would learn to swim —not a feeble stroke or two, but to be master of this river which had so nearly mastered her. "I will do it," she said. "I will swim it across and back, if it takes till December, and— bur-r-r-rh—it's cold enough now." Then it occurred to her that there was no better time to start than the present. She looked out a place where the current was not too strong, and where there were no treacherous rock-splits in the bottom, spread her wet clothing to dry in the sun, and for an hour fought the cold current at its own game.

It is not recorded how it came about, but Arthurs passed the word among the ranch hands that a certain stretch of river bank was sacred from all intrusion.

But it was in the life of the home, even more than in the joyous freedom of the out-of-doors, that Beulah found her great delight. The Arthurs, she knew, were wealthy—many times richer than her father, who passed as a wealthy man among the farmers of Plainville. But with the Arthurs wealth was merely an incident—a pleasant but by no means essential by-product of their lives. They lived simply, but well; they worked honestly, but did not slave; and in all their living and working they shed a kindliness and courtesy that communicated itself to all with whom they came in contact. The cowboys, Beulah soon discovered, were as unlike the cowboys of fiction and of her imagination as a Manitoba steer is unlike his Alberta brother; they did not carry revolvers, nor swagger in high boots, nor rip the air with their profanity; and their table manners reminded her of George and Harry Grant, and the Grants were outstanding examples of right living in the Plainville district. And Mrs. Arthurs, gentle and kind in all her doings, and yet firm and strong and calm, she was—such a woman, Beulah told herself, as her own mother might have been, had her soul not been crushed under a load of unceasing labour.

But, most of all, it was to Fred Arthurs that the heart of the young girl turned. Whether he sat over his desk at his letters, or dispensed hospitality at his table (for all who passed up or down the valley, as a matter of course, stopped for a meal at the Arthurses), or cantered across the foothills, or shouted behind his lagging herds (such shouting as it was, fit to split the canyons!), or played ball with the boys in the evening, or discussed theology with the travelling missionary, or philosophy with his book-worm neighbour from across the river, or read poetry with his wife on the Sunday afternoons, or sang with his great voice in the mellow, yellow eventide, or—most of all—when he looked at Beulah with his fine eyes, and she caught the mirrored reflection of the hunger in his soul, she felt that here was a man who had lived his life to the uttermost and would go on living it through all eternity. She only half guessed what his thoughts toward her were—she did not know that Fred and Lilian Arthurs had at last agreed that they could do better than leave their wealth to charity, and that a new will was soon to be drawn—but to her he seemed pure gold, and a gentleman to his last gesture. And she vowed one night that if ever she met a single man like Fred Arthurs she would marry him although all the canons and conventions of Christendom stood between them.

And then, quite unexpected, it came upon her, and thrilled her frame from toe to temple. Jim Travers! It had been in the background of her mind for months, the centre of the sub-conscious processes which culminated in this revelation. Yes, Fred Arthurs at twenty-five must have been such a man as Jim Travers. Jim Travers at fifty would be such a man as Fred Arthurs. She was absolutely sure of it. Jim was living his own life, seeking out that which was worth while, culling the incidental from the essential, just as Fred Arthurs must have done. She remembered with sudden joy how Jim had held a little kindness to her of greater moment than the impatient engine in the plough-field; the scores of little labours he had undertaken, not as a sacrifice, but as a privilege—as his contribution to human happiness. She would marry Jim Travers. The strange part of it was her sudden certainty that she should marry him. She found herself enveloped in a flame of possession, a feeling that he was hers—hers now, this minute, and hers for ever. Beulah was a fatalist, although she had never analyzed her own beliefs enough to know it, but she knew that Destiny had linked her life with his and that Destiny would not be balked. Her mind had been feeling its way, through the darkness of months, to this sudden ecstasy, but now that she had reached it she felt that it could never, never fail her. Her sense of possession, of mergement, was complete; she felt that already their souls had mingled irrevocably and indistinguishably.

The arrival of her mother at the Arthurses' ranch had brought fresh joy to Beulah's life. She saw the colour coming back to the old face, the frame straightening up a little, the light rekindling in the eye, the spring returning to the instep. She had not thought that her mother, after twenty-five years of unprotesting submission, had still the nerve to place a limit on that submission, and the discovery had surprised and delighted her. True, Mary Harris let it be known that she was only on a visit, and in due course would return to her home; but Beulah knew the die had been cast, and things could never again be quite as they were. And Beulah told her secret, and her mother just kissed her and let a tear or two fall in her hair.

So this morning, as the girl stretched her young limbs, rounding with life and energy, and the burnt-orange glow of sunrise suffused the room and lit the pink tissues of her slender fingers, she rested in the deep peace which, ever since her revelation, had enveloped her about. For a minute she let her mind dwell on the picture she carried in her brain, until the association became too keen and threatened to overwhelm her from very tenderness; then she sprang from her bed, and, flipping the window-blind to the top, drank in the beauty of the valley through the open window. Her bedroom had windows both to the east and the west; and it was her custom to awaken early and feast on the glory as it surged up the valley, and then, turning, watch the long waves of light sink slowly down the white mountains. And this morning, when she thought the first beams must be gilding the highest peaks, she turned to the westward window and saw the light playing under a Chinook arch across a segment of sky so soft and near she could almost feel it with extended fingers. And then a sound caught her ear, and up the trail she saw two men on horseback, a mounted policeman and another, and behind them other men driving in a buggy.

By intuition Beulah knew that a mishap had occurred. The Arthurses' ranch was the first abode of real civilization on the way out from the mountains, and it was nothing unusual for a lumberman with a chopped foot, or a prospector caught in sliding rock, or a river-driver crushed between logs, or a hunter the victim of his own marksmanship, to come limping or riding down the trail to this haven of first aid. Quickly she drew on her simple clothing and hurried downstairs, but Arthurs was already at the door. The little party came into the yard, and the policeman rode up to the door. The other horseman sat with his back to the house; his hands were chained together in front of him.

"Good-morning, Sergeant Grey," said Arthurs. "You're early out."

The sergeant saluted. The salutation was intended for Arthurs, but at the moment the policeman's eye fell on Beulah, and even the discipline of the Force could not prevent a momentary turning of the head.

"I've a badly hurt man here," he said, "a man who will need your hospitality and care for some days. There was a shooting up the

valley last night. His father is here, too, unhurt physically, but on the verge of collapse,
if I am not mistaken."

"We will bring both of them in at once,"
said Arthurs. "Beulah, will you call Lilian,
and your mother, too? They may be needed.
But who is the third?" he continued, turning
to Grey.

"A prisoner. It seems the older man overpowered him. Now let us get this poor fellow
in."

The policeman beckoned and Harris drove
the buggy up to the door. Arthurs glanced at
him with a casual "Good-morning," but the
next instant his eyes were riveted on the visitor.
"John Harris!" he exclaimed, taking a great
stride forward and extending his strong arm.
"Man, John, I'm glad to see you, but not in
these troubles."

Harris took his hand in a silent clasp, and
there was a warmth in it that set his heart
beating as it had not for years. "It's hard,
Fred," he managed to say in a dry voice, "but
it's good to have you by."

Arthurs bent over Allan, who was half sitting, half lying, in the buggy. His face was
sapped and grey in the growing light. Tenderly the three men lifted him out. "Take
him straight upstairs," said Arthurs. "It will
save moving him again." Both spare-rooms in
the house were occupied, but Arthurs led the

way into Beulah's, and they laid the wounded boy on the white bed.

Arthurs heard Beulah in the hall. "Take off his clothes, Grey," he said, and turned to the doorway. "Where's your mother, Beulah?" he asked in a low voice, closing the bedroom door behind him.

"Dressing." The girl looked in his face, and drew back with a little cry. "What's the matter, Uncle Fred? What's wrong?"

"A friend of mine has been hurt, and an old friend of your mother's. She must not see him just now. You will arrange that?"

"Yes. But I must see him—I must help."

Beulah hurried to the room where her mother was rapidly dressing. "A man has been hurt, mother," she said, with suppressed excitement. "We need hot water. Will you start a fire in the range?"

Mary Harris mistook Beulah's emotion for natural sympathy over a suffering creature, and hurried to the kitchen. Mrs. Arthurs was whispering with her husband in the hall, but a moment later joined Mary at the range.

Then Beulah entered the room. The policeman was speaking to Arthurs. "I must go into town now with my prisoner," he was saying. "I will send out a doctor at once, and in the meantime I know you will do everything possible."

Beulah turned her eyes to the bed A man

was lying there, and an old man was sitting beside it. At the second glance she recognized him, but in an instant she had herself under control. She walked with a steady step to the bed and looked for a full minute in her brother's face. Then she looked at her father.

"What have you done to him?" she said.

He threw out his hand feebly. "You do well to ask me that," he said. "I take all the blame." He raised his face slowly until his eyes met hers. They were not the eyes she had known. They were the eyes of a man who had been crushed, who had been powdered between the wheels of Fate. The old masterful quality, the old indomitable will that stirred her anger and admiration were gone, and in their place were coals of sorrow and ashes of defeat. For a moment she held back; then, with arms outstretched, she fell upon her father's breast.

And then he felt his strength return. He drew her to him as all that remained in the world; crushed her to him; then, very gently, released her a little. . . . He found his fingers threading her fine hair, as they had loved to do when she was a little child.

She sank to her knees beside him, and at last she looked up in his face. "Forgive me, my father," she whispered.

He kissed her forehead and struggled with his voice. "We all make mistakes, Beulah," he said. "I have made mine this twenty-five years, and there—there is the price!"

His words turned Beulah's thought to Allan, and the necessity for action brought her to her feet. "We must save him," she cried. "We must, and we will! Is the policeman gone? We must have the best doctors from Calgary." Looking about she found that Grey and Arthurs had left the room. They had slipped out to leave father and child alone with their emotion, but she found them at the front of the house.

She seized the policeman by the arm. "You must get us a doctor—the best doctor in the country," she pled. "We will spare nothing——" ·

"My guest, Miss Harris, Sergeant Grey," said Arthurs, and the policeman deftly converted her grasp into a handshake.

"Mr. Arthurs has told me the injured man is your brother. He shall want for nothing. And the sooner I go the sooner you will have help."

"Your prisoner seems docile enough," Arthurs remarked, as the policeman swung on to his horse.

"Rather a puzzler," said Grey. "Doesn't look the part, but was caught in the act, or next thing to it, and his revolver was found lying on the spot where the young man was shot. By the way, I had almost forgotten. One of the robbers was shot and killed. I had to leave his body, but I wish you would send a man up to stay about the place until I can get a coroner out here."

"Robbers, did you say?" demanded Beulah. "Then it was for robbery?"

"Yes, Miss Harris. It seems your father had a large sum of money on him. We have found no trace of it yet, but it is not likely that more than two were implicated, and as one was shot on the spot this other must know where the money is. We will bring it out of him in due time."

So saying he rode down to the gate, thanked the cowboy who had been keeping an eye on the prisoner, and the two started off at a smart trot down the trail.

CHAPTER XIX

BEULAH returned to the house to minister to her brother, but Mrs. Arthurs stopped her on the stairs.

"Your mother knows," she said. "They are both in the room with Allan."

Her first impulse was to rush in and complete the family circle, but some fine sense restrained her. For distraction she plunged into the task of preparing breakfast.

At length they came down. Beulah saw them on the stairs, and knew that the gulf was bridged.

"Allan is better," her mother said, when she saw the girl. "He has asked for you." And the next minute Beulah was on her knees by the white bed, caressing the locks that would fall over the pale forehead.

"How did I get here, Beulah?" he whispered. "How did we all get here? What has happened?"

"You have been hurt, Allan," she said. "You have been badly hurt, but you are going to get well again. When you are stronger we will talk about it, but at present you must lie still and rest."

"Lie still and rest," he repeated. "How good it is to lie still and rest!"

Later in the day the pain in his wound began to give much discomfort, but he was able to swallow some porridge with pure cream, and his breath came easily. His father stayed about the house, coming every little while to look in upon son and daughter, and as Allan's great constitution gave evidence of winning the fight a deep happiness came upon John Harris. He was able to sleep for a short time, and in the afternoon suggested a walk with his wife. Beulah saw that they were arm in arm as they disappeared in the trees by the river.

"I haven't told you all yet," Harris said to her. "I have done even worse than you suppose, but in some way it doesn't seem so bad to-day. Last night I was in Gethsemane."

It was strange to hear a word suggestive of religion from his lips. Harris had not renounced religion; he had merely been too busy for it. But this word showed that his mind had been travelling back over old tracks.

"And to-day we are in Olivet," she answered, tenderly. "What matters if—if everything's all right?"

"If only Allan——," he faltered.

"Allan will get well," she said. "When he could withstand the first shock he will get well. Of course he must have attention, but he is in the right place for that."

"The Arthurses are wonderful people," he ventured, after a pause. "Mary, they have found something that we missed."

"But we have found it now, John. We are going to take time to live. That is where we made our mistake."

There was another pause, broken only by the rustle of leaves and the rushing of the river.

"Beulah was right," he said, at last. "Beulah is a wonderful girl, and a beautiful."

"She will not be wanting to go back home with us," said the mother.

"So much the better. Mary, Mary, we have no home to go back to!"

She looked at him with a sudden puzzled, half-frightened expression. "No home, John? No home? You don't mean that?"

He nodded and turned his face away. "I said I hadn't told you all," he managed at length. . . . "I sold the farm."

She was sitting on a fallen log, very trim, and grey, and small, but she seemed suddenly to become smaller and greyer still.

"Sold the old farm," she repeated, mechanically.

"Yes, I sold the old farm," he said again, as if finding some delight in goading himself with the repetition. "I thought I saw a chance to make a lot of money if only I had some ready cash to turn in my hand, and I sold it. I thought I would be rich and then I would be happy. But they took the money last night. They found out about it some way, and took it, and nearly killed our boy. Mary, you worked hard all your life, and to-day you have nothing. I brought you to this."

She looked with unseeing eyes through the trees at the fast-running water. Her thoughts were with the old home, with the ideals they had cherished when they founded it, with the hardships and the sorrow, and the sickness and the pain, and the joy that had hallowed it as no other spot in all the universe—the place where their first love had nursed them in its tenderness, where they had sat hand in hand in the gathering dusk, drinking the ripple of the water and the whirr of the wild duck's wing; where she had gone down into the valley of the shadow and their little children had come into their arms. And it was gone. He had sold it. Without so much as by-your-leave from the partner of his labours and his life he had sold it and left them destitute.

She saw it all, and for the moment her heart shrank within her. But she saw, too, the futility of it all. She might have upbraided him; she might have returned in part the sorrows he had forced upon her, for he was wounded now and could not strike back. But she rose and stretched her arms toward him.

"You said I had nothing, John. You are wrong. I have you. I have everything!"
. . . "And it was to you, beloved, to you, a woman of such great soul, that I could do this thing. . . . I should be utterly wretched. . . . But I'm not." He spoke slowly and deliberately, as one having ample time, and with the diction of earlier years. "I should be scouring the valleys with a troop of men, hunting for our money. But I'm not. It seems such a puny thing, it's hardly worth the while —except for the happiness it might bring to you, and Beulah." . . .

They sat long in the sunshine of the warm autumn afternoon, living again through sweet, long-forgotten days, and already planning for their future. Harris would again exercise homestead right, and with Allan to take up land alongside they should have comfort and happiness. They would go back to the beginning; they would start over again; and this time they would not stray from the path.

When they returned to the house it was almost evening, and they found the doctor from town busy over Allan. "Would have killed nine men out of ten," he told Harris, quite frankly; "but this boy is the tenth. He's badly hurt, but he'll pull through, if we can arrest any infection. His constitution and his clean blood will save him."

Before the doctor left Arthurs inquired if

the police had any further details of the crime. Harris appeared to have lost interest in everything except the members of his family.

"Quite a mystery," said the doctor. "I understand one of the robbers was shot, and I will go on up from here to make an examination, as coroner. To-morrow the police will bring out a jury, and a formal verdict will be returned. A systematic search will also be undertaken to recover the money, as I understand that you"—turning to Harris—"suffered a heavy financial loss in addition to the injury to your son. Of course, it is impossible to say how many took part in the affair, but it is not likely the outlaws numbered more than two, in which case they are both accounted for. The one captured had no money to speak of in his possession, but he may have cached it somewhere, and when he sees the rope before him it will be likely to make him talk. They seem to have a pretty straight case against him. Not only was he captured practically in the act, but they have another important clue. He owns up to his name frankly enough, and it seems the revolver found on the scene of the crime had his initials, 'J. T.'—Jim Travers, cut in the grip. In fact, he admits the revolver is —. What's wrong, Miss Harris? Are you ill?"

Beulah's breath had stopped at the mention of Travers' name, and she staggered to a chair. Harris, too, was overcome.

"We knew him down East," Beulah explained, when she had somewhat recovered her composure. "I could not have thought it possible!"

"I didn't think he would have carried it that far," said Harris, at length, speaking very slowly and sadly. "Jim, Jim, you've made a worse mistake than mine."

Mary learned of the disclosure in a few minutes, and followed Beulah upstairs.

"You poor child!" she said, as she overtook her daughter.

"It's not me," she shot back. "It's Jim. He must be saved, some way. It's impossible to think—I won't think it, no matter what they say! Let them find what they like! . . . But he's in a hole, and we've got to get him out."

The mother shook her head with some recollection of the blindness of love. And yet her own heart refused to accept any idea of guilt on the part of Travers.

"I want to be alone, mother," said Beulah. "I want to be alone, to think. I'm going down by the river."

As she strode rapidly through the paths in the cotton-woods the girl gradually became conscious of one dominating impulse in her maze of emotions. She must see Jim. She must see him at once. She must see him alone. There were things to be said that needed—that admitted—no witness. She knew that. Ar-

thurs or one of the men would willingly ride
to town for her, or with her, but this was a task
for her alone. They must know nothing until
it was over.

Outwardly calm, but inwardly burning with
impatience, she returned to the house and
went through the form of eating supper. Then
she dallied through the evening, giving her attention to Allan until all the household, except
her mother, had gone to bed.

"I will watch with Allan to-night," her
mother said. "You need rest more than I do.
Lie down in my room and try to get some
sleep."

Her mother kissed her, and Beulah went to
her room. But not to sleep. When silence
filled all the house she slipped gently down the
stairs, through the front yard, and into the
corral. Fortunately her horse had been
stabled. She harnessed him with some difficulty in the darkness, and threw herself into
the saddle. For a hundred yards she walked
him; then she drew him off the hard road on
to the grass and loosed him into a trot. Half
a mile from the house she was swinging at a
hard gallop down the dark valley. The soft
night wind pressed its caresses on her flushed
cheek, but her heart beat fast with excitement
and impatience, and she galloped the foaming
horse to the limit of his speed. More than
once even the sure-footed ranger almost fell

over the treacherous badger-holes, but she had learned to ride like the saddle itself, and she merely tightened the rein and urged him faster.

Two hours of such violence were a safety-valve to her emotions, and both horse and rider were content to enter the little town at a walk. Here and there a coal-oil lamp shed its cube of yellow light through an unblinded window, but the streets were deserted and in utter darkness. She had now reached the point at which her general plan to see Travers must be worked out into detail, and she allowed the horse his time as she turned the matter over in her mind. She had no doubt that if she found Sergeant Grey he would permit an interview, but she shrank from making the request. She might do so as a last resort; but if possible she meant to seek out her lover—for so she thought of him—for herself. She knew that the jails in the smaller towns were crude affairs, where the prisoner was locked up and usually left without a guard. The first thing was to find the jail.

At a crossing her horse almost collided with a boy returning home from some late errand. "Oh, Mr. Boy," she said. "Come here, please, I want you to help me."

The boy approached hesitatingly, as though suspicious that some kind of trick were being played on him.

"Can you tell me," she said, in a low voice,

"where the jail is? I'll give you a dollar if you do."

"There ain't no jail here, miss," he replied frankly, evidently satisfied that the question was *bona fide*. "There's a coop, but you wouldn't give a dime to see it. It's just a kind of a shed."

"That's just what I want to find," she continued, "and I'll give you a dollar to show me where it is."

"Easy pickin'," said the boy. "Steer your horse along this way."

He led her through the main part of the town, to where a one-storey building, somewhat apart, stood aloof in the darkness.

"Some coop, ain't it?" said her guide, with boyish irony. "My dad says that's what we git fer votin' against the Gover'ment. The fire truck's in the front end, an' there's a cell with bars behind. Do you want to see that, too?"

"Yes, that's what I want to see, but I can find it myself now, thank you."

"Say, miss, you better be kerful. They've got a murd'rer in there now—Oh, say"—with a sudden change in his voice—"maybe he's somethin' to you? They ain't proved nothin' against him yet."

"Yes, he's a good deal to me," she said.

"Brother?" he demanded, with disconcerting persistence.

"No."

If her eyes could have pierced the darkness she would have seen a broad smile of understanding spreading over his young face. But it was a sympathetic smile withal. "Then I guess this dollar stands for 'beat it'?" he remarked.

"You win," she said, falling into his slang. "Also, forget it."

"I gotchuh, miss," he said, trotting off. Then he called back through the darkness, "An' I hope he gits off."

"God bless him for that," she said to herself, as she dismounted and made her way to the back of the building. She saw the outline of a door, which was undoubtedly locked, and further down the same wall was a little square window, with bars on it. There appeared to be only one cell, so there was no problem of locating the right one.

She stole up along the wall, but the window was too high for her. Searching about the littered yard she found a square tin, such as the ranchers use to carry coal-oil. Mounting this she was able to bring her face to the bars. The window was open for ventilation, and she strained her ear, but at first could hear nothing for the tumultous beating of her own heart. But at length she seemed to catch the sound of regular breathing from within.

"Jim," she said, in a low voice, listening intently. But there was no response.

"Jim," she repeated, a little louder. She fancied she heard a stir, and the sound of breathing seemed to cease.

"Jim Travers!"

"Yes!" came a quick reply. "Yes! Who is it?"

"Come to the window, Jim."

In a moment she saw the outline of his face through the darkness.

"Beulah Harris," he demanded, in his quiet voice, "what are you doing here?"

A great happiness surged about her at the sound of his voice and the warmth of his breath against her face. "I might ask the same, Jim, but such questions are embarrassing. Anyway, I am on the right side of the wall."

She saw his teeth gleam in the darkness. What a wonderful soul he was!

"But you shouldn't have come like this," he protested, and his voice was serious enough. "You are compromising yourself."

"Not I," she answered. "These bars are more inflexible than the stiffest chaperone. And I just had to see you, Jim, at once. We've got to get you out of here."

"How's Allan?"

"Getting better."

"And your father? Pretty angry at me, I guess."

"No. Father isn't angry any more. He's just sorry."

"Times are changing, Beulah. But if he wound that sack around my neck in sorrow, I don't want him at it when he's cross."

She laughed a little, mirthful ripple. Then, with sudden seriousness, "But, Jim, we shouldn't be jesting. We've got to get you out of here."

"I'm not worrying, Beulah," he answered. "They seem to have the drop on me, but I know a few things they don't. Shall I tell you what I know?"

"No."

"Why?"

"Because it would seem like arguing—like trying to prove you are innocent. And you don't need to prove anything to me. You understand? You don't need to prove *anything* to me."

She felt his eyes hot on her face through the darkness. "You don't need to prove anything to me," she repeated.

For a moment he held himself in restraint. The words were simple enough, but he knew what they meant. And this country girl, whom he had learned to like on her father's farm, had grown larger and larger in his scheme of things with the passing weeks. At first he had tried to dissuade himself, to think of it only as a passing fancy, and to remember that he was engaged in the serious business of earning enough money to build a shack on a homestead, and buy a team and a plough, and a cow and some bits of furniture. It would be a plain, simple life, but Beulah was accustomed —— What had Beulah to do with it? He scolded himself for permitting her intrusion, and turned his mind to the mellow fields where he would follow the plough until the sun dipped into the Rockies. And then he would turn the horses loose for food and rest, and in the shack the jack-pine knots would be frying in the kitchen stove, and the little table would be set, and Beulah——

And now this girl had come to him, while he was under the shadow, and because the shadow would not let him speak, and because her soul would not be bound by custom, and because her love could not be concealed, she had let him know.

"Have you thought it over, Beulah?" he said. "I have no right, as matters stand, to give or take a promise. I have no right——"

"You have no right to say 'as matters stand' as though matters had anything to do with it. They haven't Jim. No, I have not thought it over. This isn't something you think. It is something that comes to you when you don't think, or in spite of your thinking. But it's real—more real than anything you can touch or handle—more real than these bars, which are not so close as you seem to fancy——"

And then, between the iron rods across the open window, his lips met hers.

. . . "And you were seeking life, Beulah," he said at last. "Life that you should live in your own way, for the joy of living it. And——"

"And I have found it," she answered, in a voice low and thrilling with tenderness. "I have found it in you. We shall work out our destiny together, but we must keep our thought on the destiny, rather than the work. Oh, Jim, I'm just dying to see your homestead —our homestead. And are there two windows? We must have two windows, Jim— one in the east for the sun, and one in the west for the mountains."

"Our house is all window, as yet," he answered gaily. "And there isn't as much as a fence post to break the view."

"What are you doing here?" said a sharp voice, and Beulah felt as though her tin box were suddenly sinking into a great abyss. She turned with a little gasp. Sergeant Grey stood within arm's length of her.

"Oh, it's Sergeant Grey," she said, with a tone of relief. "I am Beulah Harris. And I've just been getting myself engaged to your prisoner here. Oh, it's not so awful as you think. You see, we knew each other in Manitoba, and we've really been engaged for quite a while, but he didn't know it until to-night."

For a moment the policeman retained his reserve. He remembered the girl, who had already cost him a deflected glance, and he reproached himself that he could doubt her even as he doubted, but how could he know that she had not been passing in firearms or planning a release?

"What she says is right, sergeant," said Travers. "She has just broken the news to me, and I'm the happiest man in Canada, jail or no jail."

There was no mistaking the genuine ring in Travers' voice, and the policeman was convinced. "Most extraordinary," he remarked, at length, "but entirely natural on your part, I must say. I congratulate you, sir." The officer had not forgotten the girl who clung to his arm the morning before. "Hang me, sir," he continued, "there's luck everywhere but in the Mounted Police."

He unlocked the door of the cell. "I ought to search you," he said to Beulah, "but if you'll give me your word that you have no firearms, weapons, knives, or matches, I'll admit you to this—er—drawing-room for a few minutes."

"Nothing worse than a hat-pin," she assured him. "But you must come, too," she added, placing her hand on his arm. "You must understand that."

He accompanied her into the cell, but remained in the doorway, where he suddenly developed an interest in astronomy. At length he turned quickly and faced in to the darkness.

"Speaking, not as an officer, but as a fellowman, I wish you were damned well—that is, very well—out of this, old chap," he said to Travers.

"Oh, that's all right," Jim assured him. "You couldn't help taking me up, of course, and for all your kindness you would quite cheerfully hang me if it fell to your lot. But it isn't going to."

"I stand ready to be of any service to you that is permissible."

"The inquest is to be to-morrow, isn't it?" asked Beulah. "I think you should be at the inquest, Jim."

"That's right," said the sergeant. "You may throw some new light on the case."

"I've just one request," said Travers. "You know Gardiner?"

"I've heard of him."

"Have him at the inquest."

"As a juror or witness?"

"It doesn't matter, but have him there."

"All right. I'll see to it. And now, Miss Harris, if you will permit me, I will bring your horse for you."

Grey took a conveniently long time to find the horse, but at last he appeared in the door. Beulah released her fingers from Jim's and swung herself into the saddle.

"Sergeant Grey," she said, "I think you're the second best man in the world. Goodnight."

The sergeant's military shoulders came up squarer still, and he stood at attention as she rode into the darkness.

CHAPTER XX

THE inquest party consisted of the coroner, who was the doctor that had already attended Allan; Sergeant Grey; six jurors, selected from the townspeople; the manager of the bank, whose suspicions had first been communicated to Grey; Travers; and Gardiner. In the early morning the policeman had ridden out to the ranch for Gardiner, but had met him on his way to town. News of the tragedy had reached him, he said, and he was hurrying in to see if he could be of some assistance to Travers, in arranging for a lawyer, or in any way that might be practicable. Grey told him that as yet no formal charge had been laid against Travers; that he was merely being held pending the finding of the coroner's jury, and suggested that if Gardiner would accompany him to the inquest he might be able, not only to throw some light on Travers' character, but also on his whereabouts on the night of the tragedy. To this Gardiner readily agreed.

It was noon when the party reached the Arthurses' ranch. Beulah counted them out with a field-glass while they were still miles down the valley, and a big table was set in the bunk-house where the cowboys were accommodated during the branding season. It was a matter of course that the men should be fed when they reached Arthurs'. At intervals in the setting of the table the girl returned to her field-glass, until she was quite sure of the straight figure riding beside the mounted policeman.

They swung into the yard amid a cloud of dust, the jingle of trappings, and the hearty exchange of greetings between Arthurs and his acquaintances from town. Gardiner was introduced to Arthurs, and shook hands without removing his gauntlets. He had learned that the party were to have dinner here, and he excused himself, saying that the long ride in the heat had upset him somewhat, and he thought he would be wiser to lie in the shade for an hour or two before eating. Arthurs pressed his hospitality upon him, but as Gardiner seemed fixed in his purpose he did not insist. Then the rancher walked over and shook hands with Travers. There were no signs of handcuffs now, and an outsider would not have known that the young man's position differed from that of the others present.

After the meal Gardiner joined them again, and the party, which now included Arthurs and Harris, proceeded up the valley to the scene of the tragedy. It was a great shock to Harris to find that the victim of Allan's gun was his old neighbour, Riles. He stood for a long time as one dazed by the discovery, but gradually out of the confusion a horrible fear took shape in his mind. Allan had shot this man, with whom they had an appointment at this spot; had shot him down, as far as could be shown, without excuse or provocation, before he had so much as entered the door. The body proved to be unarmed, and from its position had evidently fallen into the building after receiving the fatal charge.

The old man turned dry eyes from the gruesome thing across the warm, shimmering valleys. On the farther slopes, leagues distant through the clear air, ripening fields of wheat lay on the hillsides like patches of copper-plate, and farther still thin columns of smoke marked the points where steam-ploughs were wrapping the virgin prairie in her first black bridal of commerce. But he saw none of these. He saw Allan, and he saw bars, and a prisoner's dock. And there was something else that he would not see; he would close his eyes; he would not let its horrid gaunt ligaments thrust themselves into his vision!

After a thorough examination of the scene they laid the body in a democrat and returned to Arthurs', where the coroner held his court in the bunk-house.

Harris's evidence was first received. He found it difficult to give his story connectedly, but item by item he told of his acquaintance with Riles in the eastern province; of their decision to come west and take up more land; of the chance by which they had fallen with Gardiner, and the prospect he had laid before them of more profitable returns from another form of investment; of how his hesitation had finally been overcome by the assurance that all he need do was have his money ready—he was to be under no obligation to go any further in the transaction unless entirely satisfied; of the offer wired by the New York capitalists; of the sale of his farm for a disappointing sum, and their journey with the money to the old shanty up the valley, where they were to be met by Riles and Gardiner, and also, as they expected, by the owner of the mine, with whom they would open direct negotiations, producing the money as proof of their desire and ability to carry out their undertaking; of how they hoped the owner would be induced to accept a deposit and accompany them back to town, where an option would be secured from him for a period sufficient to enable them to turn the property over to the New York investors at a handsome profit; of how he—Harris—wearied by the long ride in the bright, thin air, had gone to sleep confidently with Allan at his side, and of how he had suddenly been

awakened by a shot and had heard Allan spring
to his feet and rush across the floor of the old
building. Then there had been another shot
—a revolver shot this time—and everything
was darkness, and he could hear only something struggling at the door. Then he told of
his own fight; of how they had fallen and rolled
about on the rotten floor, and how, in despera-
tion, he had not hesitated to use his teeth on
the hand of his assailant, who had finally
broken away and disappeared in the darkness.
Then he told the rest of his story; of his vigil
with Allan, of the loss of the money, of the capture of Travers, and finally of the arrival of the
policeman on the scene.

"Didn't it seem to you a foolish thing to go
into the hills with all that money to meet a
man you had never seen, and buy a property
you had never examined?" asked the coroner.

"It wasn't foolishness; it was stark, raving
madness, as I see it now," Harris admitted.
"But I didn't see it that way then. It looked
like a lot of easy money. I didn't care what
the coal mine was like—I didn't care whether
there was a coal mine at all or not, so long as
we made our turn-over to the New York
people."

"But did it not occur to you that the whole
thing—coal mine and mine owner and New
Yorkers and all—was simply a scheme hatched
up to induce you away into the fastnesses of

the foothills with a lot of money in your possession?"

A half-bewildered look came over Harris, as of a man gripped by a new and paralyzing thought. But he shook his head. "No, it couldn't have been that," he said. "You see, Riles was an old neighbour of mine, and Mr. Gardiner, too, I knew for a good many years. It wasn't like as if I had been dealing with strangers."

"We will go deeper into that matter after a little," said the coroner. "It's very fortunate Mr. Gardiner is here to add what light he can to the mystery. We will now adjourn to the room where the younger Mr. Harris lies and hear his evidence. It would be unwise to move him for some days yet."

They found Allan partly propped up in the white bed. His face was pale, and his hands were astonishingly thin and white, but his mind was clear, and he could talk without difficulty. He covered much the same ground as his father had done, up to the point where the elder Harris had fallen asleep in the old building.

"I can't tell you how it happened, Doctor," he said, turning his eyes, larger now in his pale face, upon the coroner, "but I think I got very homesick—I guess I was pretty tired, too—and I began thinking of things that had happened long ago, back when I was a little child, in a little sod shanty that the old shack in the valley some way seemed to bring to mind. And then I guess I fell asleep, too, but suddenly I sat up in a great fright. I'm not a coward," he said, with a faint smile. "When I'm feeling myself it takes more than a notion or a dark night to send the creeps up the back of my neck. But I own I sat up there so frightened my teeth chattered. I had a feeling that I was going to be attacked—I didn't know by what —maybe by a wild beast—but something was going to rush in through that old blanket hanging in the door and pounce on me."

The sweat was standing on Allan's face, and he sank back weakly into the pillows. Beulah placed a glass to his lips, and the doctor told him to take his time with his story. The jurors stood about the bed in silence, looking from one to the other with expressions that suggested they were almost in the presence of the supernatural. If the black bag with the money had slowly risen out of the floor someone would have quietly set it in a corner until Allan was ready to continue his evidence.

"As the minutes went by," Allan continued, after an interval, "that terrible dread grew upon me, and my sense of danger changed from fear to certainty. Something was going to attack me through that door! I raised my gun and took careful aim. I saw the blanket swing a little; then I saw the fingers of a man's hand. Then I fired.

"Perhaps I am a murderer," he continued, simply, "but before God I know no more why I fired that shot than you do."

There were deep breathing and shuffling of feet as Allan completed this part of his statement, but only the coroner found his voice. "Most remarkable evidence," he ejaculated. "Most extraordinary evidence. I have never heard anything so obviously sincere and at the same time so altogether unexplainable."

"Perhaps it's not so unexplainable," said a quiet voice; and Mary Harris made her way through the circle of men to the side of the bed. She sat down on the coverlet and took the boy's hand in hers. It mattered not how many were looking on; he was her little boy again.

"*You* will understand, Doctor, and some of you men are parents," she began. "Allan will be twenty-five years old this coming winter. A little less than twenty-five years ago my husband was obliged to leave me alone for a considerable period in our little sod shanty on the homestead where we had located down in Manitoba. There were no near neighbours, as we count distance in well-settled districts, and I was altogether alone. I stood it all right for the first day or two, but my nerves were not what they should have been, and gradually a strange, unreasoning fear came upon me. I suppose it was the immensity of the prairies, the terrible loneliness of it all, and my own state of health, but the dread grew from day to day and from night to night. I tried to busy myself, to keep my mind active, to throw off the spectre that haunted me, but day and night I was oppressed with a sense of impending danger. We had no wooden door on the house; we hadn't money to buy the boards to make one, and all my protection was a blanket hung in the doorway. I used to watch that blanket at night; I would light the lantern and sit in the corner and watch that blanket. My fear gradually pictured to itself an attack through that doorway—I didn't know by what; by white man, or Indian, or wild beast, or ghost, or worse, if that is possible; my mind could not balance things; nothing seemed too unreasonable or terrible to expect. So I took the gun, and sat in the corner, and waited.

"And then at last it came. I didn't see anything, and I didn't hear anything, but I knew it was there. I still remember how frightened and yet how cool I was in that last moment. I held the gun to my shoulder and waited for *It* to thrust itself against the blanket. In another moment I am sure I should have fired. But before that moment I heard my name called, and I knew my husband's voice, and I came out of the nightmare."

She brought her eyes slowly from the face of the doctor over the group of men assembled in the room, and then dropped them to meet

Allan's. He was breathing her name softly. "If it was a wrong thing for Allan to shoot this man," she said, "don't blame Allan for it. Let me pay any price that must be paid."

"Most extraordinary," the coroner repeated, after a silence. "It seems to account for the shooting of Riles, but it leaves us as much as ever—more than ever, I should say—in the dark concerning the disappearance of the money, and the part which has implicated the young man Travers in the affair."

The banker gave his evidence. It was not unusual, he said, for considerable sums in bank-notes to be handled among speculators and land buyers, but the amount withdrawn by Harris was so great that it had left him somewhat ill at ease, and as Sergeant Grey had happened his way he had mentioned the matter to him.

The policeman shed little new light on the case. He had followed the party into the hills as best he could, taking the off chance of something sinister afoot. He had found Harris, with his wounded son, and a prisoner, and a man dead in the doorway. He had notified the coroner and taken Travers in charge. Here his eyes met Beulah's. "I don't think there is anything more to be said," he concluded.

During the hearing of the various witnesses Gardiner had attempted an air of impersonal interest, but with no great success. His demeanour, studied though it was, betrayed a certain anxiety and impatience. He was dressed just as he had dismounted from his horse, having removed only his hat. But he smiled confidently when asked for his evidence, and told his story calmly and connectedly.

It is quite true that he was associated with Riles and Mr. Harris in the coal-mine investment. He was acting for the owner of the property, but had seen that a large profit was to be made from the turn-over, and had been glad to place the opportunity in the way of two old friends. The offer from the New York concern was entirely *bona fide;* he had the telegram in his pocket at that moment, notwithstanding the suggestion made by the coroner, which, if he might say so, he thought was hardly warranted, and would not have been made with a full knowledge of the circumstances. The owner of the mine could be produced at the proper moment, if that became necessary.

"I feel a grave responsibility in this whole matter," Gardiner protested, with some emotion. "I feel that I am, at least indirectly, responsible for the serious loss that has befallen Mr. Harris, and for the injury to his son. But when you have heard the whole circumstances you will agree that the situation was one I could not possibly have foreseen. Let me give them to you in some detail.

"The day before yesterday, in company with Riles, I met Mr. Harris and his son, and found that their money had arrived. The remittance was not as large as they expected, but I believed that I could raise some money privately, and that we would still be able to put the deal through. I advised against losing any time, as I knew that if the owner should meet anyone else interested in a proposition of a similar nature we would find it much harder to make a bargain with him. It was arranged that the two Mr. Harrises were to drive ahead, taking the money with them, and that Riles and I would follow. We were to overtake them at the old building where this unfortunate tragedy occurred. As it happened, I had a sick horse at the ranch, and, as I was delayed in getting some medicine for him, Riles suggested that he would ride out to the ranch—that is, where I live—and wait for me there. Up to that time I had no suspicions, and I agreed to that.

"Well, when I reached the ranch, I could find nothing of Riles, and, on further search, I could find nothing of Travers, who was working for me. Their riding horses were gone, and so were their saddles and bridles. I found that Travers had taken his revolver out of the house. I confess my suspicions were then somewhat aroused, but I found myself with the sick horse on my hands, and I could not very well leave the place. Of course, I never thought of anything so bad as has happened, or I would not have considered the horse, but I admit I was at a loss to understand their conduct. But when I heard, early this morning, what had happened, it was all clear to me."

During the latter part of this evidence Travers had fixed his eyes on Gardiner, but the witness had steadily avoided him. Jim was now convinced that he was the victim, not of a coincidence, but a plot. Of course, he could give his evidence, which would be directly contradictory to that of Gardiner, but he was already under suspicion, and anything he might say would be unconsciously discounted by the jurors. But he began calmly, a quiet smile still playing about his thin lips and clean teeth.

"I am sorry I cannot corroborate all the last witness has said," he commenced. "I did not leave the ranch with Riles; on the contrary, I was fishing down by the river when I saw Riles and Gardiner ride by. Gardiner was talking, and I heard him mention Mr. Harris's name. I worked for Mr. Harris not long ago, but I did not know he was in this part of the country. I heard Gardiner say——" Jim coloured a little, and stopped.

"Well, what did you hear him say?" said the coroner. "That is what we are anxious to know."

"I heard him say something about Mr. Harris losing all his money that night, in the old shanty up the river road. 'Strange things have happened up there, Riles,' he said. That made me suspicious, and I hurried back to the ranch, determined to follow them. I found that my revolver had been taken. I armed myself as best I could, and set out. When I came near the building which Gardiner had mentioned I dismounted and approached it carefully. It was very dark. Suddenly I was attacked from behind. A sack was thrown over my head, and I was overpowered, and bound. I don't know how long I was kept in that condition, but when at last the sack was removed I was in the presence of Sergeant Grey."

With the progress of Travers' narrative all eyes had turned to Gardiner, but, whatever his inward emotions, he outwardly showed no signs of discomfiture. "This seems to be a day of strange tales," he said to the coroner, "and the last we have heard is stranger than the first. Of course, it is quite absurd on the face of it. The suggestion that I would be a party to robbing Mr. Harris of twenty thousand dollars, and so balk a transaction in which I stood to make a profit of more than twice that amount, is too ridiculous for discussion. I didn't say so before, because it didn't seem to bear on the case, but I have at home a telegram which I received a few days ago from the New York investors, offering me a personal commission of twenty per cent. on the transaction if I was able to get this property for them at the price they had offered. So, from a purely selfish point of view, you see where my interests lay. But there are other reasons for this fine tale which you have just heard. To spare the feelings of some present, I intended to say nothing of them, but if I must tell what I know, why, I must tell what I know. This man Travers was a farm hand working for Harris on his farm back in Manitoba. Harris is—or was— well-to-do, and Travers accordingly mustered up an attachment for his daughter. This the young lady, it seems, was foolish enough to return. They——"

"That'll do, Gardiner," interrupted Travers, in a quiet, vibrant voice. "You are getting away from the subject."

"On the contrary, I'm getting close to the subject—a little too close for your comfort, it seems."

"I am not investigating any family closets," said the coroner. "You will have to show the connection between these matters and the inquiry we are making."

"I will do that in a moment, sir," Gardiner returned. "But I cannot show the connection until I have shown the events that are connected. Travers had trouble with Harris and had a fight with Allan. Then he and the young lady ran away. They have both been in this part of the country for some time. But

Travers' plan to inherit the Harris property was upset on account of the girl quarrelling with her parents, and his ardour seems to have cooled off noticeably. But he was as keen for the property as ever. Riles was a weakling in the hands of a man like Travers, and no doubt he betrayed the fact that Harris was taking his money with him into the hills. Then the two of them framed up the plan which has resulted in the death of one and the arrest of the other."

During these exchanges the sympathies of the jurors seemed to veer from side to side. The theories propounded were so contradictory that opinions wavered with each sentence of evidence. But a new bolt was ready for the shooting.

"Mr. Coroner," said Beulah, rising and pointing at Gardiner, "will you make that man take his gauntlets off?"

There seemed an instant recession of the blood from Gardiner's face. But it was for the instant only. "My hat is off," he said, with a smile. "Is not that sufficient?"

"Make him take them off!" Beulah insisted.

"There is no rule against wearing gauntlets in a coroner's court," said the coroner. "I do not see the point of your objection."

"Make him take them off," said Beulah.

"As the young lady insists," said the coroner, turning to Gardiner, "I suggest that you comply with her request."

"I should be glad to," said Gardiner, "but the fact is I have a sore hand. When I was giving the horse medicine the night Travers left me alone the brute nipped me a little, and I have been keeping it covered up since."

"Make him take them off," said Beulah.

"Why should you be so insistent?" said the coroner. "Surely it makes no difference——"

"Only this difference. You have heard my father's evidence of the fight in the old house. The man with whom he fought will have tooth-marks in his hand. Make him take them off. Or if you won't—look at these hands." She seized Jim's hands in hers and held them up before the coroner and the jury. "Any tooth-marks there? Now make this other man show his."

For a moment all eyes were on Travers' hands. In that moment Gardiner rushed for the open window, and in another instant would have been through it, had not the quick arm of the policeman intercepted.

"Not so fast, my man," said Grey. "Now we will see this horse-bite of yours." Gardiner made no further resistance, and he drew the glove from his hand. There was a fresh scar on the right thumb.

The coroner examined it carefully. When he spoke it was in the voice of a judge delivering sentence. "That is not a horse-bite," he said. "Those are the marks of human teeth!"

Gardiner smiled a faint smile. "Well, what are you going to do about it?" he said.

"We are going to put you in Travers' place and tender him our apologies," said the coroner.

"Very good," said Gardiner. "And do I marry the girl?"

"This is no time for levity," said the coroner, sternly. "You have escaped a murder charge only by grace of this young man's excellent constitution."

But Travers had crowded into the centre of the circle. "Gardiner," he said, "if you weren't under arrest I'd thrash you here and now. But you can at least do something to square yourself. Where is that money?"

"That's right, Jim. Everyone thinks of what is nearest his heart."

"You scoundrel! You know why it is near my heart. You have robbed Mr. Harris of all that he had spent his whole life for. You will have no chance to use that money yourself. You are sure of your living for the next twenty years. Why not show that you are not all bad—that you have some human sentiments in you? It seems as little as you can do."

"There may be something in what you say," said Gardiner. "I have a slip of paper here with the key to the secret."

He reached with his finger and thumb in his vest pocket and drew out a small folded paper.

This he unfolded very slowly and deliberately before the eyes of the onlookers. It contained a small quantity of white powder. Before any hand could reach him he had thrown his head back and swallowed it.

"Too late!" he cried, as Grey snatched the empty paper from his fingers. "Too late! Well, I guess I beat you all out, eh? And, as I said before, what are you going to do about it? Twenty years, eh, Jim? You'll be scrawny and rheumatic by that time, and the beautiful Beulah will be fat and figureless. Twenty years for you, Jim, but twenty minutes for me—and I wouldn't trade with you, damn you! I beg the pardon of the ladies present. One should never forget to be a gentleman, even when—when——"

But Gardiner's breath was beginning to come fast, and he raised his hands to his throat. A choking spell seized him, and he would have fallen had not the policeman and the coroner held him on his feet. "Let me lie down," he said, when he got his breath. "Let me lie down, can't you? Have I got to die on end, like a murderer?"

They led him to the adjoining room, where he fell upon the bed. The muscles of his great arms and neck were working in contortions, and his tongue seemed to fill his mouth.

"Most extraordinary," said the coroner. "Strychnine, doubtless. We can't do much for him, I'm afraid. We might try some mustard and hot water, Mrs. Arthurs."

"Take your time, Lil," whispered Arthurs. "You may save your country a long board bill." But Lilian Arthurs' abhorrence of Gardiner's perfidy had been overwhelmed in a wave of sympathy for a suffering fellow-being. She hurried to the kitchen, while the men of the party filed down the stairs and out into the yard. John Harris was the last to leave the house, and he walked slowly, with bare, bowed head, into the group who were excitedly discussing the amazing turn events had taken. He took no part in their conversation, but stood a little apart, plunged deep in his own inward struggle.

At last he turned and called his wife in the kitchen door. "Bring Beulah," he said.

The two women joined him. At first Harris stood with face averted, but in a moment he spoke in a clear, quiet voice.

"I haven't played the game fair with you two," he said, "and I want to say so now. Perhaps it would be truer to say that I played the wrong game. Twenty-five years have proved it was the wrong game. Now, without a penny, I can start just where I started twenty-five years ago. The only difference is that I am an old man instead of a young one. I'm going to take another homestead and start again, at the right game, if Mary will start with me."

She put her hand in his, and her eyes were bright again with the fire of youth. "You know there is only one answer, John," she whispered.

Harris called Travers over from the group of men.

"There's one thing more," he continued. "When I started I had only a wife to keep, and I don't intend to take any bigger responsibility now. Allan will be having a homestead of his own. Jim Travers, I am speaking to you! I owe you an apology for some things and an explanation for some things, but I'm going to square the debt with the only gift I have left."

The light breeze tossed the hair of Beulah's uncovered head, and the light of love and health glowed in her face and thrilled through the fine symmetry of her figure.

"Take her, Jim," he said.

"She is a godly gift," said the young man reverently.

"You think so now," said her father. "You know nothing about it. In twenty-five years you will know just how great a gift she is— or she will not be worthy of her mother."

Harris and his wife were gazing with unseeing eyes into the mountains when Arthurs handed them a letter. "It came in the mail which the boys brought out this morning," he said, "and I forgot all about it until this minute."

It was from Bradshaw. Harris opened it

indifferently, but the first few lines aroused his interest, and he read it eagerly to the end.

"My dear Harris," it ran, "on receipt of your telegram I immediately opened negotiations through my connections looking to a sale of your farm with its crop and equipment, complete as a going concern. I succeeded in getting an offer of the $40,000 you set on it, and had all the papers drawn up, when I discovered that among us we had made a serious omission. You will remember that, a good many years ago, when you were taking on some fresh obligations, you transferred the homestead into your wife's name. I assured the purchaser that there would be no difficulty about getting title from your wife, but as all the buildings are on the homestead quarter he would agree to nothing better than paying $20,000 for the rest of your land, leaving the homestead quarter, with the buildings, stock, and implements, out of the transaction. As his price seemed a fair one for the balance of the property, and as I assumed your need of the money was urgent, I closed a deal on that basis, cashed the agreement, and remitted the proceeds to you at once by wire. I trust my actions in the matter meet with your approval.

"Yours sincerely,

"GEORGE BRADSHAW."

[342]

THE HOMESTEADERS

Harris placed the letter in the hands of his wife. She tried to read it, but a great happiness enveloped her as a flood and the typewritten characters seemed to swim before her. "What does it mean, John?" she asked, noting his restrained excitement. "What does it mean?"

"It means that the homestead quarter was not sold—after all—that it is still yours, with the buildings, and machinery, and stock, and this year's crop just ready for cutting."

She raised her eyes to his. "Still ours, John, you mean. Still ours."

In the rapid succession of events everyone seemed to have forgotten, or disregarded, Gardiner. But at this moment the doctor came rushing out of the house.

"Gardiner's gone!" he exclaimed, as he came up to the men.

Some of the party removed their hats.

"Oh, not that way—not that way!" exclaimed the doctor. "I mean he's gone—skipped—beat it, if you understand. Most extraordinary! I was taking his pulse. It was about normal, and he seemed resting easier, so I slipped downstairs for the antidote. When I went back—I was only gone a moment—there wasn't sight or sound of him."

The men stared at each other for a moment; then followed the doctor in a race for Gardiner's room. They found it as he said. There was neither sight nor sound of Gardiner.

Sergeant Grey conducted a swift examination, not of Gardiner's room, but of the one in which Allan was lying. He was rewarded by finding the little slip of paper, with a few crystals of powder still clinging to it. The coroner examined the crystals through his magnifying-glass; then, somewhat dubiously, raised them on a moistened finger to his tongue, and after a moment's hesitation swallowed in an impressive, scholarly fashion.

"*Saccharum album!*" he exclaimed. "Common white sugar! Most extraordinary!"

But Sergeant Grey was at the open window. It was only an eight-foot drop to the soft earth, and to the policeman there was no longer any mystery in Gardiner's disappearance. The mock suicide was a carefully-planned ruse to be employed by Gardiner if the worst came to the worst.

At that moment the sound of horse's hoofs was heard on the gravelly road, and three hundred yards away Gardiner dashed through a gap in the trees that skirted the base of the hills. He was on the policeman's horse, and riding like wild fire.

"I want all of you men, and a horse for each," said Grey, quickly, turning upon them like a general marshalling his officers. "There are a dozen different trails he may fellow, and we must put a man on each. I will give immediate pursuit, in the hope of riding him down before he can throw us off the scent, and I will leave it to you, Mr. Arthurs, to organize the posse and scour the whole country until he is located."

At Grey's first words two men had rushed to the corral, and were already saddling horses. The first and fastest was placed at the command of the policeman, and in a minute he, too, was riding break-neck into the hills. But the delay was enough to give Gardiner almost a mile's lead, and the Government horse was a match for any on the ranch.

Grey knew that the main road, if followed far enough, dwindled into a pack trail, which in turn seemed to lose itself in the fastnesses of the mountains, but in reality opened into a pass leading through the range. He gave Gardiner credit for knowing as much, and concluded that the fugitive would make a bolt straight through the mountains. There was no time to watch for tracks; his chance to ride his man down depended entirely upon speed. If he miscalculated, and Gardiner, instead of making for the pass, sought refuge in the mountains, the posse would certainly locate him or starve him into surrender. So the officer urged his horse to the limit and galloped straight into the mountain battlements ahead of him.

An hour's hard riding brought him into a tremendously rough country, where the trail at times was nothing more than a narrow defile or ledge, and sheer walls of rock rose thousands of feet above, their giant edges cutting the blue sky like the teeth of a mighty saw. Far below, a ribbon of green and white, the river rolled in its canyon. Here and there a thin stream of water sprayed down the mountain side, cutting a damp, treacherous belt across the trail. But at one such spot Grey's heart leaped within him, for there, unmistakably clear in the thin soil and soft rock, were the marks of a horse's shoe, not an hour old. A few minutes later he saw Gardiner swinging round a spur of rock half a mile further up the pass.

The policeman began to watch the moist spots for the tell-tale hoof-prints, and invariably their evidence revealed itself. He knew now that he had guessed Gardiner's course correctly, and it was a matter of minutes until he should ride him down. He wondered whether the man was armed or not; it would be an easy trick to hide behind a rock and pick the policeman off as he rode by.

Suddenly, at a turn in the path, his eye caught a sight which made him throw his horse back on his tracks. A sheer precipice fell away a thousand feet below him, and beetling cliffs cut off the sky above. Across the path trickled a little stream. And there in the stream, so clear they could not be misread, were the marks cut by a horse's feet *sliding over the precipice.*

THE HOMESTEADERS

The policeman dismounted carefully. There was scarcely room for him to pass his horse on the narrow ledge. Where the stream had worn it it sloped downwards at an uncomfortable angle. He knelt beside it and traced the marks of the shoe-calks with his finger. They led over the edge. Eighteen inches down the mountain side was a fresh scar where steel had struck a projecting corner of rock.

A thousand feet below the green water slid and swirled in the bed of the canyon.

THE END.